By C. S. Lewis

The Abolition of Man

Mere Christianity

The Great Divorce

The Problem of Pain

The Weight of Glory and Other Addresses

The Screwtape Letters (with "Screwtape Proposes a Toast")

Miracles

The Case for Christianity

The Lion, the Witch and the Wardrobe

Prince Caspian

The Voyage of the Dawn Treader

The Silver Chair

The Magician's Nephew

The Horse and His Boy

The Last Battle

Perelandra

That Hideous Strength

Out of the Silent Planet

The Joyful Christian

George Macdonald: An Anthology

C. S. Lewis: Letters to Children

C. S. Lewis

PERELANDRA

A Novel

SCRIBNER
NEW YORK LONDON TORONTO SYDNEY

SCRIBNER
1230 Avenue of the Americas
New York, NY 10020

First Scribner trade paperback edition 2003
SCRIBNER and design are trademarks
of Macmillan Library reference USA, Inc., used under license
by Simon & Schuster, the publisher of this work.

For information about special discounts for bulk purchases,
please contact Simon & Schuster Special Sales:
1-800-456-6798 or business@simonandschuster.com

Designed by Brooke Koven
Set in Sabon

Manufactured in the United States of America

7   9   10   8   6

Library of Congress Cataloging-in-Publication Data is available.

ISBN-13: 978-0-684-83365-1
ISBN-10:   0-684-83365-4
ISBN-13: 978-0-7432-3491-7 (Pbk)
ISBN-10:   0-7432-3491-X (Pbk)

To Some Ladies *at* Wantage

PREFACE

This story can be read by itself but is also a sequel to *Out of the Silent Planet* in which some account was given of Ransom's adventures in Mars—or, as its inhabitants call it, *Malacandra*. All the human characters in this book are purely fictitious and none of them is allegorical.

C.S.L.

I

As I left the railway station at Worchester and set out on the three-mile walk to Ransom's cottage, I reflected that no one on that platform could possibly guess the truth about the man I was going to visit. The flat heath which spread out before me (for the village lies all behind and to the north of the station) looked an ordinary heath. The gloomy five-o'clock sky was such as you might see on any autumn afternoon. The few houses and the clumps of red or yellowish trees were in no way remarkable. Who could imagine that a little farther on in that quiet landscape I should meet and shake by the hand a man who had lived and eaten and drunk in a world forty million miles distant from London, who had seen this Earth from where it looks like a mere point of green fire, and who had spoken face to face with a creature whose life began before our own planet was inhabitable?

For Ransom had met other things in Mars besides the Martians. He had met the creatures called *eldila,* and specially that great eldil who is the ruler of Mars or, in their speech, the *Oyarsa* of *Malacandra.* The eldila are very different from any planetary creatures. Their physical organism, if organism it can be called, is quite unlike either the human or the Martian. They do not eat, breed, breathe, or suffer natural death, and to that extent resemble thinking minerals more than they resemble anything we should recognise as an animal. Though they appear on planets and may even seem to our senses to be sometimes resident in them, the precise spatial location of an eldil at any moment presents great problems. They themselves regard space (or "Deep Heaven") as their true habitat, and the planets are to them not closed worlds but merely moving points—perhaps even interruptions—in what we know as the Solar System and they as the Field of Arbol.

At present I was going to see Ransom in answer to a wire which had said "Come down Thursday if possible. Business." I guessed what sort of business he meant, and that was why I kept on telling myself that it would be perfectly delightful to spend a night with Ransom and also kept on feeling that I was not enjoying the prospect as much as I ought to. It was the eldila that were my trouble. I could just get used to the fact that Ransom had been to Mars . . . but to have met an eldil, to have spoken with something whose life appeared to be practically unending. . . . Even the journey to Mars was bad enough. A man who has been in another world does not come back unchanged. One can't put the difference into words. When the man is a friend it may become painful: the old footing is not easy to recover. But much worse my growing conviction that, since his return, the eldila were not leaving him alone. Little things in his conversation, little mannerisms, accidental allusions which he made and then drew back with an awkward apology, all suggested that he was keeping strange company; that there were—well, Visitors— at that cottage.

As I plodded along the empty, unfenced road which runs across the middle of Worchester Common I tried to dispel my growing sense of *malaise* by analysing it. What, after all, was I afraid of? The moment I had put this question I regretted it. I was shocked to find that I had mentally used the word "afraid." Up till then I had tried to pretend that I was feeling only distaste, or embarrassment, or even boredom. But the mere word *afraid* had let the cat out of the bag. I realised now that my emotion was neither more, nor less, nor other, than Fear. And I realised that I was afraid of two things—afraid that sooner or later I myself might meet an eldil, and afraid that I might get "drawn in." I suppose every one knows this fear of getting "drawn in"—the moment at which a man realises that what had seemed mere speculations are on the point of landing him in the Communist Party or the Christian Church—the sense that a door has just slammed and left him on the inside. The thing was such sheer bad luck. Ransom himself had been taken to Mars (or Malacandra) against his will and almost by accident, and I had become connected with his affair by another accident. Yet here we were both getting more and more involved in what I could only describe as interplanetary politics. As to my intense wish never to come into contact with the eldila myself, I am not sure whether I can make you understand it. It was something more than a prudent desire to avoid creatures alien in kind, very powerful, and very intelligent. The truth was that all I heard about them served to connect two things which one's mind tends to keep separate, and that connecting gave one a sort of shock. We tend to think about non-human intelligences in two distinct categories which we label "scientific" and "supernatural" respectively. We think, in one mood, of Mr. Wells' Martians (very unlike the real Malacandrians, by the bye), or his Selenites. In quite a different mood we let our minds loose on the possibility of angels, ghosts, fairies, and the like. But the very moment we are compelled to recognise a creature in either class as *real* the distinction begins to get blurred: and when it is a creature like an eldil the distinction vanishes altogether. These things were not animals—to that extent one had to classify them with the second group; but they had some kind of material vehicle whose presence could (in principle) be scientifically verified. To that extent they belonged to the first group. The distinction between natural and supernatural, in fact, broke down; and when it had done so, one realised how great a comfort it had been—how it had eased the burden of intolerable strangeness which this universe imposes on us by dividing it into two halves and encouraging the mind never to think of both in the same context. What price we may have paid for this comfort in the way of false security and accepted confusion of thought is another matter.

"This is a long, dreary road," I thought to myself. "Thank goodness I haven't anything to carry." And then, with a start of realisation, I remembered that I ought to be carrying a pack, containing my things for the night. I swore to myself. I must have left the thing in the train. Will you believe me when I say that my immediate impulse was to turn back to the station and "do something about it"? Of course there was nothing to be done which could not equally well be done by ringing up from the cottage. That train, with my pack in it, must by this time be miles away.

I realise that now as clearly as you do. But at the moment it seemed perfectly obvious that I must retrace my steps, and I had indeed begun to do so before reason or conscience awoke and set me once more plodding forwards. In doing this I discovered more clearly than before how very little I wanted to do it. It was such hard work that I felt as if I were walking against a headwind; but in fact it was one of those still, dead evenings when no twig stirs, and beginning to be a little foggy.

The farther I went the more impossible I found it to think about anything except these eldila. What, after all, did Ransom really know about them? By his own account the sorts which he had met did not usually visit our own planet—or had only begun to do so since his return from Mars. We had eldila of our own, he said, Tellurian eldils, but they were of a different kind and mostly hostile to man. That, in fact, was why our world was cut off from communication with the other planets. He described us as being in a state of siege, as being, in fact, an enemy-occupied territory, held down by eldils who were at war both with us and with the eldils of "Deep Heaven," or "space." Like the bacteria on the microscopic level, so these co-inhabiting pests on the macroscopic permeate our whole life invisibly and are the real explanation of that fatal bent which is the main lesson of history. If all this were true, then, of course, we should welcome the fact that eldila of a better kind had at last broken the frontier (it is, they say, at the Moon's orbit) and were beginning to visit us. Always assuming that Ransom's account was the correct one.

A nasty idea occurred to me. Why should not Ransom be a dupe? If something from outer space were trying to invade our planet, what better smoke-screen could it put up than this very story of Ransom's? Was there the slightest evidence, after all, for the existence of the supposed maleficent eldils on this earth? How if my friend were the unwitting bridge, the Trojan Horse, whereby some possible invader were effecting its landing on Tellus? And then once more, just as when I had discovered that I had no pack, the impulse to go no farther returned to me. "Go back, go back," it whispered to me, "send him a wire, tell him you were ill, say you'll come some other time—anything." The strength of the feeling astonished me. I stood still for a few moments telling myself not to be a fool, and when I finally resumed my walk I was wondering whether this might be the beginning of a nervous breakdown. No sooner had this idea occurred to me than it also became a new reason for not visiting Ransom. Obviously, I wasn't fit for any such jumpy "business" as his telegram almost certainly referred to. I wasn't even fit to spend an ordinary week-end away from home. My only sensible course was to turn back at once and get safe home, before I lost my memory or became hysterical, and to put myself in the hands of a doctor. It was sheer madness to go on.

I was now coming to the end of the heath and going down a small hill, with a copse on my left and some apparently deserted industrial buildings on my right. At the bottom the evening mist was partly thick. "They call it a breakdown *at first*," I thought. Wasn't there some mental disease in which quite ordinary objects looked to the patient unbelievably ominous? . . . looked, in fact, just as that abandoned factory looks to me now? Great bulbous shapes of cement, strange brickwork bogeys, glowered at me over dry scrubby grass pock-marked with grey pools and intersected with the remains of a light railway. I was reminded of things which Ransom had seen in that other world: only there, they were people. Long spindle-like giants whom he called Sorns. What made it worse was that he regarded them as good people—very much nicer, in fact, than our own race. He was in league with them! How did I know he was even a dupe? He might be something worse . . . and again I came to a standstill.

The reader, not knowing Ransom, will not understand how contrary to all reason this idea was. The rational part of my mind, even at that moment, knew perfectly well that even if the whole universe were crazy and hostile, Ransom was sane and wholesome and honest. And this part of my mind in the end sent me forward—but with a reluctance and a difficulty I can hardly put into words. What enabled me to go on was the knowledge (deep down inside me) that I was getting nearer at every stride to the one friend: but I *felt* that I was getting nearer to the one enemy—the traitor, the sorcerer, the man in league with "them" . . . walking into the trap with my eyes open, like a fool. "They call it a breakdown at first," said my mind, "and send you to a nursing home; later on they move you to an asylum."

I was past the dead factory now, down in the fog, where it was very cold. Then came a moment—the first one—of absolute terror and I had to bite my lips to keep myself from screaming. It was only a cat that had run across the road, but I found myself completely unnerved. "Soon you will really be screaming," said my inner tormentor, "running round and round, screaming, and you won't be able to stop it."

There was a little empty house by the side of the road, with most of the windows boarded up and one staring like the eye of a dead fish. Please understand that at ordinary times the idea of a "haunted house" means no more to me than it does to you. No more; but also, no less. At that moment it was nothing so definite as the thought of a ghost that came to me. It was just the *word* "haunted." "Haunted" . . . "haunting" . . . what a quality there is in that first syllable! Would not a child who had never heard the word before and did not know its meaning shudder at the mere sound if, as the day was closing in, it heard one of its elders say to another "This house is haunted"?

At last I came to the cross-roads by the little Wesleyan chapel where I had to turn to the left under the beech trees. I ought to be seeing the lights from Ransom's windows by now—or was it past black-out time? My watch had stopped, and I didn't know. It was dark enough but that might be due to the fog and the trees. It wasn't the dark I was afraid of, you understand. We have all known times when inanimate objects seemed to have almost a facial expression, and it was the expression of this bit of road which I did not like. "It's not true," said my mind, "that people who are really going mad never think they're going mad." Suppose that real insanity had chosen this place in which to begin? In that case, of course, the black enmity of those dripping trees—their horrible expectancy—would be a hallucination. But that did not make it any better. To think that the spectre you see is an illusion does not rob him of his terrors: it simply adds the further terror of madness itself—and then on top of that the horrible surmise that those whom the rest call mad have, all along, been the only people who see the world as it really is.

This was upon me now. I staggered on into the cold and the darkness, already half convinced that I must be entering what is called Madness. But each moment my opinion about sanity changed. Had it ever been more than a convention—a comfortable set of blinkers, an agreed mode of wishful thinking, which excluded from our view the full strangeness and malevolence of the universe we are compelled to inhabit? The things I had begun to know during the last few months of my acquaintance with Ransom already amounted to more than "sanity" would admit; but I had come much too far to dismiss them as unreal. I doubted his interpretation, or his good faith. I did not doubt the existence of the things he had met in Mars—the Pfifltriggi, the Hrossa, and the Sorns—nor of these interplanetary eldila. I did not even doubt the reality of that mysterious being whom the eldila call Maleldil and to whom they appear to give a total obedience such as no Tellurian dictator can command. I knew what Ransom supposed Maleldil to be.

Surely that was the cottage. It was very well blacked-out. A childish, whining thought arose on my mind: why was he not out at the gate to welcome me? An even more childish thought followed it. Perhaps he *was* in the garden waiting for me, hiding. Perhaps he would jump on me from behind. Perhaps I should see a figure that looked like Ransom standing with its back to me and when I spoke to it, it would turn round and show a face that was not human at all. . . .

I have naturally no wish to enlarge on this phase of my story. The state of mind I was in was one which I look back on with humiliation. I would have passed it over if I did not think that some account of it was necessary for a full understanding of what follows—and, perhaps, of some other things as well. At all events, I *can't* really describe how I reached the front door of the cottage. Somehow or other, despite the loathing and dismay that pulled me back and a sort of invisible wall of resistance that met me in the face, fighting for each step, and almost shrieking as a harmless spray of the hedge touched my face, I managed to get through the gate and up the little path. And there I was, drumming on the door and wringing the handle and shouting to him to let me in as if my life depended on it.

There was no reply—not a sound except the echo of the sounds I had been making myself. There was only something white fluttering on the knocker. I guessed, of course, that it was a note. In striking a match to read it by, I discovered how very shaky my hands had become; and when the match went out I realised how dark the evening had grown. After several attempts I read the thing. "Sorry. Had to go up to Cambridge. Shan't be back till the late train. Eatables in larder and bed made up in your usual room. Don't wait supper for me unless you feel like it—E. R." And immediately the impulse to retreat, which had already assailed me several times, leaped upon me with a sort of demoniac violence. Here was my retreat left open, positively inviting me. Now was my chance. If anyone expected me to go into that house and sit there alone for several hours, they were mistaken! But then, as the thought of the return journey began to take shape in my mind, I faltered. The idea of setting out to traverse the avenue of beech trees again (it was really dark now) with this house behind me (one had the absurd feeling that it could follow one) was not attractive. And then, I hope, something better came into my mind—some rag of sanity and some reluctance to let Ransom down. At least I could try the door to see if it were really unlocked. I did. And it was. Next moment, I hardly know how, I found myself inside and let it slam behind me.

It was quite dark, and warm. I groped a few paces forward, hit my shin violently against something, and fell. I sat still for a few seconds nursing my leg. I thought I knew the layout of Ransom's hall-sitting-room pretty well and couldn't imagine what I had blundered into. Presently I groped in my pocket, got out my matches, and tried to strike a light. The head of the match flew off. I stamped on it and sniffed to make sure it was not smouldering on the carpet. As soon as I sniffed I became aware of a strange smell in the room. I could not for the life of me make out what it was. It had an unlikeness to ordinary domestic smells as great as that of some chemicals, but it was not a chemical kind of smell at all. Then I struck another match. It flickered and went out almost at once—not unnaturally, since I was sitting on the door-mat and there are few front doors even in better built houses than Ransom's country cottage which do not admit a draught. I had seen nothing by it except the palm of my own hand hollowed in an attempt to guard the flame. Obviously I must get away from the door. I rose gingerly and felt my way forward. I came at once to an obstacle—something smooth and very cold that rose a little higher than my knees. As I touched it I realised that it was the source of the smell. I groped my way along this to the left and finally came to the end of it. It seemed to present several surfaces and I couldn't picture the shape. It was not a table, for it had no top. One's hand groped along the rim of a kind of low wall—the thumb on the outside and the fingers down inside the enclosed space. If it had felt like wood I should have supposed it to be a large packing-case. But it was not wood. I thought for a moment that it was wet, but soon decided that I was mistaking coldness for moisture. When I reached the end of it I struck my third match.

I saw something white and semi-transparent—rather like ice. A great big thing, very long: a kind of box, an open box: and of a disquieting shape which I did not immediately recognise. It was big enough to put a man into. Then I took a step back, lifting the lighted match higher to get a more comprehensive view, and instantly tripped over something behind me. I found myself sprawling in darkness, not on the carpet, but on more of the cold substance with the odd smell. How many of the infernal things were there?

I was just preparing to rise again and hunt systematically round the room for a candle when I heard Ransom's name pronounced; and almost, but not quite, simultaneously I saw the thing I had feared so long to see. I heard Ransom's name pronounced: but I should not like to say I heard a voice pronounce it. The sound was quite astonishingly unlike a voice. It was perfectly articulate: it was even, I suppose, rather beautiful. But it was, if you understand me, inorganic. We feel the difference between animal voices (including those of the human animal) and all other noises pretty clearly, I fancy, though it is hard to define. Blood and lungs and the warm, moist cavity of the mouth are somehow indicated in every Voice. Here they were not. The two syllables sounded more as if they were played on an instrument than as if they were spoken: and yet they did not sound mechanical either. A machine is something we make out of natural materials; this was more as if rock or crystal or light had spoken of itself. And it went through me from chest to groin like the thrill that goes through you when you think you have lost your hold while climbing a cliff.

That was what I heard. What I saw was simply a very faint rod or pillar of light. I don't think it made a circle of light either on the floor or the ceiling, but I am not sure of this. It certainly had very little power of illuminating its surroundings. So far, all is plain sailing. But it had two other characteristics which are less easy to grasp. One was its colour. Since I saw the thing I must obviously have seen it either white or coloured; but no efforts of my memory can conjure up the faintest image of what that colour was. I try blue, and gold, and violet, and red, but none of them will fit. How it is possible to have a visual experience which immediately and ever after becomes impossible to remember, I do not attempt to explain. The other was its angle. It was not at right angles to the floor. But as soon as I have said this, I hasten to add that this way of putting it is a later reconstruction. What one actually felt at the moment was that the column of light was vertical but the floor was not horizontal—the whole room seemed to have heeled over as if it were on board ship. The impression, however produced, was that this creature had reference to some horizontal, to some whole system of directions, based outside the Earth, and that its mere presence imposed that alien system on me and abolished the terrestrial horizontal.

I had no doubt at all that I was seeing an eldil, and little doubt that I was seeing the archon of Mars, the Oyarsa of Malacandra. And now that the thing had happened I was no longer in a condition of abject panic. My sensations were, it is true, in some ways very unpleasant. The fact that it was quite obviously not organic—the knowledge that intelligence was somehow located in this homogeneous cylinder of light but not related to it as our consciousness is related to our brains and nerves—was profoundly disturbing.[1] It would not fit into our categories. The response which we ordinarily make to a living creature and that which we make to an inanimate object were here both equally inappropriate. On the other hand, all those doubts which I had felt before I entered the cottage as to whether these creatures were friend or foe, and whether Ransom were a pioneer or a dupe, had for the moment vanished. My fear was now of another kind. I felt sure that the creature was what we call "good," but I wasn't sure whether I liked "goodness" so much as I had supposed. This is a very terrible experience. As long as what you are afraid of is something evil, you may still hope that the good may come to your rescue. But suppose you struggle through to the good and find that it also is dreadful? How if food itself turns out to be the very thing you can't eat, and home the very place you can't live, and your very comforter the person who makes you uncomfortable? Then, indeed, there is no rescue possible: the last card has been played. For a

---

1. In the text I naturally keep to what I thought and felt at the time, since this alone is first-hand evidence: but there is obviously room for much further speculation about the form in which *eldila* appear to our senses. The only serious considerations of the problem so far are to be sought in the early seventeenth century. As a starting point for future investigation I recommend the following from Natvilcius (*De Aethereo at aerio Corpore,* Basel. 1627, II. xii.); *liquet simplicem flammam sensibus nostris subjectam non esse corpus proprie dictum angeli vel daemonis, sed potius aut illius corporis sensorium aut superficiem corporis in coelesti dispositione locorum supra cogitationes humanas existentis.* ("It appears that the homogeneous flame perceived by our senses is not the body, properly so called, of an angel or daemon, but rather either the sensorium of that body or the surface of a body which exists after a manner beyond our conception in the celestial frame of special references.") By the "celestial frame of references" I take him to mean what we should now call "multi-dimensional space." Not, of course, that Natvilcius knew anything about multidimensional geometry, but that he had reached empirically what mathematics has since reached on theoretical grounds.

second or two I was nearly in that condition. Here at last was a bit of that world from beyond the world, which I had always supposed that I loved and desired, breaking through and appearing to my senses: and I didn't like it, I wanted it to go away. I wanted every possible distance, gulf, curtain, blanket, and barrier to be placed between it and me. But I did not fall quite into the gulf. Oddly enough my very sense of helplessness saved me and steadied me. For now I was quite obviously "drawn in." The struggle was over. The next decision did not lie with me.

Then, like a noise from a different world, came the opening of the door and the sound of boots on the door-mat, and I saw, silhouetted against the greyness of the night in the open doorway, a figure which I recognised as Ransom. The speaking which was not a voice came again out of the rod of light, and Ransom, instead of moving, stood still and answered it. Both speeches were in a strange polysyllabic language which I had not heard before. I make no attempt to excuse the feelings which awoke in me when I heard the unhuman sound addressing my friend and my friend answering it in the unhuman language. They are, in fact, inexcusable; but if you think they are improbable at such a juncture, I must tell you plainly that you have read neither history nor your own heart to much effect. They were feelings of resentment, horror, and jealousy. It was in my mind to shout out, "Leave your familiar alone, you damned magician, and attend to Me."

What I actually said was, "Oh, Ransom. Thank God you've come."

2

The door was slammed (for the second time that night) and after a moment's groping Ransom had found and lit a candle. I glanced quickly round and could see no one but ourselves. The most noticeable thing in the room was the big white object. I recognised the shape well enough this time. It was a large coffin-shaped casket, open. On the floor beside it lay its lid, and it was doubtless this that I had tripped over. Both were made of the same white material, like ice, but more cloudy and less shining.

"By Jove, I'm glad to see you," said Ransom, advancing and shaking hands with me. "I'd hoped to be able to meet you at the station, but everything has had to be arranged in such a hurry and I found at the last moment that I'd got to go up to Cambridge. I never intended to leave you to make *that* journey alone." Then, seeing, I suppose, that I was still staring at him rather stupidly, he added, "I say—you're *all right,* aren't you? You got through the barrage without any damage?"

"The barrage?—I don't understand."

"I was thinking you would have met some difficulties in getting here."

"Oh, *that!*" said I. "You mean it wasn't just my nerves? There really was something in the way?"

"Yes. They didn't want you to get here. I was afraid something of the sort might happen but there was no time to do anything about it. I was pretty sure you'd get through somehow."

"By *they* you mean the others—our own eldila?"

"Of course. They've got wind of what's on hand. . . ."

I interrupted him. "To tell you the truth, Ransom," I said, "I'm getting more worried every day about the whole business. It came into my head as I was on my way here——"

"Oh, they'll put all sorts of things into your head if you let them," said Ransom lightly. "The best plan is to take no notice and keep straight on. Don't try to answer them. They like drawing you into an interminable argument."

"But, look here," said I. "This isn't child's play. Are you quite certain that this Dark Lord, this depraved Oyarsa of Tellus, really exists? Do you know for certain either that there are two sides, or which side is ours?"

He fixed me suddenly with one of his mild, but strangely formidable, glances.

"You are in *real* doubt about either, are you?" he asked.

"No," said I, after a pause, and felt rather ashamed.

"That's all right, then," said Ransom cheerfully. "Now let's get some supper and I'll explain as we go along."

"What's that coffin affair?" I asked as we moved into the kitchen.

"That is what I'm to travel in."

"Ransom!" I exclaimed. "He—it—the eldil—is not going to take you back to Malacandra?"

"Don't!" said he. "Oh, Lewis, you don't understand. Take me back to Malacandra? If only he would! I'd give anything I possess . . . just to look down one of those gorges again and see the blue, blue water winding in and out among the woods. Or to be up on top—to see a Sorn go gliding along the slopes. Or to be back there of an evening when Jupiter was rising, too bright to look at, and all the asteroids like a Milky Way, with each star in it as bright as Venus looks from Earth! And the smells! It is hardly ever out of my mind. You'd expect it to be worse at night when Malacandra is up and I can actually see it. But it isn't then that I get the real twinge. It's on hot summer days—looking up at the deep blue and that thinking that *in there,* millions of miles deep where I can never, never get back to it, there's a place I know, and flowers at that very moment growing over Meldilorn, and friends of mine, going about their business, who would welcome me back. No. No such luck. It's not Malacandra I'm being sent to. It's Perelandra."

"That's what we call Venus, isn't it?"

"Yes."

"And you say you're being sent."

"Yes. If you remember, before I left Malacandra the Oyarsa hinted to me that my going there at all might be the beginning of a whole new phase in the life of the Solar System—the Field of Arbol. It might mean, he said, that the isolation of our world, the siege, was beginning to draw to an end."

"Yes. I remember."

"Well, it really does look as if something of the sort were afoot. For one thing, the two sides, as you call them, have begun to appear much more clearly, much less mixed, here on Earth, in our own human affairs—to show in something a little more like their true colours."

"I see that all right."

"The other thing is this. The black archon—our own bent Oyarsa—is meditating some sort of attack on Perelandra."

"But is he at large like that in the Solar System? Can he get there?"

"That's just the point. He can't get there in his own person, in his own photosome or whatever we should call it. As you know, he was driven back within these bounds centuries before any human life existed on our planet. If he ventured to show himself outside the Moon's orbit he'd be driven back again—by main force. That would be a different kind of war. You or I could contribute no more to it than a flea could contribute to the defence of Moscow. No. He must be attempting Perelandra in some different way."

"And where do you come in?"

"Well—simply I've been ordered there."

"By the—by Oyarsa, you mean?"

"No. The order comes from much higher up. They all do, you know, in the long run."

"And what have you got to do when you get there?"

"I haven't been told."

"You are just part of the Oyarsa's *entourage?*"

"Oh, no. He isn't going to be there. He is to transport me to Venus—to deliver me there. After that, as far as I know, I shall be alone."

"But, look here, Ransom—I mean . . ." my voice trailed away.

"I know!" said he with one of his singularly disarming smiles. "You are feeling the absurdity of it. Dr. Elwin Ransom setting out single-handed to combat powers and principalities. You may even be wondering if I've got megalomania."

"I didn't mean that quite," said I.

"Oh, but I think you did. At any rate that is what I have been feeling myself ever since that thing was sprung on me. But when you come to think of it, is it odder than what all of us have to do every day? When the Bible used that very expression about fighting with principalities and powers and depraved hypersomatic beings at great heights (our translation is very misleading at that point, by the way) it meant that quite ordinary people were to do the fighting."

"Oh, I dare say," said I. "But that's rather different. That refers to a moral conflict."

Ransom threw back his head and laughed. "Oh, Lewis, Lewis," he said, "you are inimitable, simply inimitable!"

"Say what you like, Ransom, there *is* a difference."

"Yes. There is. But not a difference that makes it megalomania to think that any of us might have to fight either way. I'll tell you how I look at it. Haven't you noticed how in our own little war here on earth, there are different phases, and while any one phase is going on people get into the habit of thinking and behaving as if it was going to be permanent? But really the thing is changing under your hands all the time, and neither your assets nor your dangers this year are the same as the year before. Now your idea that ordinary people will never have to meet the Dark Eldila in any form except a psychological or moral form—as temptations or the like—is simply an idea that held good for a certain phase of the cosmic war: the phase of the great siege, the phase which gave to our planet its name of Thulcandra, the *silent* planet. But supposing that phase is passing? In the next phase it may be anyone's job to meet them . . . well, in some quite different mode."

"I see."

"Don't imagine I've been selected to go to Perelandra because I'm anyone in particular. One never can see, or not till long afterwards, why *any* one was selected for *any* job. And when one does, it is usually some reason that leaves no room for vanity. Certainly, it is never for what the man himself would have regarded as his chief qualifications. I rather fancy I am being sent because those two blackguards who kidnapped me and took me to Malacandra, did something which they never intended: namely, gave a human being a chance to learn that language."

"What language do you mean?"

"*Hressa-Hlab,* of course. The language I learned in Malacandra."

"But surely you don't imagine they will speak the same language on Venus?"

"Didn't I tell you about that?" said Ransom, leaning forward. We were now at table and had nearly finished our cold meat and beer and tea. "I'm surprised I didn't, for I found out two or three months ago, and scientifically it is one of the most interesting things about the whole affair. It appears we were quite mistaken in thinking *Hressa-Hlab* the peculiar speech of Mars. It is really what may be called Old Solar, *Hlab-Eribol-ef-Cordi.*"

"What on earth do you mean?"

"I mean that there was originally a common speech for all rational creatures inhabiting the planets of our system: those that were ever inhabited, I mean—what the eldils call the Low Worlds. Most of them, of course, have never been inhabited and never will be. At least not what we'd call inhabited. That original speech was lost on Thulcandra, our own world, when our whole tragedy took place. No human language now known in the world is descended from it."

"But what about the other two languages on Mars?"

"I admit I don't understand about them. One thing I do know, and I believe I could prove it on purely philological grounds. They are incomparably less ancient than *Hressa-Hlab,* specially *Surnibur,* the speech of the Sorns. I believe it could be shown that *Surnibur* is, by Malacandrian standards, quite a modern development. I doubt if its birth can be put further back than a date which would fall within our Cambrian Period."

"And you think you will find *Hressa-Hlab,* or Old Solar, spoken on Venus?"

"Yes. I shall arrive knowing the language. It saves a lot of trouble— though, as a philologist I find it rather disappointing."

"But you've no idea what you are to do, or what conditions you will find?"

"No idea at all what I'm to do. There are jobs, you know, where it is essential that one should *not* know too much beforehand . . . things one might have to say which one couldn't say effectively if one had prepared them. As to conditions, well, I don't know much. It will be warm: I'm to go naked. Our astronomers don't know anything about the surface of Perelandra at all. The outer layer of her atmosphere is too thick. The main problem, apparently, is whether she revolves on her own axis or not, and at what speed. There are two schools of thought. There's a man called Schiaparelli who thinks she revolves once on herself in the same time it takes her to go once round Arbol—I mean, the Sun. The other people think she revolves on her own axis once in every twenty-three hours. That's one of the things I shall find out."

"If Schiaparelli is right there'd be perpetual day on one side of her and perpetual night on the other?"

He nodded, musing. "It'd be a funny frontier," he said presently. "Just think of it. You'd come to a country of eternal twilight, getting colder and darker every mile you went. And then presently you wouldn't be able to go further because there'd be no more air. I wonder can you stand in the day, just on the right side of the frontier, and look *into* the night which you can never reach? And perhaps see a star or two—the only place you *could* see them, for of course in the Day-Lands they would never be visible. . . . Of course if they have a scientific civilisation they may have diving-suits or things like submarines on wheels for going into the Night."

His eyes sparkled, and even I who had been mainly thinking of how I should miss him and wondering what chances there were of my ever seeing him again, felt a vicarious thrill of wonder and of longing to know. Presently he spoke again.

"You haven't yet asked me where *you* come in," he said.

"Do you mean I'm to go too?" said I, with a thrill of exactly the opposite kind.

"Not at all. I mean you are to pack me up, and to stand by to unpack me when I return—if all goes well."

"Pack you? Oh, I'd forgotten about that coffin affair. Ransom, how on earth are you going to travel in that thing? What's the motive power? What about air—and food—and water? There's only just room for you to lie in it."

"The Oyarsa of Malacandra himself will be the motive power. He will simply move it to Venus. Don't ask me how. I have no idea what organs or instruments they use. But a creature who has kept a planet in its orbit for several billions of years will be able to manage a packing-case!"

"But what will you eat? How will you breathe?"

"He tells me I shall need to do neither. I shall be in some state of suspended animation, as far as I can make out. I can't understand him when he tries to describe it. But that's his affair."

"Do you feel quite happy about it?" said I, for a sort of horror was beginning once more to creep over me.

"If you mean, Does my reason accept the view that he will (accidents apart) deliver me safe on the surface of Perelandra?—the answer is Yes," said Ransom. "If you mean, Do my nerves and my imagination respond to this view?—I'm afraid the answer is No. One can believe in anæsthetics and yet feel in a panic when they actually put the mask over your face. I think I feel as a man who believes in the future life feels when he is taken out to face a firing party. Perhaps it's good practice."

"And I'm to pack you into that accursed thing?" said I.

"Yes," said Ransom. "That's the first step. We must get out into the garden as soon as the sun is up and point it so that there are no trees or buildings in the way. Across the cabbage bed will do. Then I get in—with a bandage across my eyes, for those walls won't keep out all the sunlight once I'm beyond the air—and you screw me down. After that, I think you'll just see it glide off."

"And then?"

"Well, then comes the difficult part. You must hold yourself in readiness to come down here again the moment you are summoned, to take off the lid and let me out when I return."

"When do you expect to return?"

"Nobody can say. Six months—a year—twenty years. That's the trouble. I'm afraid I'm laying a pretty heavy burden on you."

"I might be dead."

"I know. I'm afraid part of your burden is to select a successor: at once, too. There are four or five people whom we can trust."

"What will the summons be?"

"Oyarsa will give it. It won't be mistakable for anything else. You needn't bother about that side of it. One other point. I've no particular reason to suppose I shall come back wounded. But just in case—if you can find a doctor whom we can let into the secret, it might be just as well to bring him with you when you come down to let me out."

"Would Humphrey do?"

"The very man. And now for some more personal matters. I've had to leave you out of my will, and I'd like you to know why."

"My dear chap, I never thought about your will till this moment."

"Of course not. But I'd like to have left you something. The reason I haven't, is this. I'm going to disappear. It is possible I may not come back. It's just conceivable there might be a murder trial, and if so one can't be too careful. I mean, for your sake. And now for one or two other private arrangements."

We laid our heads together and for a long time we talked about those matters which one usually discusses with relatives and not with friends. I got to know a lot more about Ransom than I had known before, and from the number of odd people whom he recommended to my care, "If ever I happened to be able to do anything," I came to realise the extent and intimacy of his charities. With every sentence the shadow of approaching separation and a kind of graveyard gloom began to settle more emphatically upon us. I found myself noticing and loving all sorts of little mannerisms and expressions in him such as we notice always in a woman we love, but notice in a man only as the last hours of his leave run out or the date of the probably fatal operation draws near. I felt our nature's incurable incredulity; and could hardly believe that what was now so close, so tangible and (in a sense) so much at my command, would in a few hours be wholly inaccessible, an image—soon, even an elusive image—in my memory. And finally a sort of shyness fell between us because each knew what the other was feeling. It had got very cold.

"We must be going soon," said Ransom.

"Not till he—the Oyarsa—comes back," said I—though, indeed, now that the thing was so near I wished it to be over.

"He has never left us," said Ransom, "he has been in the cottage all the time."

"You mean he has been waiting in the next room all these hours?"

"Not waiting. They never have that experience. You and I are conscious of waiting, because we have a body that grows tired or restless, and therefore a sense of cumulative duration. Also we can distinguish duties and spare time and therefore have a conception of leisure. It is not like that with him. He has been here all this time, but you can no more call it *waiting* than you can call the whole of his existence *waiting*. You might as well say that a tree in a wood was waiting, or the sunlight waiting on the side of a hill." Ransom yawned. "I'm tired," he said, "and so are you. I shall sleep well in that coffin of mine. Come. Let us lug it out."

We went in to the next room and I was made to stand before the featureless flame which did not wait but just was, and there, with Ransom as our interpreter, I was in some fashion presented and with my own tongue sworn in to this great business. Then we took down the blackout and let in the grey, comfortless morning. Between us we carried out the casket and the lid, so cold they seemed to burn our fingers. There was a heavy dew on the grass and my feet were soaked through at once. The eldil was with us, outside there, on the little lawn; hardly visible to my eyes at all in the daylight. Ransom showed me the clasps of the lid and how it was to be fastened on, and then there was some miserable hanging about, and then the final moment when he went back into the house and reappeared, naked; a tall, white, shivering, weary scarecrow of a man at that pale, raw hour. When he had got into the hideous box he made me tie a thick black bandage round his eyes and head. Then he lay down. I had no thoughts of the planet Venus now and no real belief that I should see him again. If I had dared I would have gone back on the whole scheme: but the other thing—the creature that did not wait—was there, and the fear of it was upon me. With feelings that have since often returned to me in nightmare I fastened the cold lid down on top of the living man and stood back. Next moment I was alone. I didn't see how it went. I went back indoors and was sick. A few hours later I shut up the cottage and returned to Oxford.

Then the months went past and grew to a year and a little more than a year, and we had raids and bad news and hopes deferred and all the earth became full of darkness and cruel habitations, till the night when Oyarsa came to me again. After that there was a journey in haste for Humphrey and me, standings in crowded corridors and waitings at small hours on windy platforms, and finally the moment when we stood in clear early sunlight in the little wilderness of deep weeds which Ransom's garden had now become and saw a black speck against the sunrise and then, almost silently, the casket had glided down between us. We flung ourselves upon it and had the lid off in about a minute and a half.

"Good God! All smashed to bits," I cried at my first glance of the interior.

"Wait a moment," said Humphrey. And as he spoke the figure in the coffin began to stir and then sat up, shaking off as it did so a mass of red things which had covered its head and shoulders and which I had momentarily mistaken for ruin and blood. As they streamed off him and were caught in the wind I perceived them to be flowers. He blinked for a second or so, then called us by our names, gave each of us a hand, and stepped out on the grass.

"How are you both?" he said. "You're looking rather knocked up."

I was silent for a moment, astonished at the form which had risen from that narrow house—almost a new Ransom, glowing with health and rounded with muscle and seemingly ten years younger. In the old days he had been beginning to show a few grey hairs; but now the beard which swept his chest was pure gold.

"Hullo, you've cut your foot," said Humphrey: and I saw now that Ransom was bleeding from the heel.

"Ugh, it's cold down here," said Ransom. "I hope you've got the boiler going and some hot water—and some clothes."

"Yes," said I, as we followed him into the house. "Humphrey thought of all that. I'm afraid I shouldn't have."

Ransom was now in the bathroom, with the door open, veiled in clouds of steam, and Humphrey and I were talking to him from the landing. Our questions were more numerous than he could answer.

"That idea of Schiaparelli's is all wrong," he shouted. "They have an ordinary day and night there," and "No, my heel doesn't hurt—or, at least, it's only just begun to," and "Thanks, any old clothes. Leave them on the chair" and "No thanks. I don't somehow feel like bacon or eggs or anything of that kind. No fruit, you say? Oh well, no matter. Bread or porridge or something" and "I'll be down in five minutes now."

He kept on asking if we were really all right and seemed to think we looked ill. I went down to get the breakfast, and Humphrey said he would stay and examine and dress the cut on Ransom's heel. When he rejoined me I was looking at one of the red petals which had come in the casket.

"That's rather a beautiful flower," said I, handing it to him.

"Yes," said Humphrey, studying it with the hands and eyes of a scientist. "What extraordinary delicacy! It makes an English violet seem like a coarse weed."

"Let's put some of them in water."

"Not much good. Look—it's withered already."

"How do you think he is?"

"Tip-top general. But I don't quite like that heel. He says the hæmorrhage has been going on for a long time."

Ransom joined us, fully dressed, and I poured out the tea. And all that day and far into the night he told us the story that follows.

3

What it is like to travel in a celestial coffin was a thing that Ransom never described. He said he couldn't. But odd hints about that journey have come out at one time or another when he was talking of quite different matters.

According to his own account he was not what we call conscious, and yet at the same time the experience was a very positive one with a quality of its own. On one occasion, someone had been talking about "seeing life" in the popular sense of knocking about the world and getting to know people, and B. who was present (and who is an Anthroposophist) said something I can't quite remember about "seeing life" in a very different sense. I think he was referring to some system of meditation which claimed to make "the form of Life itself" visible to the inner eye. At any rate Ransom let himself in for a long cross-examination by failing to conceal the fact that he attached some very definite idea to this. He even went so far—under extreme pressure—as to say that life appeared to him, in that condition, as a "coloured shape." Asked "what colour," he gave a curious look and could only say "what colours! yes, what colours!" But then he spoiled it all by adding, "of course it wasn't colour at all really. I mean, not what we'd call colour," and shutting up completely for the rest of the evening. Another hint came out when a sceptical friend of ours called McPhee was arguing against the Christian doctrine of the resurrection of the human body. I was his victim at the moment and he was pressing on me in his Scots way with such questions as "So you think you're going to have guts and palate for ever in a world where there'll be no eating, and genital organs in a world without copulation? Man, ye'll have a grand time of it!" when Ransom suddenly burst out with great excitement, "Oh, don't you see, you ass, that there's a difference between a trans-sensuous life and a non-sensuous life?" That, of course, directed McPhee's fire to him. What emerged was that in Ransom's opinion the present functions and appetites of the body would disappear, not because they were atrophied but because they were, as he said, "engulfed." He used the word "trans-sexual" I remember and began to hunt about for some similar words to apply to eating (after rejecting "trans-gastronomic"), and since he was not the only philologist present, that diverted the conversation into different channels. But I am pretty sure he was thinking of something he had experienced on his voyage to Venus. But perhaps the most mysterious thing he ever said about it was this. I was questioning him on the subject—which he doesn't often allow—and had incautiously said, "Of course I realise it's all rather too vague for you to put into words," when he took me up rather sharply, for such a patient man, by saying, "On the contrary, it is words that are vague. The reason why the thing can't be expressed is that it's too *definite* for language." And that is about all I can tell you of his journey. One thing is certain, that he came back from Venus even more changed than he had come back from Mars. But of course that may have been because of what happened to him after his landing.

To that landing, as Ransom narrated it to me, I will now proceed. He seems to have been awakened (if that is the right word) from his indescribable celestial state by the sensation of falling—in other words, when he was near enough to Venus to feel Venus as something in the downward direction. The next thing he noticed was that he was very warm on one side and very cold on the other, though neither sensation was so extreme as to be really painful. Anyway, both were soon swallowed up in the prodigious white light from below which began to penetrate through the semi-opaque walls of the casket. This steadily increased and became distressing in spite of the fact that his eyes were protected. There is no doubt this was the *albedo,* the outer veil of very dense atmosphere with which Venus is surrounded and which reflects the sun's rays with intense power. For some obscure reason he was not conscious, as he had been on his approach to Mars, of his own rapidly increasing weight. When the white light was just about to become unbearable, it disappeared altogether, and very soon after the cold on his left side and the heat on his right began to decrease and to be replaced by an equable warmth. I take it he was now in the outer layer of the Perelandrian atmosphere—at first in a pale, and later in a tinted, twilight. The prevailing colour, as far as he could see through the sides of the casket, was golden or coppery. By this time he must have been very near the surface of the planet, with the length of the casket at right angles to that surface—falling feet downwards like a man in a lift. The sensation of falling—helpless as he was and unable to move his arms—became frightening. Then suddenly there came a great green darkness, an unidentifiable noise—the first message from the new world—and a marked drop in temperature. He seemed now to have assumed a horizontal position and also, to his great surprise, to be moving not downwards but upwards; though, at the moment, he judged this to be an illusion. All this time he must have been making faint, unconscious efforts to move his limbs, for now he suddenly found that the sides of his prison-house yielded to pressure. He *was* moving his limbs, encumbered with some viscous substance. Where was the casket? His sensations were very confused. Sometimes he seemed to be falling, sometimes to be soaring upwards, and then again to be moving in the horizontal plane. The viscous substance was white. There seemed to be less of it every moment . . . white, cloudy stuff just like the casket, only not solid. With a horrible shock he realised that it *was* the casket, the casket melting, dissolving away, giving place to an indescribable confusion of colour—a rich, varied world in which nothing, for the moment, seemed palpable. There was no casket now. He was turned out—deposited—solitary. He was in Perelandra.

His first impression was of nothing more definite than of something slanted—as though he were looking at a photograph which had been taken when the camera was not held level. And even this lasted only for an instant. The slant was replaced by a different slant; then two slants rushed together and made a peak, and the peak flattened suddenly into a horizontal line, and the horizontal line tilted and became the edge of a vast gleaming slope which rushed furiously towards him. At the same moment he felt that he was being lifted. Up and up he soared till it seemed as if he must reach the burning dome of gold that hung above him instead of a sky. Then he was at a summit; but almost before his glance had taken in a huge valley that yawned beneath him—shining green like glass and marbled with streaks of scummy white—he was rushing down into that valley at perhaps thirty miles an hour. And now he realised that there was a delicious coolness over every part of him except his head, that his feet rested on nothing, and that he had for some time been performing unconsciously the actions of a swimmer. He was riding the foamless swell of an ocean, fresh and cool after the fierce temperatures of Heaven, but warm by earthly standards—as warm as a shallow bay with sandy bottom in a sub-tropical climate. As he rushed smoothly up the great convex hillside of the next wave he got a mouthful of the water. It was hardly at all flavoured with salt; it was drink-able—like fresh water and only, by an infinitesimal degree, less insipid. Though he had not been aware of thirst till now, his drink gave him a quite astonishing pleasure. It was almost like meeting Pleasure itself for the first time. He buried his flushed face in the green translucence, and when he withdrew it, found himself once more on the top of a wave.

There was no land in sight. The sky was pure, flat gold like the background of a medieval picture. It looked very distant—as far off as a cirrhus cloud looks from earth. The ocean was gold too, in the offing, flecked with innumerable shadows. The nearer waves, though golden where their summits caught the light, were green on their slopes: first emerald, and lower down a lustrous bottle green, deepening to blue where they passed beneath the shadow of other waves.

All this he saw in a flash; then he was speeding down once more into the trough. He had somehow turned on his back. He saw the golden roof of that world quivering with a rapid variation of paler lights as a ceiling quivers at the reflected sunlight from the bath-water when you step into your bath on a summer morning. He guessed that this was the reflection of the waves wherein he swam. It is a phenomenon observable three days out of five in the planet of love. The queen of those seas views herself continually in a celestial mirror.

Up again to the crest, and still no sight of land. Something that looked like clouds—or could it be ships?—far away on his left. Then down, down, down—he thought he would never reach the end of it . . . this time he noticed how dim the light was. Such tepid revelry in water—such glorious bathing, as one would have called it on earth, suggested as its natural accompaniment a blazing sun. But here there was no such thing. The water gleamed, the sky burned with gold, but all was rich and dim, and his eyes fed upon it undazzled and unaching. The very names of green and gold, which he used perforce in describing the scene, are too harsh for the tenderness, the muted iridescence, of that warm, maternal, delicately gorgeous world. It was mild to look upon as evening, warm like summer noon, gentle and winning like early dawn. It was altogether pleasurable. He sighed.

There was a wave ahead of him now so high that it was dreadful. We speak idly in our own world of seas mountain high when they are not much more than mast high. But this was the real thing. If the huge shape had been a hill of land and not of water he might have spent a whole forenoon or longer walking the slope before he reached the summit. It gathered him into itself and hurled him up to that elevation in a matter of seconds. But before he reached the top, he almost cried out in terror. For this wave had not a smooth top like the others. A horrible crest appeared; jagged and billowy and fantastic shapes, unnatural, even unliquid, in appearance, sprouted from the ridge. Rocks? Foam? Beasts? The question hardly had time to flash through his mind before the thing was upon him. Involuntarily he shut his eyes. Then he found himself once more rushing downhill. Whatever it was, it had gone past him. But it had been something. He had been struck in the face. Dabbing with his hands he found no blood. He had been struck by something soft which did him no harm but merely stung like a lash because of the speed at which he met it. He turned round on his back again—already, as he did so, soaring thousands of feet aloft to the high water of the next ridge. Far down below him in a vast momentary valley he saw the thing that had missed him. It was an irregularly shaped object with many curves and re-entrants. It was variegated in colours like a patch-work quilt— flame-colour, ultramarine, crimson, orange, gamboge, and violet. He could not say more about it for the whole glimpse lasted so short a time. Whatever the thing was, it was floating, for it rushed up the slope of the opposite wave and over the summit and out of sight. It sat to the water like a skin, curving as the water curved. It took the wave's shape at the top, so that for a moment half of it was already out of sight beyond the ridge and the other half still lying on the hither slope. It behaved rather like a mat of weeds on a river—a mat of weeds that takes on every con- tour of the little ripples you make by rowing past it—but on a very dif- ferent scale. This thing might have been thirty acres or more in area.

Words are slow. You must not lose sight of the fact that his whole life on Venus up till now had lasted less than five minutes. He was not in the least tired, and not yet seriously alarmed as to his power of surviving in such a world. He had confidence in those who had sent him there, and for the meantime the coolness of the water and the freedom of his limbs were still a novelty and a delight; but more than all these was something else at which I have already hinted and which can hardly be put into words—the strange sense of excessive pleasure which seemed somehow to be communicated to him through all his senses at once. I use the word "excessive" because Ransom himself could only describe it by saying that for his first few days on Perelandra he was haunted, not by a feeling of guilt, but by surprise that he had no such feeling. There was an exu- berance or prodigality of sweetness about the mere act of living which our race finds it difficult not to associate with forbidden and extravagant actions. Yet it is a violent world too. Hardly had he lost sight of the floating object when his eyes were stabbed by an unendurable light. A grading, blue-to-violet illumination made the golden sky seem dark by comparison and in a moment of time revealed more of the new planet than he had yet seen. He saw the waste of waves spread illimitably before him, and far away, at the very end of the world, against the sky, a single smooth column of ghastly green standing up, the one thing fixed and vertical in this universe of shifting slopes. Then the rich twilight rushed back (now seeming almost darkness) and he heard thunder. But it has a different *timbre* from terrestrial thunder, more resonance, and even, when distant, a kind of tinkling. It is the laugh, rather than the roar, of heaven. Another flash followed, and another, and then the storm was all about him. Enormous purple clouds came driving between him and the golden sky, and with no preliminary drops a rain such as he never experienced began to fall. There were no lines in it; the water above him seemed only less continuous than the sea, and he found it difficult to breathe. The flashes were incessant. In between them, when he looked in any direction except that of the clouds, he saw a completely changed world. It was like being at the centre of a rainbow, or in a cloud of multi-coloured steam. The water which now filled the air was turning sea and sky into a bedlam of flaming and writhing transparencies. He was dazzled and now for the first time a little frightened. In the flashes he saw, as before, only the endless sea and the still green column at the end of the world. No land anywhere—not the suggestion of a shore from one horizon to the other.

The thunder was ear-splitting and it was difficult to get enough air. All sorts of things seemed to be coming down in the rain—living things apparently. They looked like preternaturally airy and graceful frogs— sublimated frogs—and had the colour of dragon-flies, but he was in no plight to make careful observations. He was beginning to feel the first symptoms of exhaustion and was completely confused by the riot of colours in the atmosphere. How long this state of affairs lasted he could not say, but the next thing that he remembers noticing with any accuracy was that the swell was decreasing. He got the impression of being near the end of a range of water-mountains and looking down into lower country. For a long time he never reached this lower country; what had seemed, by comparison with the seas which he had met on his first arrival, to be calm water, always turned out to be only slightly smaller waves when he rushed down into them. There seemed to be a good many of the big floating objects about. And these, again, from some distance looked like an archipelago, but always, as he drew nearer and found the roughness of the water they were riding, they became more like a fleet. But in the end there was no doubt that the swell was subsiding. The rain stopped. The waves were merely of Atlantic height. The rainbow colours grew fainter and more transparent and the golden sky first showed timidly through them and then established itself again from horizon to horizon. The waves grew smaller still. He began to breathe freely. But he was now really tired, and beginning to find leisure to be afraid.

One of the great patches of floating stuff was sidling down a wave not more than a few hundred yards away. He eyed it eagerly, wondering whether he could climb on to one of these things for rest. He strongly suspected that they would prove mere mats of weed, or the topmost branches of submarine forests, incapable of supporting him. But while he thought this, the particular one on which his eyes were fixed crept up a wave and came between him and the sky. It was not flat. From its tawny surface a whole series of feathery and billowy shapes arose, very unequal in height; they looked darkish against the dim glow of the golden roof. Then they all tilted one way as the thing which carried them curled over the crown of the water and dipped out of sight. But here was another, not thirty yards away and bearing down on him. He struck out towards it, noticing as he did so how sore and feeble his arms were and feeling his first thrill of true fear. As he approached it he saw that it ended in a fringe of undoubtedly vegetable matter; it trailed, in fact, a dark red skirt of tubes and strings and bladders. He grabbed at them and found he was not yet near enough. He began swimming desperately, for the thing was gliding past him at some ten miles an hour. He grabbed again and got a handful of whip-like red strings, but they pulled out of his hand and almost cut him. Then he thrust himself right in among them, snatching wildly straight before him. For one second he was in a kind of vegetable broth of gurgling tubes and exploding bladders; next moment his hands caught something firmer ahead, something almost like very soft wood. Then, with the breath nearly knocked out of him and a bruised knee, he found himself lying face downward on a resistant surface. He pulled himself an inch or so further. Yes—there was no doubt now; one did not go through; it was something one could lie on.

It seems that he must have remained lying on his face, doing nothing and thinking nothing for a very long time. When he next began to take any notice of his surroundings he was, at all events, well rested. His first discovery was that he lay on a dry surface, which on examination turned out to consist of something very like heather, except for the colour which was coppery. Burrowing idly with his fingers he found something friable like dry soil, but very little of it, for almost at once he came upon a base of tough interlocked fibres. Then he rolled round on his back, and in doing so discovered the extreme resilience of the surface on which he lay. It was something much more than the pliancy of the heatherlike vegetation, and felt more as if the whole floating island beneath the vegetation were a kind of mattress. He turned and looked "inland"—if that is the right word—and for one instant what he saw looked very like a country.

He was looking up a long lonely valley with a copper-coloured floor bordered on each side by gentle slopes clothed in a kind of many-coloured forest. But even as he took this in, it became a long copper-coloured ridge with the forest sloping *down* on each side of it. Of course he ought to have been prepared for this, but he says that it gave him an almost sickening shock. The thing had looked, in that first glance, so like a real country that he had forgotten it was floating—an island if you like, with hills and valleys, but hills and valleys which changed places every minute so that only a cinematograph could make a contour map of it. And that is the nature of the floating islands of Perelandra. A photograph, omitting the colours and the perpetual variation of shape, would make them look deceptively like landscapes in our own world, but the reality is very different; for they are dry and fruitful like land but their only shape is the inconstant shape of the water beneath them. Yet the land-like appearance proved hard to resist. Although he had now grasped with his brain what was happening, Ransom had not yet grasped it with his muscles and nerves. He rose to take a few paces inland—and downhill, as it was at the moment of his rising—and immediately found himself flung down on his face, unhurt because of the softness of the weed. He scrambled to his feet—saw that he now had a steep slope to ascend—and fell a second time. A blessed relaxation of the strain in which he had been living since his arrival dissolved him into weak laughter. He rolled to and fro on the soft fragrant surface in a real schoolboy fit of the giggles.

This passed. And then for the next hour or two he was teaching himself to walk. It was much harder than getting your sea-legs on a ship, for whatever the sea is doing the deck of the ship remains a plane. But this was like learning to walk on water itself. It took him several hours to get a hundred yards away from the edge, or coast, of the floating island; and he was proud when he could go five paces without a fall, arms outstretched, knees bent in readiness for sudden change of balance, his whole body swaying and tense like that of one who is learning to walk the tightrope. Perhaps he would have learned more quickly if his falls had not been so soft, if it had not been so pleasant, having fallen, to lie still and gaze at the golden roof and hear the endless soothing noise of the water and breathe in the curiously delightful smell of the herbage. And then, too, it was so strange, after rolling head over heels down into some little dell, to open his eyes and find himself seated on the central mountain peak of the whole island looking down like Robinson Crusoe on field and forest to the shores in every direction, that a man could hardly help sitting there a few minutes longer—and then being detained again because, even as he made to rise, mountain and valley alike had been obliterated and the whole island had become a level plain.

At long last he reached the wooded part. There was an undergrowth of feathery vegetation, about the height of gooseberry bushes, coloured like sea anemones. Above this were the taller growths—strange trees with tube-like trunks of grey and purple spreading rich canopies above his head, in which orange, silver, and blue were the predominant colours. Here, with the aid of the tree trunks, he could keep his feet more easily. The smells in the forest were beyond all that he had ever conceived. To say that they made him feel hungry and thirsty would be misleading; almost, they created a new kind of hunger and thirst, a longing that seemed to flow over from the body into the soul and which was a heaven to feel. Again and again he stood still, clinging to some branch to steady himself, and breathed it all in, as if breathing had become a kind of ritual. And at the same time the forest landscape furnished what would have been a dozen landscapes on earth—now level wood with trees as vertical as towers, now a deep bottom where it was surprising not to find a stream, now a wood growing on a hillside, and now again, a hilltop whence one looked down through slanted boles at the distant sea. Save for the inorganic sound of waves there was utter silence about him. The sense of his solitude became intense without becoming at all painful—only adding, as it were, a last touch of wildness to the unearthly pleasures that surrounded him. If he had any fear now, it was a faint apprehension that his reason might be in danger. There was something in Perelandra that might overload a human brain.

Now he had come to a part of the wood where great globes of yellow fruit hung from the trees—clustered as toy-balloons are clustered on the back of the balloon-man and about the same size. He picked one of them and turned it over and over. The rind was smooth and firm and seemed impossible to tear open. Then by accident one of his fingers punctured it and went through into coldness. After a moment's hesitation he put the little aperture to his lips. He had meant to extract the smallest, experimental sip, but the first taste put his caution all to flight. It was, of course, a taste, just as his thirst and hunger had been thirst and hunger. But then it was so different from every other taste that it seemed mere pedantry to call it a taste at all. It was like the discovery of a totally new *genus* of pleasures, something unheard of among men, out of all reckoning, beyond all covenant. For one draught of this on earth wars would be fought and nations betrayed. It could not be classified. He could never tell us, when he came back to the world of men, whether it was sharp or sweet, savoury or voluptuous, creamy or piercing. "Not like that" was all he could ever say to such inquiries. As he let the empty gourd fall from his hand and was about to pluck a second one, it came into his head that he was now neither hungry nor thirsty.

And yet to repeat a pleasure so intense and almost so spiritual seemed an obvious thing to do. His reason, or what we commonly take to be reason in our own world, was all in favour of tasting this miracle again; the childlike innocence of fruit, the labours he had undergone, the uncertainty of the future, all seemed to commend the action. Yet something seemed opposed to this "reason." It is difficult to suppose that this opposition came from desire, for what desire would turn from so much deliciousness? But for whatever cause, it appeared to him better not to taste again. Perhaps the experience had been so complete that repetition would be a vulgarity—like asking to hear the same symphony twice in a day.

As he stood pondering over this and wondering how often in his life on earth he had reiterated pleasures not through desire, but in the teeth of desire and in obedience to a spurious rationalism, he noticed that the light was changing. It was darker behind him than it had been; ahead, the sky and sea shone through the wood with a changed intensity. To step out of the forest would have been a minute's work on earth; on this undulating island it took him longer, and when he finally emerged into the open an extraordinary spectacle met his eyes. All day there had been no variation at any point in the golden roof to mark the sun's position, but now the whole of one half-heaven revealed it. The orb itself remained invisible, but on the rim of the sea rested an arc of green so luminous that he could not look at it, and beyond that, spreading almost to the zenith, a great fan of colour like a peacock's tail. Looking over his shoulder he saw the whole island ablaze with blue, and across it and beyond it, even to the ends of the world, his own enormous shadow. The sea, far calmer now than he had yet seen it, smoked towards heaven in huge dolomites and elephants of blue and purple vapour, and a light wind, full of sweetness, lifted the hair on his forehead. The day was burning to death. Each moment the waters grew more level; something not far removed from silence began to be felt. He sat down cross-legged on the edge of the island, the desolate lord, it seemed, of this solemnity. For the first time it crossed his mind that he might have been sent to an uninhabited world, and the terror added, as it were, a razor-edge to all that profusion of pleasure.

Once more, a phenomenon which reason might have anticipated took him by surprise. To be naked yet warm, to wander among summer fruits and lie in sweet heather—all this had led him to count on a twilit night, a mild midsummer greyness. But before the great apocalyptic colours had died out in the west, the eastern heaven was black. A few moments, and the blackness had reached the western horizon. A little reddish light lingered at the zenith for a time, during which he crawled back to the woods. It was already, in common parlance, "too dark to see your way." But before he had lain down among the trees the real night had come—seamless darkness, not like night but like being in a coalcellar, darkness in which his own hand held before his face was totally invisible. Absolute blackness, the undimensioned, the impenetrable, pressed on his eyeballs. There is no moon in that land, no star pierces the golden roof. But the darkness was warm. Sweet new scents came stealing out of it. The world had no size now. Its boundaries were the length and breadth of his own body and the little patch of soft fragrance which made his hammock, swaying ever more and more gently. Night covered him like a blanket and kept all loneliness from him. The blackness might have been his own room. Sleep came like a fruit which falls into the hand almost before you have touched the stem.

4

At Ransom's waking something happened to him which perhaps never happens to a man until he is out of his own world: he saw reality, and thought it was a dream. He opened his eyes and saw a strange heraldically coloured tree loaded with yellow fruits and silver leaves. Round the base of the indigo stem was coiled a small dragon covered with scales of red gold. He recognised the garden of the Hesperides at once. "This is the most vivid dream I have ever had," he thought. By some means or other he then realised that he was awake; but extreme comfort and some trance-like quality, both in the sleep which had just left him and in the experience to which he had awaked, kept him lying motionless. He remembered how in the very different world called Malacandra—that cold, archaic world, as it now seemed to him—he had met the original of the Cyclops, a giant in a cave and a shepherd. Were all the things which appeared as mythology on earth scattered through other worlds as realities? Then the realisation came to him "You are in an unknown planet, naked and alone, and that may be a dangerous animal." But he was not badly frightened. He knew that the ferocity of terrestrial animals was, by cosmic standards, an exception, and had found kindness in stranger creatures than this. But he lay quiet a little longer and looked at it. It was a creature of the lizard type, about the size of a St. Bernard dog, with a serrated back. Its eyes were open.

Presently he ventured to rise on one elbow. The creature went on looking at him. He noticed that the island was perfectly level. He sat up and saw, between the stems of the trees, that they were in calm water. The sea looked like gilded glass. He resumed his study of the dragon.

Could this be a rational animal—a *hnau* as they said in Malacandra—and the very thing he had been sent there to meet? It did not look like one, but it was worth trying. Speaking in the Old Solar tongue he formed his first sentence—and his own voice sounded to him unfamiliar.

"Stranger," he said, "I have been sent to your world through the Heaven by the servants of Maleldil. Do you give me welcome?"

The thing looked at him very hard and perhaps very wisely. Then, for the first time, it shut its eyes. This seemed an unpromising start. Ransom decided to rise to his feet. The dragon reopened its eyes. He stood looking at it while you could count to twenty, very uncertain how to proceed. Then he saw that it was beginning to uncoil itself. By a great effort of will he stood his ground; whether the thing were rational or irrational, flight could hardly help him for long. It detached itself from the tree, gave itself a shake, and opened two shining reptilian wings—bluish gold and bat-like. When it had shaken these and closed them again, it gave Ransom another long stare, and at last, half waddling and half crawling, made its way to the edge of the island and buried its long metallic-looking snout in the water. When it had drunk it raised its head and gave a kind of croaking bleat which was not entirely unmusical. Then it turned, looked yet again at Ransom, and finally approached him. "It's madness to *wait* for it," said the false reason, but Ransom set his teeth and stood. It came right up and began nudging him with its cold snout about his knees. He was in great perplexity. Was it rational and was this how it talked? Was it irrational but friendly—and if so, how should he respond? You could hardly stroke a creature with scales! Or was it merely scratching itself against him? At that moment, with a suddenness which convinced him it was only a beast, it seemed to forget all about him, turned away, and began tearing up the herbage with great avidity. Feeling that honour was now satisfied, he also turned away back to the woods.

There were trees near him loaded with the fruit which he had already tasted, but his attention was diverted by a strange appearance a little farther off. Amid the darker foliage of a greenish-grey thicket something seemed to be sparkling. The impression, caught out of the corner of his eye, had been that of a greenhouse roof with the sun on it. Now that he looked at it squarely it still suggested glass, but glass in perpetual motion. Light seemed to be coming and going in a spasmodic fashion. Just as he was moving to investigate this phenomenon he was startled by a touch on his left leg. The beast had followed him. It was once more nosing and nudging. Ransom quickened his pace. So did the dragon. He stopped; so did it. When he went on again it accompanied him so closely that its side pressed against his thighs and sometimes its

cold, hard, heavy foot descended on his. The arrangement was so little
to his satisfaction that he was beginning to wonder seriously how he
could put an end to it when suddenly his whole attention was attracted
by something else. Over his head there hung from a hairy tube-like
branch a great spherical object, almost transparent, and shining. It held
an area of reflected light in it and at one place a suggestion of rainbow
colouring. So this was the explanation of the glass-like appearance in the
wood. And looking round he perceived innumerable shimmering globes
of the same kind in every direction. He began to examine the nearest one
attentively. At first he thought it was moving, then he thought it was not.
Moved by a natural impulse he put out his hand to touch it. Immediately
his head, face, and shoulders were drenched with what seemed (in that
warm world) an ice-cold shower bath, and his nostrils filled with a
sharp, shrill, exquisite scent that somehow brought to his mind the verse
in Pope, "die of a rose in aromatic pain." Such was the refreshment that
he seemed to himself to have been, till now, but half awake. When he
opened his eyes—which had closed involuntarily at the shock of moisture—all the colours about him seemed richer and the dimness of that
world seemed clarified. A re-enchantment fell upon him. The golden
beast at his side seemed no longer either a danger or a nuisance. If a
naked man and a wise dragon were indeed the sole inhabitants of this
floating paradise, then this also was fitting, for at that moment he had a
sensation not of following an adventure but of enacting a myth. To be
the figure that he was in this unearthly pattern appeared sufficient.

He turned again to the tree. The thing that had drenched him was
quite vanished. The tube or branch, deprived of its pendent globe, now
ended in a little quivering orifice from which there hung a bead of crystal moisture. He looked round in some bewilderment. The grove was
still full of its iridescent fruit but now he perceived that there was a slow
continual movement. A second later he had mastered the phenomenon.
Each of the bright spheres was very gradually increasing in size, and
each, on reaching a certain dimension, vanished with a faint noise, and
in its place there was a momentary dampness on the soil and a soon-
fading, delicious fragrance and coldness in the air. In fact, the things
were not fruit at all but bubbles. The trees (he christened them at that
moment) were bubble-trees. Their life, apparently, consisted in drawing
up water from the ocean and then expelling it in this form, but enriched
by its short sojourn in their sappy innards. He sat down to feed his eyes
upon the spectacle. Now that he knew the secret he could explain to
himself why this wood looked and felt so different from every other part
of the island. Each bubble, looked at individually, could be seen to
emerge from its parent-branch as a mere bead, the size of a pea, and

swell and burst; but looking at the wood as a whole, one was conscious only of a continual faint disturbance of light, an elusive interference with the prevailing Perelandrian silence, an unusual coolness in the air, and a fresher quality in the perfume. To a man born in our world it felt a more out-door place than the open parts of the island, or even the sea. Looking at a fine cluster of the bubbles which hung above his head he thought how easy it would be to get up and plunge oneself through the whole lot of them and to feel, all at once, that magical refreshment multiplied tenfold. But he was restrained by the same sort of feeling which had restrained him over-night from tasting a second gourd. He had always disliked the people who encored a favourite air in the opera—"That just spoils it" had been his comment. But this now appeared to him as a principle of far wider application and deeper moment. This itch to have things over again, as if life were a film that could be unrolled twice or even made to work backwards . . . was it possibly the root of all evil? No: of course the love of money was called that. But money itself—perhaps one valued it chiefly as a defence against chance, a security for being able to have things over again, a means of arresting the unrolling of the film.

He was startled from his meditation by the physical discomfort of some weight on his knees. The dragon had lain down and deposited its long, heavy head across them. "Do you know," he said to it in English, "that you are a considerable nuisance?" It never moved. He decided that he had better try and make friends with it. He stroked the hard dry head, but the creature took no notice. Then his hand passed lower down and found softer surface, or even a chink in the mail. Ah . . . that was where it liked being tickled. It grunted and shot out a long cylindrical slate-coloured tongue to lick him. It rolled round on its back revealing an almost white belly, which Ransom kneaded with his toes. His acquaintance with the dragon prospered exceedingly. In the end it went to sleep.

He rose and got a second shower from a bubble-tree. This made him feel so fresh and alert that he began to think of food. He had forgotten whereabouts on the island the yellow gourds were to be found, and so as he set out to look for them he discovered that it was difficult to walk. For a moment he wondered whether the liquid in the bubbles had some intoxicating quality, but a glance around assured him of the real reason. The plain of copper-coloured heather before him, even as he watched, swelled into a low hill and the low hill moved in his direction. Spellbound anew at the sight of land rolling towards him, like water, in a wave, he forgot to adjust himself to the movement and lost his feet. Picking himself up, he proceeded more carefully. This time there was no doubt about it. The sea was rising. Where two neighbouring woods made a vista to the edge of this living raft he could see troubled water, and the warm wind was now strong enough to ruffle his hair. He made his way gingerly towards the coast, but before he reached it he passed some bushes which carried a rich crop of oval green berries, about three times the size of almonds. He picked one and broke it in two. The flesh was dryish and bread-like, something of the same kind as a banana. It turned out to be good to eat. It did not give the orgiastic and almost alarming pleasure of the gourds, but rather the specific pleasure of plain food—the delight of munching and being nourished, a "Sober certainty of waking bliss." A man, or at least a man like Ransom, felt he ought to say grace over it; and so he presently did. The gourds would have required rather an oratorio or a mystical meditation. But the meal had its unexpected high lights. Every now and then one struck a berry which had a bright red centre: and these were so savoury, so memorable among a thousand tastes, that he would have begun to look for them and to feed on them only, but that he was once more forbidden by that same inner adviser which had already spoken to him twice since he came to Perelandra. "Now on earth," thought Ransom, "they'd soon discover how to breed these redhearts, and they'd cost a great deal more than the others." Money, in fact, would provide the means of saying *encore* in a voice that could not be disobeyed.

When he had finished his meal he went down to the water's edge to drink, but before he arrived there it was already "up" to the water's edge. The island at that moment was a little valley of bright land nestling between hills of green water, and as he lay on his belly to drink he had the extraordinary experience of dipping his mouth in a sea that was higher than the shore. Then he sat upright for a bit with his legs dangling over the edge among the red weeds that fringed this little country. His solitude became a more persistent element in his consciousness. What had he been brought here to do? A wild fancy came into his head that this empty world had been waiting for him as for its first inhabitant, that he was singled out to be the founder, the beginner. It was strange that the utter loneliness through all these hours had not troubled him so much as one night of it on Malacandra. He thought the difference lay in this, that mere chance, or what he took for chance, had turned him adrift in Mars, but here he knew that he was part of a plan. He was no longer unattached, no longer on the outside.

As his country climbed the smooth mountains of dimly lustrous water he had frequent opportunity to see that many other islands were close at hand. They varied from his own island and from one another in their colouring more than he would have thought possible. It was a wonder to see these big mats or carpets of land tossing all around him like yachts in harbour on a rough day—their trees each moment at a different angle just as the masts of the yachts would be. It was a wonder to see some edge of vivid green or velvety crimson come creeping over the top of a wave far above him and then wait till the whole country unrolled itself down the wave's side for him to study. Sometimes his own land and a neighbouring land would be on opposite slopes of a trough, with only a narrow strait of water between them; and then, for the moment, you were cheated with the semblance of a terrestrial landscape. It looked exactly as though you were in a well-wooded valley with a river at the bottom of it. But while you watched, that seeming river did the impossible. It thrust itself up so that the land on either side sloped downwards from it; and then up farther still and shouldered half the landscape out of sight beyond its ridge; and became a huge greeny-gold hog's back of water hanging in the sky and threatening to engulf your own land, which now was concave and reeled backwards to the next roller, and rushing upwards, became convex again.

A clanging, whirring noise startled him. For a moment he fancied he was in Europe and that a plane was flying low over his head. Then he recognised his friend the dragon. Its tail was streaked out straight behind it so that it looked like a flying worm, and it was heading for an island about half a mile away. Following its course with his eyes, he saw two long lines of winged objects, dark against the gold firmament, approaching the same island from the left and the right. But they were not bat-winged reptiles. Peering hard into the distance, he decided that they were birds, and a musical chattering noise, presently wafted to him by a change of the wind, confirmed this belief. They must have been a little larger than swans. Their steady approach to the same island for which the dragon was heading fixed his attention and filled him with a vague feeling of expectation. What followed next raised this to positive excitement. He became aware of some creamily foamed disturbance in the water, much nearer, and making for the same island. A whole fleet of objects was moving in formation. He rose to his feet. Then the lift of a wave cut them off from his sight. Next moment they were visible again, hundreds of feet below him. Silver-coloured objects, all alive with circling and frisking movements . . . he lost them again, and swore. In such a very uneventful world they had become important. Ah . . . ! here they were again. Fish certainly. Very large, obese, dolphin-like fish, two long lines together, some of them spouting columns of rainbow-coloured water from their noses, and one leader. There was something queer about the leader, some sort of projection or malformation on the back. If only the things would remain visible for more than fifty seconds at a time! They had almost reached that other island now, and the birds were all descending to meet them at its edge. There was the leader again, with his hump or pillar on his back. A moment of wild incredulity followed, and then Ransom was balanced, with legs wide apart, on the utmost fringe of his own island and shouting for all he was worth. For at the very moment when the leading fish had reached that neighbouring land, the land had risen up on a wave between him and the sky; and he had seen, in perfect and unmistakable silhouette, the thing on the fish's back reveal itself as a human form—a human form which stepped ashore, turned with a slight inclination of its body towards the fish and then vanished from sight as the whole island slid over the shoulder of the billow. With beating heart Ransom waited till it was in view again. This time it was not between him and the sky. For a second or so the human figure was undiscoverable. A stab of something like despair pierced him. Then he picked it out again—a tiny darkish shape moving slowly between him and a patch of blue vegetation. He waved and gesticulated and shouted till his throat was hoarse, but it took no notice of him. Every now and then he lost sight of it. Even when he found it again, he sometimes doubted whether it were not an optical illusion—some chance figuration of foliage which his intense desire had assimilated to the shape of a man. But always, just before he had despaired, it would become unmistakable again. Then his eyes began to grow tired and he knew that the longer he looked the less he would see. But he went on looking none the less.

At last, from mere exhaustion, he sat down. The solitude, which up till now had been scarcely painful, had become a horror. Any return to it was a possibility he dared not face. The drugging and entrancing beauty had vanished from his surroundings; take that one human form away and all the rest of this world was now pure nightmare, a horrible cell or trap in which he was imprisoned. The suspicion that he was beginning to suffer from hallucinations crossed his mind. He had a picture of living for ever and ever on this hideous island, always really alone but always haunted by the phantoms of human beings, who would come up to him with smiles and outstretched hands, and then fade away as he approached them. Bowing his head on his knees, he set his teeth and endeavoured to restore some order in his mind. At first he found he was merely listening to his own breathing and counting the beats of his heart; but he tried again and presently succeeded. And then, like revelation, came the very simple idea that if he wished to attract the attention of this man-like creature he must wait till he was on the crest of a wave and then stand up so that it would see him outlined against the sky.

Three times he waited till the shore whereon he stood became a ridge, and rose, swaying to the movement of his strange country, gesticulating. The fourth time he succeeded. The neighbouring island was, of course, lying for the moment beneath him like a valley. Quite unmistakably the small dark figure waved back. It detached itself from a confusing background of greenish vegetation and began running towards him—that is, towards the nearer coast of its own island—across an orange-coloured field. It ran easily: the heaving surface of the field did not seem to trouble it. Then his own land reeled downwards and backwards and a great wall of water pushed its way up between the two countries and cut each off from sight of the other. A moment later, and Ransom, from the valley in which he now stood, saw the orange-coloured land pouring itself like a moving hillside down the slightly convex slope of a wave far above him. The creature was still running. The width of water between the two islands was about thirty feet, and the creature was less than a hundred yards away from him. He knew now that it was not merely man-like, but a man—a green man on an orange field, green like the beautifully coloured green beetle in an English garden, running downhill towards him with easy strides and very swiftly. Then the seas lifted his own land and the green man became a foreshortened figure far below him, like an actor seen from the gallery at Covent Garden. Ransom stood on the very brink of his island, straining his body forward and shouting. The green man looked up. He was apparently shouting too, with his hands arched about his mouth; but the roar of the seas smothered the noise and the next moment Ransom's island dropped into the trough of the wave and the high green ridge of sea cut off his view. It was maddening. He was tortured with the fear that the distance between the islands might be increasing. Thank God: here came the orange land over the crest following him down into the pit. And there was the stranger, now on the very shore, face to face with him. For one second the alien eyes looked at his full of love and welcome. Then the whole face changed: a shock as of disappointment and astonishment passed over it. Ransom realised, not without a disappointment of his own, that he had been mistaken for someone else. The running, the waving, the shouts, had not been intended for him. And the green man was not a man at all, but a woman.

It is difficult to say why this surprised him so. Granted the human form, he was presumably as likely to meet a female as a male. But it did surprise him, so that only when the two islands once more began to fall apart into separate wave-valleys did he realise that he had said nothing to her, but stood staring like a fool. And now that she was out of sight he found his brain on fire with doubts. Was *this* what he had been sent to meet? He had been expecting wonders, had been prepared for wonders, but not prepared for a goddess carved apparently out of green stone, yet alive. And then it flashed across his mind—he had not noticed it while the scene was before him—that she had been strangely accompanied. She had stood up amidst a throng of beasts and birds as a tall sapling stands among bushes—big pigeon-coloured birds and flame-coloured birds, and dragons, and beaver-like creatures about the size of rats, and heraldic-looking fish in the sea at her feet. Or had he imagined that? Was this the beginning of the hallucinations he had feared? Or another myth coming out into the world of fact—perhaps a more terrible myth, of Circe or Alcina? And the expression on her face . . . what had she expected to find that made the finding of him such a disappointment?

The other island became visible again. He had been right about the animals. They surrounded her ten or twenty deep, all facing her, most of them motionless, but some of them finding their places, as at a cere-mony, with delicate noiseless movements. The birds were in long lines and more of them seemed to be alighting on the island every moment and joining these lines. From a wood of bubble-trees behind her half a dozen creatures like very short-legged and elongated pigs—the dachs-hunds of the pig world—were waddling up to join the assembly. Tiny frog-like beasts, like those he had seen falling in the rain, kept leaping about her, sometimes higher than her head, sometimes alighting on her shoulders; their colours were so vivid that at first he mistook them for kingfishers. Amidst all this she stood looking at him; her feet together, her arms hanging at her sides, her stare level and unafraid, communicat-ing nothing. Ransom determined to speak, using the Old Solar tongue. "I am from another world," he began and then stopped. The Green Lady had done something for which he was quite unprepared. She raised her arm and pointed at him: not as in menace, but as though inviting the other creatures to behold him. At the same moment her face changed again, and for a second he thought she was going to cry. Instead she burst into laughter—peal upon peal of laughter till her whole body shook with it, till she bent almost double, with her hands resting on her knees, still laughing and repeatedly pointing at him. The animals, like our own dogs in similar circumstances, dimly understood that there was merriment afoot; all manner of gambolling, wing-clapping, snorting, and standing upon hind legs began to be displayed. And still the Green Lady laughed till yet again the wave divided them and she was out of sight.

Ransom was thunderstruck. Had the eldila sent him to meet an idiot? Or an evil spirit that mocked men? Or was it after all a hallucina-tion?—for this was just how a hallucination might be expected to behave. Then an idea occurred to him which would have taken much longer, perhaps, to occur to me or you. It might not be she who was mad but he who was ridiculous. He glanced down at himself. Certainly his legs presented an odd spectacle, for one was brownish-red (like the flanks of a Titian satyr) and the other was white—by comparison, almost a leprous white. As far as self-inspection could go, he had the same parti-coloured appearance all over—no unnatural result of his one-sided exposure to the sun during the voyage. Had this been the joke? He felt a momentary impatience with the creature who could mar the meeting of two worlds with laughter at such a triviality. Then he smiled in spite of himself at the very undistinguished career he was having on Perelandra. For dangers he had been prepared; but to be first a disappointment and then an absurdity . . . Hullo! Here were the Lady and her island in sight again.

She had recovered from her laughter and sat with her legs trailing in the sea, half unconsciously caressing a gazelle-like creature which had thrust its soft nose under her arm. It was difficult to believe that she had ever laughed, ever done anything but sit on the shore of her floating isle. Never had Ransom seen a face so calm, and so unearthly, despite the full humanity of every feature. He decided afterwards that the unearthly quality was due to the complete absence of that element of resignation which mixes, in however slight a degree, with all profound stillness in terrestrial faces. This was a calm which no storm had ever preceded. It might be idiocy, it might be immortality, it might be some condition of mind to which terrestrial experience offered no clue at all. A curious and rather horrifying sensation crept over him. On the ancient planet Malacandra he had met creatures who were not even remotely human in form but who had turned out, on further acquaintance, to be rational and friendly. Under an alien exterior he had discovered a heart like his own. Was he now to have the reverse experience? For now he realised that the word "human" refers to something more than the bodily form or even to the rational mind. It refers also to that community of blood and experience which unites all men and women on the Earth. But this creature was not of his race; no windings, however intricate, of any genealogical tree, could ever establish a connection between himself and her. In that sense, not one drop in her veins was "human." The universe had produced her species and his quite independently.

All this passed through his mind very quickly, and was speedily interrupted by his consciousness that the light was changing. At first he thought that the green Creature had, of herself, begun to turn bluish and to shine with a strange electric radiance. Then he noticed that the whole landscape was a blaze of blue and purple—and almost at the same time that the two islands were not so close together as they had been. He glanced at the sky. The many-coloured furnace of the short-lived evening was kindled all about him. In a few minutes it would be pitch black . . . and the islands were drifting apart. Speaking slowly in that ancient language, he cried out to her, "I am a stranger. I come in peace. Is it your will that I swim over to your land?"

The Green Lady looked quickly at him with an expression of curiosity.

"What is 'peace'?" she asked.

Ransom could have danced with impatience. Already it was visibly darker and there was no doubt now that the distance between the islands was increasing. Just as he was about to speak again a wave rose between them and once more she was out of sight; and as that wave hung above him, shining purple in the light of the sunset, he noticed how dark the sky beyond it had become. It was already through a kind of twilight that he looked down from the next ridge upon the other island far below him. He flung himself into the water. For some seconds he found a difficulty in getting clear of the shore. Then he seemed to succeed and struck out. Almost at once he found himself back again among the red weeds and bladders. A moment or two of violent struggling followed and then he was free—and swimming steadily—and then, almost without warning, swimming in total darkness. He swam on, but despair of finding the other land, or even of saving his life, now gripped him. The perpetual change of the great swell abolished all sense of direction. It could only be by chance that he would land anywhere. Indeed, he judged from the time he had already been in the water that he must have been swimming *along* the space between the islands instead of across it. He tried to alter his course; then doubted the wisdom of this, tried to return to his original course, and became so confused that he could not be sure he had done either. He kept on telling himself that he must keep his head. He was beginning to be tired. He gave up all attempts to guide himself. Suddenly, a long time after, he felt vegetation sliding past him. He gripped and pulled. Delicious smells of fruit and flowers came to him out of the darkness. He pulled harder still on his aching arms. Finally, he found himself, safe and panting, on the dry, sweet-scented, undulating surface of an island.

5

Ransom must have fallen asleep almost as soon as he landed, for he remembered nothing more till what seemed the song of a bird broke in upon his dreams. Opening his eyes, he saw that it was a bird indeed, a long-legged bird like a very small stork, singing rather like a canary. Full daylight—or what passes for such in Perelandra—was all about him, and in his heart such a premonition of good adventure as made him sit up forthwith and brought him, a moment later, to his feet. He stretched his arms and looked around. He was not on the orange-coloured island, but on the same island which had been his home ever since he came to this planet. He was floating in a dead calm and therefore had no difficulty in making his way to the shore. And there he stopped in astonishment. The Lady's island was floating beside his, divided only by five feet or so of water. The whole look of the world had changed. There was no expanse of sea now visible—only a flat wooded landscape as far as the eye could reach in every direction. Some ten or twelve of the islands, in fact, were here lying together and making a short-lived continent. And there walking before him, as if on the other side of a brook, was the Lady herself—walking with her head a little bowed and her hands occupied in plaiting together some blue flowers. She was singing to herself in a low voice but stopped and turned as he hailed her and looked him full in the face.

"I was young yesterday," she began, but he did not hear the rest of her speech. The meeting, now that it had actually come about, proved overwhelming. You must not misunderstand the story at this point. What overwhelmed him was not in the least the fact that she, like himself, was totally naked. Embarrassment and desire were both a thousand miles away from his experience: and if he was a little ashamed of his own body, that was a shame which had nothing to do with difference of sex and turned only on the fact that he knew his body to be a little ugly and a little ridiculous. Still less was her colour a source of horror to him. In her own world that green was beautiful and fitting; it was his pasty white and angry sunburn which were the monstrosity. It was neither of these; but he found himself unnerved. He had to ask her presently to repeat what she had been saying.

"I was young yesterday," she said. "When I laughed at you. Now I know that the people in your world do not like to be laughed at."

"You say you were young?"

"Yes."

"Are you not young to-day also?"

She appeared to be thinking for a few moments, so intently that the flowers dropped, unregarded, from her hand.

"I see it now," she said presently. "It is very strange to say one is young at the moment one is speaking. But to-morrow I shall be older. And then I shall say I was young to-day. You are quite right. This is great wisdom you are bringing, O Piebald Man."

"What do you mean?"

"This looking backward and forward along the line and seeing how a day has one appearance as it comes to you, and another when you are in it, and a third when it has gone past. Like the waves."

"But you are very little older than yesterday."

"How do you know that?"

"I mean," said Ransom, "a night is not a very long time."

She thought again, and then spoke suddenly, her face lightening. "I see it now," she said. "You think times have lengths. A night is always a night whatever you do in it, as from this tree to that is always so many paces whether you take them quickly or slowly. I suppose that is true in a way. But the waves do not always come at equal distances. I see that you come from a wise world . . . if this is wise. I have never done it before—stepping out of life into the Alongside and looking at oneself living as if one were not alive. Do they all do that in your world, Piebald?"

"What do you know about other worlds?" said Ransom.

"I know this. Beyond the roof it is all Deep Heaven, the high place. And the low is not really spread out as it seems to be" (here she indicated the whole landscape) "but is rolled up into little balls: little lumps of the low swimming in the high. And the oldest and greatest of them have on them that which we have never seen nor heard and cannot at all understand. But on the younger Maleldil has made to grow the things like us, that breathe and breed."

"How have you found all this out? Your roof is so dense that your people cannot see through into Deep Heaven and look at the other worlds."

Up till now her face had been grave. At this point she clapped her hands and a smile such as Ransom had never seen changed her. One does not see that smile here except in children, but there was nothing of the child about it there.

"Oh, I see it," she said. "I am older now. Your world has no roof. You look right out into the high place and see the great dance with your own eyes. You live always in that terror and that delight, and what we must only believe you can behold. Is not this a wonderful invention of Maleldil's? When I was young I could imagine no beauty but this of our own world. But He can think of all, and all different."

"That is one of the things that is bewildering me," said Ransom. "That you are not different. You are shaped like the women of my own kind. I had not expected that. I have been in one other world beside my own. But the creatures there are not at all like you and me."

"What is bewildering about it?"

"I do not see why different worlds should bring forth like creatures. Do different trees bring forth like fruit?"

"But that other world was older than yours," she said.

"How do you know that?" asked Ransom in amazement.

"Maleldil is telling me," answered the woman. And as she spoke the landscape had become different, though with a difference none of the senses would identify. The light was dim, the air gentle, and all Ransom's body was bathed in bliss, but the garden world where he stood seemed to be packed quite full, and as if an unendurable pressure had been laid upon his shoulders, his legs failed him and he half sank, half fell, into a sitting position.

"It all comes into my mind now," she continued. "I see the big furry creatures, and the white giants—what is it you called them?—the Sorns, and the blue rivers. Oh, what a strong pleasure it would be to see them with my outward eyes, to touch them, and the stronger because there are no more of that kind to come. It is only in the ancient worlds they linger yet."

"Why?" said Ransom in a whisper, looking up at her.

"You must know that better than I," she said. "For was it not in your own world that all this happened?"

"All what?"

"I thought it would be you who would tell me of it," said the woman, now in her turn bewildered.

"What are you talking about?" said Ransom.

"I mean," said she, "that in your world Maleldil first took Himself this form, the form of your race and mine."

"You know that?" said Ransom sharply. Those who have had a dream which is very beautiful but from which, nevertheless, they have ardently desired to awake, will understand his sensations.

"Yes, I know that Maleldil has made me older to that amount since we began speaking." The expression on her face was such as he had never seen, and could not steadily look at. The whole of this adventure seemed to be slipping out of his hands. There was a long silence. He stooped down to the water and drank before he spoke again.

"Oh, my Lady," he said, "why do you say that such creatures linger only in the ancient worlds?"

"Are you so young?" she answered. "How could they come again? Since our Beloved became a man, how should Reason in any world take on another form? Do you not understand? That is all over. Among times there is a time that turns a corner and everything this side of it is new. Times do not go backward."

"And can one little world like mine be the corner?"

"I do not understand. Corner with us is not the name of a size."

"And do you," said Ransom with some hesitation—"and do you know *why* He came thus to my world?"

All through this part of the conversation he found it difficult to look higher than her feet, so that her answer was merely a voice in the air above him. "Yes," said the voice. "I know the reason. But it is not the reason you know. There was more than one reason, and there is one I know and cannot tell to you, and another that you know and cannot tell to me."

"And after this," said Ransom, "it will all be men."

"You say it as if you were sorry."

"I think," said Ransom, "I have no more understanding than a beast. I do not well know what I am saying. But I loved the furry people whom I met in Malacandra, that old world. Are they to be swept away? Are they only rubbish in the Deep Heaven?"

"I do not know what *rubbish* means," she answered, "nor what you are saying. You do not mean they are worse because they come early in the history and do not come again? They are their own part of the history and not another. We are on this side of the wave and they on the far side. All is new."

One of Ransom's difficulties was an inability to be quite sure who was speaking at any moment in this conversation. It may (or may not) have been due to the fact that he could not look long at her face. And now he wanted the conversation to end. He had "had enough"—not in the half-comic sense whereby we use those words to mean that a man has had too much, but in the plain sense. He had had his fill, like a man who has slept or eaten enough. Even an hour ago, he would have found it difficult to express this quite bluntly; but now it came naturally to him to say:

"I do not wish to talk any more. But I would like to come over to your island so that we may meet again when we wish."

"Which do you call my island?" said the Lady.

"The one you are on," said Ransom. "What else?"

"Come," she said, with a gesture that made that whole world a house and her a hostess. He slid into the water and scrambled out beside her. Then he bowed, a little clumsily as all modern men do, and walked away from her into a neighbouring wood. He found his legs unsteady and they ached a little; in fact a curious physical exhaustion possessed him. He sat down to rest for a few minutes and fell immediately into dreamless sleep.

He awoke completely refreshed but with a sense of insecurity. This had nothing to do with the fact that he found himself, on waking, strangely attended. At his feet, and with its snout partially resting upon them, lay the dragon; it had one eye shut and one open. As he rose on his elbow and looked about him he found that he had another custodian at his head: a furred animal something like a wallaby but yellow. It was the yellowest thing he had ever seen. As soon as he moved both beasts began nudging him. They would not leave him alone till he rose, and when he had risen they would not let him walk in any direction but one. The dragon was much too heavy for him to shove it out of the way, and the yellow beast danced round him in a fashion that headed him off every direction but the one it wanted him to go. He yielded to their pressure and allowed himself to be shepherded, first through a wood of higher and browner trees than he had yet seen and then across a small open space and into a kind of alley of bubble-trees and beyond that into large fields of silver flowers that grew waist-high. And then he saw that they had been bringing him to be shown to their mistress. She was standing a few yards away, motionless but not apparently disengaged— doing something with her mind, perhaps even with her muscles, that he did not understand. It was the first time he had looked steadily at her, himself unobserved, and she seemed more strange to him than before. There was no category in the terrestrial mind which would fit her.

Opposites met in her and were fused in a fashion for which we have no images. One way of putting it would be to say that neither our sacred nor our profane art could make her portrait. Beautiful, naked, shameless, young—she was obviously a goddess: but then the face, the face so calm that it escaped insipidity by the very concentration of its mildness, the face that was like the sudden coldness and stillness of a church when we enter it from a hot street—that made her a Madonna. The alert, inner silence which looked out from those eyes overawed him; yet at any moment she might laugh like a child, or run like Artemis or dance like a Mænad. All this against the golden sky which looked as if it were only an arm's length above her head. The beasts raced forward to greet her, and as they rushed through the feathery vegetation they startled from it masses of the frogs, so that it looked as if huge drops of vividly coloured dew were being tossed in the air. She turned as they approached her and welcomed them, and once again the picture was half like many earthly scenes but in its total effect unlike them all. It was not really like a woman making much of a horse, nor yet a child playing with a puppy. There was in her face an authority, in her caresses a condescension, which by taking seriously the inferiority of her adorers made them somehow less inferior—raised them from the status of pets to that of slaves. As Ransom reached her she stooped and whispered something in the ear of the yellow creature, and then, addressing the dragon, bleated to it almost in its own voice. Both of them, having received their congé, darted back into the woods.

"The beasts in your world seem almost rational," said Ransom.

"We make them older every day," she answered. "Is not that what it means to be a beast?"

But Ransom clung to her use of the word *we*.

"That is what I have come to speak to you about," he said. "Maleldil has sent me to your world for some purpose. Do you know what it is?"

She stood for a moment almost like one listening and then answered "No."

"Then you must take me to your home and show me to your people."

"People? I do not know what you are saying."

"Your kindred—the others of your kind."

"Do you mean the King?"

"Yes. If you have a King, I had better be brought before him."

"I cannot do that," she answered. "I do not know where to find him."

"To your own home then."

"What is *home*?"

"The place where people live together and have their possessions and bring up their children."

She spread out her hands to indicate all that was in sight. "This is my home," she said.

"Do you live here alone?" asked Ransom.

"What is *alone*?"

Ransom tried a fresh start. "Bring me where I shall meet others of your kind."

"If you mean the King, I have already told you I do not know where he is. When we were young—many days ago—we were leaping from island to island, and when he was on one and I was on another the waves rose and we were driven apart."

"But can you take me to some other of your kind? The King cannot be the only one."

"He is the only one. Did you not know?"

"But there must be others of your kind—your brothers and sisters, your kindred, your friends."

"I do not know what these words mean."

"Who is this King?" said Ransom in desperation.

"He is himself, he is the King," said she. "How can one answer such a question?"

"Look here," said Ransom. "You must have had a mother. Is she alive? Where is she? When did you see her last?"

"I have a mother?" said the Green Lady, looking full at him with eyes of untroubled wonder. "What do you mean? I *am* the Mother." And once again there fell upon Ransom the feeling that it was not she, or not she only, who had spoken. No other sound came to his ears, for the sea and the air were still, but a phantom sense of vast choral music was all about him. The awe which her apparently witless replies had been dissipating for the last few minutes returned upon him.

"I do not understand," he said.

"Nor I," answered the Lady. "Only my spirit praises Maleldil who comes down from Deep Heaven into this lowness and will make me to be blessed by all the times that are rolling towards us. It is He who is strong and makes me strong and fills empty worlds with good creatures."

"If you are a mother, where are your children?"

"Not yet," she answered.

"Who will be their father?"

"The King—who else?"

"But the King—had he no father?"

"He *is* the Father."

"You mean," said Ransom slowly, "that you and he are the only two of your kind in the whole world?"

"Of course." Then presently her face changed. "Oh, how young I have been," she said. "I see it now. I had known that there were many creatures in that ancient world of the Hrossa and the Sorns. But I had forgotten that yours also was an older world than ours. I see—there are many of you by now. I had been thinking that of you also there were only two. I thought you were the King and Father of your world. But there are children of children of children by now, and you perhaps are one of these."

"Yes," said Ransom.

"Greet your Lady and Mother well from me when you return to your own world," said the Green Woman. And now for the first time there was a note of deliberate courtesy, even of ceremony, in her speech. Ransom understood. She knew now at last that she was not addressing an equal. She was a queen sending a message to a queen through a commoner, and her manner to him was henceforward more gracious. He found it difficult to make his next answer.

"Our Mother and Lady is dead," he said.

"What is *dead*?"

"With us they go away after a time. Maleldil takes the soul out of them and puts it somewhere else—in Deep Heaven, we hope. They call it death."

"Do not wonder, O Piebald Man, that your world should have been chosen for time's corner. You live looking out always on heaven itself, and as if this were not enough Maleldil takes you all thither in the end. You are favoured beyond all worlds."

Ransom shook his head. "No. It is not like that," he said.

"I wonder," said the woman, "if you were sent here to teach us *death*."

"You don't understand," he said. "It is not like that. It is horrible. It has a foul smell. Maleldil Himself wept when He saw it." Both his voice and his facial expression were apparently something new to her. He saw the shock, not of horror, but of utter bewilderment, on her face for one instant and then, without effort, the ocean of her peace swallowed it up as if it had never been, and she asked him what he meant.

"You could never understand, Lady," he replied. "But in our world not all events are pleasing or welcome. There may be such a thing that you would cut off both your arms and your legs to prevent it happening—and yet it happens: with us."

"But how can one wish any of those waves not to reach us which Maleldil is rolling towards us?"

Against his better judgment Ransom found himself goaded into argument.

"But even you," he said, "when you first saw me, I know now you were expecting and hoping that I was the King. When you found I was not, your face changed. Was *that* event not unwelcome? Did you not wish it to be otherwise?"

"Oh," said the Lady. She turned aside with her head bowed and her hands clasped in an intensity of thought. She looked up and said, "You make me grow older more quickly than I can bear," and walked a little farther off. Ransom wondered what he had done. It was suddenly borne in upon him that her purity and peace were not, as they had seemed, things settled and inevitable like the purity and peace of an animal—that they were alive and therefore breakable, a balance maintained by a mind and therefore, at least in theory, able to be lost. There is no reason why a man on a smooth road should lose his balance on a bicycle; but he could. There was no reason why she should step out of her happiness into the psychology of our own race; but neither was there any wall between to prevent her doing so. The sense of precariousness terrified him: but when she looked at him again he changed that word to Adventure, and then all words died out of his mind. Once more he could not look steadily at her. He knew now what the old painters were trying to represent when they invented the halo. Gaiety and gravity together, a splendour as of martyrdom yet with no pain in it at all, seemed to pour from her countenance. Yet when she spoke her words were a disappointment.

"I have been so young till this moment that all my life now seems to have been a kind of sleep. I have thought that I was being carried, and behold, I was walking."

Ransom asked what she meant.

"What you have made me see," answered the Lady, "is as plain as the sky, but I never saw it before. Yet it has happened every day. One goes into the forest to pick food and already the thought of one fruit rather than another has grown up in one's mind. Then, it may be, one finds a different fruit and not the fruit one thought of. One joy was expected and another is given. But this I had never noticed before—that the very moment of the finding there is in the mind a kind of thrusting back, or setting aside. The picture of the fruit you have *not* found is still, for a moment, before you. And if you wished—if it were possible to wish—you could keep it there. You could send your soul after the good you had expected, instead of turning it to the good you had got. You could refuse the real good; you could make the real fruit taste insipid by thinking of the other."

Ransom interrupted. "That is hardly the same thing as finding a stranger when you wanted your husband."

"Oh, that is how I came to understand the whole thing. You and the King differ more than two kinds of fruit. The joy of finding him again and the joy of all the new knowledge I have had from you are more unlike than two tastes; and when the difference is as great as that, and each of the two things so great, then the first picture does stay in the mind quite a long time—many beats of the heart—after the other good has come. And this, O Piebald, is the glory and wonder you have made me see; that it is I, I myself, who turn from the good expected to the given good. Out of my own heart I do it. One can conceive a heart which did not: which clung to the good it had first thought of and turned the good which was given it into no good."

"I don't see the wonder and the glory of it," said Ransom.

Her eyes flashed upon him such a triumphant flight above his thoughts as would have been scorn in earthly eyes; but in that world it was not scorn.

"I thought," she said, "that I was carried in the will of Him I love, but now I see that I walk with it. I thought that the good things He sent me drew me into them as the waves lift the islands; but now I see that it is I who plunge into them with my own legs and arms, as when we go swimming. I feel as if I were living in that roofless world of yours where men walk undefended beneath naked heaven. It is a delight with terror in it! One's own self to be walking from one good to another, walking beside Him as Himself may walk, not even holding hands. How has He made me so separate from Himself? How did it enter His mind to conceive such a thing? The world is so much larger than I thought. I thought we went along paths—but it seems there are no paths. The going itself is the path."

"And have you no fear," said Ransom, "that it will ever be hard to turn your heart from the thing you wanted to the thing Maleldil sends?"

"I see," said the Lady presently. "The wave you plunge into may be very swift and great. You may need all your force to swim into it. You mean, He might send me a good like that?"

"Yes—or like a wave so swift and great that all your force was too little."

"It often happens that way in swimming," said the Lady. "Is not that part of the delight?"

"But are you happy without the King? Do you not *want* the King?"

"Want him?" she said. "How could there be anything I did not want?"

There was something in her replies that began to repel Ransom.

"You can't want him very much if you are happy without him," he said: and was immediately surprised at the sulkiness of his own voice.

"Why?" asked the Lady. "And why, O Piebald, are you making little hills and valleys in your forehead and why do you give a little lift of your shoulders? Are these the signs of something in your world?"

"They mean nothing," said Ransom hastily. It was a small lie; but there it would not do. It tore him as he uttered it, like a vomit. It became of infinite importance. The silver meadow and the golden sky seemed to fling it back at him. As if stunned by some measureless anger in the very air he stammered an emendation: "They mean nothing I could explain to you." The Lady was looking at him with a new and more judicial expression. Perhaps in the presence of the first mother's son she had ever seen, she was already dimly forecasting the problems that might arise when she had children of her own.

"We have talked enough now," she said at last. At first he thought she was going to turn away and leave him. Then, when she did not move, he bowed and drew back a step or two. She still said nothing and seemed to have forgotten about him. He turned and retraced his way through the deep vegetation until they were out of sight of each other. The audience was at an end.

6

As soon as the Lady was out of sight Ransom's first impulse was to run his hands through his hair, to expel the breath from his lungs in a long whistle, to light a cigarette, to put his hands in his pockets, and in general, to go through all that ritual of relaxation which a man performs on finding himself alone after a rather trying interview. But he had no cigarettes and no pockets: nor indeed did he feel himself alone. That sense of being in Someone's Presence which had descended on him with such unbearable pressure during the very first moments of his conversation with the Lady did not disappear when he had left her. It was, if anything, increased. Her society had been, in some degree, a protection against it, and her absence left him not to solitude but to a more formidable kind of privacy. At first it was almost intolerable; as he put it to us, in telling the story, "There seemed no *room*." But later on, he discovered that it was intolerable only at certain moments—at just those moments in fact (symbolised by his impulse to smoke and to put his hands in his pockets) when a man asserts his independence and feels that now at last he's on his own. When you felt like that, then the very air seemed too crowded to breathe; a complete fulness seemed to be excluding you from a place which, nevertheless, you were unable to leave. But when you gave in to the thing, gave yourself up to it, there was no burden to be borne. It became not a load but a medium, a sort of splendour as of eatable, drinkable, breathable gold, which fed and carried you and not only poured into you but out from you as well. Taken the wrong way, it suffocated; taken the right way, it made terrestrial life seem, by comparison, a vacuum. At first, of course, the wrong moments occurred pretty often. But like a man who has a wound that hurts him in certain positions and who gradually learns to avoid those positions, Ransom learned not to make that inner gesture. His day became better and better as the hours passed.

During the course of the day he explored the island pretty thoroughly. The sea was still calm and it would have been possible in many directions to have reached neighbouring islands by a mere jump. He was placed, however, at the edge of this temporary archipelago, and from one shore he found himself looking out on the open sea. They were lying, or else very slowly drifting, in the neighbourhood of the huge green column which he had seen a few moments after his arrival in Perelandra. He had an excellent view of this object at about a mile's distance. It was clearly a mountainous island. The column turned out to be really a cluster of columns—that is, of crags much higher than they were broad, rather like exaggerated dolomites, but smoother; so much smoother in fact that it might be truer to describe them as pillars from the Giant's Causeway magnified to the height of mountains. This huge upright mass did not, however, rise directly from the sea. The island had a base of rough country, but with smoother land at the coast, and a hint of valleys with vegetation in them between the ridges, and even of steeper and narrower valleys which ran some way up between the central crags. It was certainly land, real fixed land with its roots in the solid surface of the planet. He could dimly make out the texture of true rock from where he sat. Some of it was inhabitable land. He felt a great desire to explore it. It looked as if a landing would present no difficulties, and even the great mountain itself might turn out to be climbable.

He did not see the Lady again that day. Early next morning, after he had amused himself by swimming for a little and eaten his first meal, he was again seated on the shore looking out towards the Fixed Land. Suddenly he heard her voice behind him and looked around. She had come forth from the woods with some beasts, as usual, following her. Her words had been words of greeting, but she showed no disposition to talk. She came and stood on the edge of the floating island beside him and looked with him towards the Fixed Land.

"I will go there," she said at last.

"May I go with you?" asked Ransom.

"If you will," said the Lady. "But you see it is the Fixed Land."

"That is why I wish to tread on it," said Ransom. "In my world all the lands are fixed, and it would give me pleasure to walk in such a land again."

She gave a sudden exclamation of surprise and stared at him.

"Where, then, do you live in your world?" she asked.

"On the lands."

"But you said they are all fixed."

"Yes. We live on the fixed lands."

For the first time since they had met, something not quite unlike an expression of horror or disgust passed over her face.

"But what do you do during the nights?"

"During the nights?" said Ransom in bewilderment. "Why, we sleep, of course."

"But where?"

"Where we live. On the land."

She remained in deep thought so long that Ransom feared she was never going to speak again. When she did, her voice was hushed and once more tranquil, though the note of joy had not yet returned to it.

"He has never bidden you not to," she said, less as a question than as a statement.

"No," said Ransom.

"There can, then, be different laws in different worlds."

"Is there a law in your world not to sleep in a Fixed Land?"

"Yes," said the Lady. "He does not wish us to dwell there. We may land on them and walk on them, for the world is ours. But to stay there—to sleep and awake there . . ." she ended with a shudder.

"You couldn't have that law in our world," said Ransom. "There *are* no floating lands with us."

"How many of you are there?" asked the Lady suddenly.

Ransom found that he didn't know the population of the Earth, but contrived to give her some idea of many millions. He had expected her to be astonished, but it appeared that numbers did not interest her. "How do you all find room on your Fixed Land?" she asked.

"There is not one fixed land, but many," he answered. "And they are big: almost as big as the sea."

"How do you endure it?" she burst out. "Almost half your world empty and dead. Loads and loads of land, all tied down. Does not the very thought of it crush you?"

"Not at all," said Ransom. "The very thought of a world which was all sea like yours would make my people unhappy and afraid."

"Where will this end?" said the Lady, speaking more to herself than to him. "I have grown so old in these last few hours that all my life before seems only like the stem of a tree, and now I am like the branches shooting out in every direction. They are getting so wide apart that I can hardly bear it. First to have learned that I walk from good to good with my own feet . . . that was a stretch enough. But now it seems that good is not the same in all worlds; that Maleldil has forbidden in one what He allows in another."

"Perhaps my world is wrong about this," said Ransom rather feebly, for he was dismayed at what he had done.

"It is not so," said she. "Maleldil Himself has told me now. And it could not be so, if your world has no floating lands. But He is not telling me why He has forbidden it to us."

"There's probably some good reason," began Ransom, when he was interrupted by her sudden laughter.

"Oh, Piebald, Piebald," she said, still laughing. "How often the people of your race speak!"

"I'm sorry," said Ransom, a little put out.

"What are you sorry for?"

"I am sorry if you think I talk too much."

"Too much? How can I tell what would be too much for you to talk?"

"In our world when they say a man talks much they mean they wish him to be silent."

"If that is what they mean, why do they not say it?"

"What made you laugh?" asked Ransom, finding her question too hard.

"I laughed, Piebald, because you were wondering, as I was, about this law which Maleldil has made for one world and not for another. And you had nothing to say about it and yet made the nothing up into words."

"I *had* something to say, though," said Ransom almost under his breath. "At least," he added in a louder voice, "this forbidding is no hardship in such a world as yours."

"That also is a strange thing to say," replied the Lady. "Who thought of its being hard? The beasts would not think it hard if I told them to walk on their heads. It would become their delight to walk on their heads. I am His beast, and all His biddings are joys. It is not that which makes me thoughtful. But it was coming into my mind to wonder whether there are two kinds of bidding."

"Some of our wise men have said . . ." began Ransom, when she interrupted him.

"Let us wait and ask the King," she said. "For I think, Piebald, you do not know much more about this than I do."

"Yes, the King, by all means," said Ransom. "If only we can find him." Then, quite involuntarily, he added in English, "By Jove! What was that?" She also had exclaimed. Something like a shooting star seemed to have streaked across the sky, far away on their left, and some seconds later an indeterminate noise reached their ears.

"What was that?" he asked again, this time in Old Solar.

"Something has fallen out of Deep Heaven," said the Lady. Her face showed wonder and curiosity: but on earth we so rarely see these emotions without some admixture of defensive fear that her expression seemed strange to him.

"I think you're right," said he. "Hullo! What's this?" The calm sea had swelled and all the weeds at the edge of their island were in movement. A single wave passed under their island and all was still again.

"Something has certainly fallen into the sea," said the Lady. Then she resumed the conversation as if nothing had happened.

"It was to look for the King that I had resolved to go over to-day to the Fixed Land. He is on none of these islands here, for I have searched them all. But if we climbed high up on the Fixed Land and looked about, then we should see a long way. We could see if there are any other islands near us."

"Let us do this," said Ransom. "If we can swim so far."

"We shall ride," said the Lady. Then she knelt down on the shore—and such grace was in all her movements that it was a wonder to see her kneel—and gave three low calls all on the same note. At first no result was visible. But soon Ransom saw broken water coming rapidly towards them. A moment later and the sea beside the island was a mass of the large silver fishes: spouting, curling their bodies, pressing upon one another to get nearer, and the nearest ones nosing the land. They had not only the colour but the smoothness of silver. The biggest were about nine feet long and all were thick-set and powerful-looking. They were very unlike any terrestrial species, for the base of the head was noticeably wider than the foremost part of the trunk. But then the trunk itself grew thicker again towards the tail. Without this tailward bulge they would have looked like giant tadpoles. As it was, they suggested rather pot-bellied and narrow-chested old men with very big heads. The Lady seemed to take a long time in selecting two of them. But the moment she had done so the others all fell back for a few yards and the two successful candidates wheeled round and lay still with their tails to the shore, gently moving their fins. "Now, Piebald, like this," she said, and seated herself astride the narrow part of the right-hand fish. Ransom followed her example. The great head in front of him served instead of shoulders so that there was no danger of sliding off. He watched his hostess. She gave her fish a slight kick with her heels. He did the same to his. A moment later they were gliding out to sea at about six miles an hour. The air over the water was cooler and the breeze lifted his hair. In a world where he had as yet only swum and walked, the fish's progress gave the impression of quite an exhilarating speed. He glanced back and saw the feathery and billowy mass of the islands receding and the sky growing larger and more emphatically golden. Ahead, the fantastically shaped and coloured mountain dominated his whole field of vision. He noticed with interest that the whole school of rejected fish were still with them—some following, but the majority gambolling in wide extended wings to left and right.

"Do they always follow like this?" he asked.

"Do the beasts not follow in your world?" she replied. "We cannot ride more than two. It would be hard if those we did not choose were not even allowed to follow."

"Was that why you took so long to choose the two fish, Lady?"

"Of course," said the Lady. "I try not to choose the same fish too often."

The land came towards them apace and what had seemed level coastline began to open into bays and thrust itself forward into promontories. And now they were near enough to see that in this apparently calm ocean there was an invisible swell, a very faint rise and fall of water on the beach. A moment later the fishes lacked depth to swim any further, and following the Green Lady's example, Ransom slipped both his legs to one side of his fish and groped down with his toes. Oh, ecstasy!—they touched solid pebbles. He had not realised till now that he was pining for "fixed land." He looked up. Down to the bay in which they were landing ran a steep narrow valley with low cliffs and outcroppings of a reddish rock and, lower down, banks of some kind of moss and a few trees. The trees might almost have been terrestrial: planted in any southern country of our own world they would not have seemed remarkable to anyone except a trained botanist. Best of all, down the middle of the valley—and welcome to Ransom's eyes and ears as a glimpse of home or of heaven—ran a little stream, a dark translucent stream where a man might hope for trout.

"You love this land, Piebald?" said the Lady, glancing at him.

"Yes," said he, "it is like my own world."

They began to walk up the valley to its head. When they were under the trees the resemblance of an earthly country was diminished, for there is so much less light in that world that the glade which would have cast only a little shadow cast a forest gloom. It was about a quarter of a mile to the top of the valley, where it narrowed into a mere cleft between low rocks. With one or two grips and a leap the Lady was up these, and Ransom followed. He was amazed at her strength. They emerged into a steep upland covered with a kind of turf which would have been very like grass but that there was more blue in it. It seemed to be closely cropped and dotted with white fluffy objects as far as the eye could reach.

"Flowers?" asked Ransom. The Lady laughed.

"No. These are the Piebalds. I named you after them." He was puzzled for a moment but presently the objects began to move, and soon to move quickly towards the human pair whom they had apparently winded—for they were already so high that there was a strong breeze. In a moment they were bounding all about the Lady and welcoming her. They were white beasts with black spots—about the size of sheep but with ears so much larger, noses so much mobile, and tails so much longer, that the general impression was rather of enormous mice. Their claw-like or almost hand-like paws were clearly built for climbing, and the bluish turf was their food. After a proper interchange of courtesies with these creatures, Ransom and the Lady continued their journey. The circle of golden sea below them was now spread out in an enormous expanse and the green rock pillars above seemed almost to overhang. But it was a long and stiff climb to their base. The temperature here was much lower, though it was still warm. The silence was also noticeable. Down below, on the islands, though one had not remarked it at the time, there must have been a continual background of water noises, bubble noises, and the movement of beasts.

They were now entering into a kind of bay or re-entrant of turf between two of the green pillars. Seen from below these had appeared to touch one another; but now, though they had gone in so deep between two of them that most of the view was cut off on either hand, there was still room for a battalion to march in line. The slope grew steeper every moment; and as it grew steeper the space between the pillars also grew narrower. Soon they were scrambling on hands and knees in a place where the green walls hemmed them in so that they must go in single file, and Ransom, looking up, could hardly see the sky overhead. Finally they were faced with a little bit of real rock work—a neck of stone about eight feet high which joined, like a gum of rock, the roots of the two monstrous teeth of the mountain. "I'd give a good deal to have a pair of trousers on," thought Ransom to himself as he looked at it. The Lady, who was ahead, stood on tiptoe and raised her arms to catch a projection on the lip of the ridge. Then he saw her pull, apparently intending to lift her whole weight on her arms and swing herself to the top in a single movement. "Look here, you can't do it that way," he began, speaking inadvertently in English, but before he had time to correct himself she was standing on the edge above him. He did not see exactly how it was done, but there was no sign that she had taken any unusual exertion. His own climb was a less dignified affair, and it was a panting and perspiring man with a smudge of blood on his knee who finally stood beside her. She was inquisitive about the blood, and when he had explained the phenomenon to her as well as he could, wanted to scrape a little skin off her own knee to see if the same would happen. This led him to try to explain to her what was meant by pain, which only made her more anxious to try the experiment. But at the last moment Maleldil apparently told her not to.

Ransom now turned to survey their surroundings. High overhead, and seeming by perspective to lean inwards towards each other at the top and almost to shut out the sky, rose the immense piers of rock—not two or three of them, but nine. Some of them, like those two between which they had entered the circle, were close together. Others were many yards apart. They surrounded a roughly oval plateau of perhaps seven acres, covered with a finer turf than any known on our planet and dotted with tiny crimson flowers. A high, singing wind carried, as it were, a cooled and refined quintessence of all the scents from the richer world below, and kept these in continual agitation. Glimpses of the far-spread sea, visible between pillars, made one continually conscious of great height; and Ransom's eyes, long accustomed to the medley of curves and colours in the floating islands, rested on the pure lines and stable masses of this place with great refreshment. He took a few paces forward into the cathedral spaciousness of the plateau, and when he spoke his voice woke echoes.

"Oh, this is good," he said. "But perhaps you—you to whom it is forbidden—do not feel it so." But a glance at the Lady's face told him he was wrong. He did not know what was in her mind; but her face, as once or twice before, seemed to shine with something before which he dropped his eyes. "Let us examine the sea," she said presently.

They made the circle of the plateau methodically. Behind them lay the group of islands from which they had set out that morning. Seen from this altitude it was larger even than Ransom had supposed. The richness of its colours—its orange, its silver, its purple and (to his surprise) its glossy blacks—made it seem almost heraldic. It was from this direction that the wind came; the smell of those islands, though faint, was like the sound of running water to a thirsty man. But on every other side they saw nothing but the ocean. At least, they saw no islands. But when they had made almost the whole circuit, Ransom shouted and the Lady pointed almost at the same moment. About two miles off, dark against the coppery-green of the water, there was some small round object. If he had been looking down on an earthly sea Ransom would have taken it, at first sight, for a buoy.

"I do not know what it is," said the Lady. "Unless it is the thing that fell out of Deep Heaven this morning."

"I wish I had a pair of field glasses," thought Ransom, for the Lady's words had awakened in him a sudden suspicion. And the longer he stared at the dark blob the more his suspicion was confirmed. It appeared to be perfectly spherical; and he thought he had seen something like it before.

You have already heard that Ransom had been in that world which men call Mars but whose true name is Malacandra. But he had not been taken thither by the eldila. He had been taken by men, and taken in a space-ship, a hollow sphere of glass and steel. He had, in fact, been kidnapped by men who thought that the ruling powers of Malacandra demanded a human sacrifice. The whole thing had been a misunderstanding. The great Oyarsa who has governed Mars from the beginning (and whom my own eyes beheld, in a sense, in the hall of Ransom's cottage) had done him no harm and meant him none. But his chief captor, Professor Weston, had meant plenty of harm. He was a man obsessed with the idea which is at this moment circulating all over our planet in obscure works of "scientifiction," in little Interplanetary Societies and Rocketry Clubs, and between the covers of monstrous magazines, ignored or mocked by the intellectuals, but ready, if ever the power is put into its hands, to open a new chapter of misery for the universe. It is the idea that humanity, having now sufficiently corrupted the planet where it arose, must at all costs contrive to seed itself over a larger area: that the vast astronomical distances which are God's quarantine regulations, must somehow be overcome. This for a start. But beyond this lies the sweet poison of the false infinite—the wild dream that planet after planet, system after system, in the end galaxy after galaxy, can be forced to sustain, everywhere and for ever, the sort of life which is contained in the loins of our own species—a dream begotten by the hatred of death upon the fear of true immortality, fondled in secret by thousands of ignorant men and hundreds who are not ignorant. The destruction or enslavement of other species in the universe, if such there are, is to these minds a welcome corollary. In Professor Weston the power had at last met the dream. The great physicist had discovered a motive power for his space-ship. And that little black object, now floating beneath him on the sinless waters of Perelandra, looked to Ransom more like the spaceship every moment. "So that," he thought, "that is why I have been sent here. He failed on Malacandra and now he is coming here. And it's up to me to do something about it." A terrible sense of inadequacy swept over him. Last time—in Mars—Weston had had only one accomplice. But he had had firearms. And how many accomplices might he have this time? And in Mars he had been foiled not by Ransom but by the eldila, and specially the great eldil, the Oyarsa, of that world. He turned quickly to the Lady.

"I have seen no eldila in your world," he said.

"Eldila?" she repeated as if it were a new name to her.

"Yes. Elidila," said Ransom, "the great and ancient servants of Maleldil. The creatures that neither breed nor breathe. Whose bodies are made of light. Whom we can hardly see. Who ought to be obeyed."

She mused for a moment and then spoke. "Sweetly and gently this time Maleldil makes me older. He shows me all the natures of these blessed creatures. But there is no obeying them *now*, not in this world. That is all the old order, Piebald, the far side of the wave that has rolled past us and will not come again. That very ancient world to which you journeyed was put under the eldila. In your own world also they ruled once: but not since our Beloved became a Man. In your world they linger still. But in our world, which is the first of worlds to wake after the great change, they have no power. There is nothing now between us and Him. They have grown less and we have increased. And now Maleldil puts it into my mind that this is their glory and their joy. They received us—us things of the low worlds, who breed and breathe—as weak and small beasts whom their lightest touch could destroy; and their glory was to cherish us and make us older till we were older than they—till they could fall at our feet. It is a joy we shall not have. However I teach the beasts they will never be better than I. But it is a joy beyond all. Not that it is better joy than ours. Every joy is beyond all others. The fruit we are eating is always the best fruit of all."

"There have been eldila who did not think it a joy," said Ransom.

"How?"

"You spoke yesterday, Lady, of clinging to the old good instead of taking the good that came."

"Yes—for a few heart-beats."

"There was an eldil who clung longer—who has been clinging since before the worlds were made."

"But the old good would cease to be a good at all if he did that."

"Yes. It has ceased. And still he clings."

She stared at him in wonder and was about to speak, but he interrupted her.

"There is no time to explain," he said.

"No time? What has happened to the time?" she asked.

"Listen," he said. "That thing down there has come through Deep Heaven from my world. There is a man in it: perhaps many men——"

"Look," she said, "it is turning into two—one big and one small."

Ransom saw that a small black object had detached itself from the space-ship and was beginning to move uncertainly away from it. It puzzled him for a moment. Then it dawned on him that Weston—if it was Weston—probably knew the watery surface he had to expect on Venus and had brought some kind of collapsible boat. But could it be that he had not reckoned with tides or storms and did not foresee that it might be impossible for him ever to recover the space-ship? It was not like Weston to cut off his own retreat. And Ransom certainly did not wish Weston's retreat to be cut off. A Weston who could not, even if he chose, return to Earth, was an insoluble problem. Anyway, what could he, Ransom, possibly do without support from the eldila? He began to smart under a sense of injustice. What was the good of sending him—a mere scholar—to cope with a situation of this sort? Any ordinary pugilist, or, better still, any man who could make good use of a tommy-gun, would have been more to the purpose. If only they could find this King whom the Green Woman kept on talking about. . . .

But while these thoughts were passing through his mind he became aware of a dim murmuring or growling sound which had gradually been encroaching on the silence for some time. "Look," said the Lady suddenly, and pointed to the mass of islands. Their surface was no longer level. At the same moment he realised that the noise was that of waves: small waves as yet, but definitely beginning to foam on the rocky headlands of the Fixed Island. "The sea is rising," said the Lady. "We must go down and leave this land at once. Soon the waves will be too great—and I must not be here by night."

"Not that way," shouted Ransom. "Not where you will meet the man from my world."

"Why?" said the Lady. "I am Lady and Mother of this world. If the King is not here, who else should greet a stranger?"

"I will meet him."

"It is not your world, Piebald," she replied.

"You do not understand," said Ransom. "This man—he is a friend of that eldil of whom I told you—one of those who cling to the wrong good."

"Then I must explain it to him," said the Lady. "Let us go and make him older," and with that she slung herself down the rocky edge of the plateau and began descending the mountain slope. Ransom took longer to manage the rocks; but once his feet were again on the turf he began running as fast as he could. The Lady cried out in surprise as he flashed past her, but he took no notice. He could now see clearly which bay the little boat was making for and his attention was fully occupied in directing his course and making sure of his feet. There was only one man in the boat. Down and down the long slope he raced. Now he was in a fold: now in a winding valley which momentarily cut off the sight of the sea. Now at last he was in the cove itself. He glanced back and saw to his dismay that the Lady had also been running and was only a few yards behind. He glanced forward again. There were waves, though not yet very large ones, breaking on the pebbly beach. A man in shirt and shorts and a pith helmet was ankle-deep in the water, wading ashore and pulling after him a little canvas punt. It was certainly Weston, though his face had something about it which seemed subtly unfamiliar. It seemed to Ransom of vital importance to prevent a meeting between Weston and the Lady. He had seen Weston murder an inhabitant of Malacandra. He turned back, stretching out both arms to bar her way and shouting "Go back!" She was too near. For a second she was almost in his arms. Then she stood back from him, panting from the race, surprised, her mouth opened to speak. But at that moment he heard Weston's voice, from behind him, saying in English, "May I ask you, Dr. Ransom, what is the meaning of this?"

7

In all the circumstances it would have been reasonable to expect that Weston would be much more taken aback at Ransom's presence than Ransom could be at his. But if he were, he showed no sign of it, and Ransom could hardly help admiring the massive egoism which enabled this man in the very moment of his arrival on an unknown world to stand there unmoved in all his authoritative vulgarity, his arms akimbo, his face scowling, and his feet planted as solidly on that unearthly soil as if he had been standing with his back to the fire in his own study. Then, with a shock, he noticed that Weston was speaking to the Lady in the Old Solar language with perfect fluency. On Malacandra, partly from incapacity, and much more from his contempt for the inhabitants, he had never acquired more than a smattering of it. Here was an inexplicable and disquieting novelty. Ransom felt that his only advantage had been taken from him. He felt that he was now in the presence of the incalculable. If the scales had been suddenly weighted in this one respect, what might come next?

He awoke from his abstraction to find that Weston and the Lady had been conversing fluently, but without mutual understanding. "It is no use," she was saying. "You and I are not old enough to speak together, it seems. The sea is rising; let us go back to the islands. Will he come with us, Piebald?"

"Where are the two fishes?" said Ransom.

"They will be waiting in the next bay," said the Lady.

"Quick, then," said Ransom to her; and then, in answer to her look: "No, he will not come." She did not, presumably, understand his urgency, but her eye was on the sea and she understood her own reason for haste. She had already begun to ascend the side of the valley, with Ransom following her, when Weston shouted, "No, you don't." Ransom turned and found himself covered by a revolver. The sudden heat which swept over his body was the only sign by which he knew that he was frightened. His head remained clear.

"Are you going to begin in this world also by murdering one of its inhabitants?" he asked.

"What are you saying?" asked the Lady, pausing and looking back at the two men with a puzzled, tranquil face.

"Stay where you are, Ransom," said the Professor. "That native can go where she likes; the sooner the better."

Ransom was about to implore her to make good her escape when he realised that no imploring was needed. He had irrationally supposed that she would understand the situation; but apparently she saw nothing more than two strangers talking about something which she did not at the moment understand—that, and her own necessity of leaving the Fixed Land at once.

"You and he do not come with me, Piebald?" she asked.

"No," said Ransom, without turning round. "It may be that you and I shall not meet soon again. Greet the King for me if you find him and speak of me always to Maleldil. I stay here."

"We shall meet when Maleldil pleases," she answered, "or if not, some greater good will happen to us instead." Then he heard her footsteps behind him for a few seconds, and then he heard them no more and knew he was alone with Weston.

"You allowed yourself to use the word Murder just now, Dr. Ransom," said the Professor, "in reference to an accident that occurred when we were in Malacandra. In any case, the creature killed was not a human being. Allow me to tell you that I consider the seduction of a native girl as an almost equally unfortunate way of introducing civilisation to a new planet."

"Seduction?" said Ransom. "Oh, I see. You thought I was making love to her."

"When I find a naked civilised man embracing a naked savage woman in a solitary place, that is the name I give to it."

"I wasn't embracing her," said Ransom dully, for the whole business of defending himself on this score seemed at that moment a mere weariness of the spirit. "And no one wears clothes here. But what does it matter? Get on with the job that brings you to Perelandra."

"You ask me to believe that you have been living here with that woman under these conditions in a state of sexless innocence?"

"Oh, sexless!" said Ransom disgustedly. "All right, if you like. It's about as good a description of living in Perelandra as it would be to say that a man had forgotten water because Niagara Falls didn't immediately give him the idea of making it into cups of tea. But you're right enough if you mean that I have had no more thought of desiring her than—than . . ." Comparisons failed him and his voice died. Then he began again: "But don't say I'm asking you to believe it, or to believe anything. I am asking you nothing but to begin and end as soon as possible whatever butcheries and robberies you have come to do."

Weston eyed him for a moment with a curious expression: then, unexpectedly, he returned his revolver to its holster.

"Ransom," he said, "you do me a great injustice."

For several seconds there was silence between them. Long breakers with white woolpacks of foam on them were now rolling into the cove exactly as on earth.

"Yes," said Weston at last, "and I will begin with a frank admission. You may make what capital of it you please. I shall not be deterred. I deliberately say that I was, in some respects, mistaken—seriously mistaken—in my conception of the whole interplanetary problem when I went to Malacandra."

Partly from the relaxation which followed the disappearance of the pistol, and partly from the elaborate air of magnanimity with which the great scientist spoke, Ransom felt very much inclined to laugh. But it occurred to him that this was possibly the first occasion in his whole life in which Weston had ever acknowledged himself in the wrong, and that even the false dawn of humility, which is still ninety-nine per cent of arrogance, ought not to be rebuffed—or not by him.

"Well, that's very handsome," he said. "How do you mean?"

"I'll tell you presently," said Weston. "In the meantime I must get my things ashore." Between them they beached the punt, and began carrying Weston's primus-stove and tins and tent and other packages to a spot about two hundred yards inland. Ransom, who knew all the paraphernalia to be needless, made no objection, and in about a quarter of an hour something like an encampment had been established in a mossy place under some blue-trunked silver-leaved trees beside a rivulet. Both men sat down and Ransom listened at first with interest, then with amazement, and finally with incredulity. Weston cleared his throat, threw out his chest, and assumed his lecturing manner. Throughout the conversation that followed, Ransom was filled with a sense of crazy irrelevance. Here were two human beings, thrown together in an alien world under conditions of inconceivable strangeness: the one separated from his spaceship, the other newly released from the threat of instant death. Was it sane—was it imaginable—that they should find themselves at once engaged in a philosophical argument which might just as well have occurred in a Cambridge combination room? Yet that, apparently, was what Weston insisted upon. He showed no interest in the fate of his space-ship; he even seemed to feel no curiosity about Ransom's presence on Venus. Could it be that he had travelled more than thirty million miles of space in search of—conversation? But as he went on talking, Ransom felt himself more and more in the presence of a monomaniac. Like an actor who cannot think of anything but his celebrity, or a lover who can think of nothing but his mistress, tense, tedious, and unescapable, the scientist pursued his fixed idea.

"The tragedy of my life," he said, "and indeed of the modern intellectual world in general, is the rigid specialisation of knowledge entailed by the growing complexity of what is known. It is my own share in that tragedy that an early devotion to physics has prevented me from paying any proper attention to Biology until I reached the fifties. To do myself justice, I should make it clear that the false humanist ideal of knowledge as an end in itself never appealed to me. I always wanted to know in order to achieve utility. At first, that utility naturally appeared to me in a personal form—I wanted scholarships, an income, and that generally recognised position in the world without which a man has no leverage. When those were attained, I began to look farther: to the utility of the human race!"

He paused as he rounded his period and Ransom nodded to him to proceed.

"The utility of the human race," continued Weston, "in the long run depends rigidly on the possibility of interplanetary, and even inter-sidereal, travel. That problem I solved. The key of human destiny was placed in my hands. It would be unnecessary—and painful to us both—to remind you how it was wrenched from me in Malacandra by a member of a hostile intelligent species whose existence, I admit, I had not anticipated."

"Not hostile exactly," said Ransom, "but go on."

"The rigours of our return journey from Malacandra led to a serious breakdown in my health——"

"Mine too," said Ransom.

Weston looked somewhat taken aback at the interruption and went on. "During my convalescence I had that leisure for reflection which I had denied myself for many years. In particular I reflected on the objections you had felt to that liquidation of the non-human inhabitants of Malacandra which was, of course, the necessary preliminary to its occupation by our own species. The traditional and, if I may say so, the humanitarian form in which you advanced those objections had till then concealed from me their true strength. That strength I now began to perceive. I began to see that my own exclusive devotion to human utility was really based on an unconscious dualism."

"What do you mean?"

"I mean that all my life I had been making a wholly unscientific dichotomy or antithesis between Man and Nature—had conceived myself fighting *for* Man against his non-human environment. During my illness I plunged into Biology, and particularly into what may be called biological philosophy. Hitherto, as a physicist, I had been content to regard Life as a subject outside my scope. The conflicting views of those who drew a sharp line between the organic and the inorganic and those who held that what we call Life was inherent in matter from the very beginning had not interested me. Now it did. I saw almost at once that I could admit no break, no discontinuity, in the unfolding of the cosmic process. I became a convinced believer in emergent evolution. All is one. The stuff of mind, the unconsciously purposive dynamism, is present from the very beginning."

Here he paused. Ransom had heard this sort of thing pretty often before and wondered when his companion was coming to the point. When Weston resumed it was with an even deeper solemnity of tone.

"The majestic spectacle of this blind, inarticulate purposiveness thrusting its way upward and ever upward in an endless unity of differentiated achievements towards an ever-increasing complexity of organisation, towards spontaneity and spirituality, swept away all my old conception of a duty to Man as such. Man in himself is nothing. The forward movement of Life—the growing spirituality—is everything. I say to you quite freely, Ransom, that I should have been wrong in liquidating the Malacandrians. It was a mere prejudice that made me prefer our own race to theirs. To spread spirituality, not to spread the human race, is henceforth my mission. This sets the coping-stone on my career. I worked first for myself; then for science; then for humanity; but now at last for Spirit itself—I might say, borrowing language which will be more familiar to you, the Holy Spirit."

"Now what exactly do you mean by that?" asked Ransom.

"I mean," said Weston, "that nothing now divides you and me except a few outworn theological technicalities with which organised religion has unhappily allowed itself to get incrusted. But I have penetrated that crust. The Meaning beneath it is as true and living as ever. If you will excuse me for putting it that way, the essential truth of the religious view of life finds a remarkable witness in the fact that it enabled you, on Malacandra, to grasp, in your own mythical and imaginative fashion, a truth which was hidden from me."

"I don't know much about what people call the religious view of life," said Ransom, wrinkling his brow. "You see, I'm a Christian. And what we mean by the Holy Ghost is *not* a blind, inarticulate purposiveness."

"My dear Ransom," said Weston, "I understand you perfectly. I have no doubt that my phraseology will seem strange to you, and perhaps even shocking. Early and revered associations may have put it out of your power to recognise in this new form the very same truths which religion has so long preserved and which science is now at last rediscovering. But whether you can see it or not, believe me, we are talking about exactly the same thing."

"I'm not at all sure that we are."

"That, if you will permit me to say so, is one of the real weaknesses of organised religion—that adherence to formulæ, that failure to recognise one's own friends. God is a spirit, Ransom. Get hold of that. You're familiar with that already. Stick to it. God is a spirit."

"Well, of course. But what then?"

"What then? Why, spirit—mind—freedom—spontaneity—that's what I'm talking about. That is the goal towards which the whole cosmic process is moving. The final disengagement of that freedom, that spirituality, is the work to which I dedicate my own life and the life of humanity. The goal, Ransom, the goal: think of it! *Pure* spirit: the final vortex of self-thinking, self-originating activity."

"Final?" said Ransom. "You mean it doesn't yet exist?"

"Ah," said Weston, "I see what's bothering you. Of course I know. Religion pictures it as being there from the beginning. But surely that is not a real difference? To make it one, would be to take time too seriously. When it has once been attained, you might then say it had been at the beginning just as well as at the end. Time is one of the things it will transcend."

"By the way," said Ransom, "is it in any sense at all personal—is it alive?"

An indescribable expression passed over Weston's face. He moved a little nearer to Ransom and began speaking in a lower voice.

"That's what none of them understand," he said. It was such a gangster's or a schoolboy's whisper and so unlike his usual orotund lecturing style that Ransom for a moment felt a sensation almost of disgust.

"Yes," said Weston, "I couldn't have believed, myself, till recently. Not a person, of course. Anthropomorphism is one of the childish diseases of popular religion" (here he had resumed his public manner), "but the opposite extreme of excessive abstraction has perhaps in the aggregate proved more disastrous. Call it a Force. A great, inscrutable

Force, pouring up into us from the dark bases of being. A Force that can choose its instruments. It is only lately, Ransom, that I've learned from actual experience something which you have believed all your life as part of your religion." Here he suddenly subsided again into a whisper—a croaking whisper unlike his usual voice. "Guided," he said. "Chosen. Guided. I've become conscious that I'm a man set apart. Why did I do physics? Why did I discover the Weston rays? Why did I go to Malacandra? It—the Force—has pushed me on all the time. I'm being guided. I know now that I am the greatest scientist the world has yet produced. I've been made so for a purpose. It is through me that Spirit itself is at this moment pushing on to its goal."

"Look here," said Ransom, "one wants to be careful about this sort of thing. There are spirits and spirits you know."

"Eh?" said Weston. "What are you talking about?"

"I mean a thing might be a spirit and not good for you."

"But I thought you agreed that Spirit was the good—the end of the whole process? I thought you religious people were all out for spirituality? What is the point of asceticism—fasts and celibacy and all that? Didn't we agree that God is a spirit? Don't you worship Him because He is pure spirit?"

"Good heavens, no! We worship Him because He is wise and good. There's nothing specially fine about simply being a spirit. The Devil is a spirit."

"Now your mentioning the Devil is very interesting," said Weston, who had by this time quite recovered his normal manner. "It is a most interesting thing in popular religion, this tendency to fissiparate, to breed pairs of opposites: heaven and hell, God and Devil. I need hardly say that in my view no real dualism in the universe is admissible; and on that ground I should have been disposed, even a few weeks ago, to reject these pairs of doublets as pure mythology. It would have been a profound error. The cause of this universal religious tendency is to be sought much deeper. The doublets are really portraits of Spirit, of cosmic energy—self-portraits, indeed, for it is the Life-Force itself which has deposited them in our brains."

"What on earth do you mean?" said Ransom. As he spoke he rose to his feet and began pacing to and fro. A quite appalling weariness and malaise had descended upon him.

"*Your* Devil and *your* God," said Weston, "are both pictures of the same Force. Your heaven is a picture of the perfect spirituality ahead; your hell a picture of the urge or *nisus* which is driving us on to it from behind. Hence the static peace of the one and the fire and darkness of the other. The next stage of emergent evolution, beckoning us forward, is

God; the transcended stage behind, ejecting us, is the Devil. Your own religion, after all, says that the devils are fallen angels."

"And you are saying precisely the opposite, as far as I can make out—that angels are devils who've risen in the world."

"It comes to the same thing," said Weston.

There was another long pause. "Look here," said Ransom, "it's easy to misunderstand one another on a point like this. What you are saying sounds to me like the most horrible mistake a man could fall into. But that may be because in the effort to accommodate it to my supposed 'religious views,' you're saying a good deal more than you mean. It's only a metaphor, isn't it, all this about spirits and forces? I expect all you really mean is that you feel it your duty to work for the spread of civilisation and knowledge and that kind of thing." He had tried to keep out of his voice the involuntary anxiety which he had begun to feel. Next moment he recoiled in horror at the cackling laughter, almost an infantile or senile laughter, with which Weston replied.

"There you go, there you go," he said. "Like all you religious people. You talk and talk about these things all your life, and the moment you meet the reality you get frightened."

"What proof," said Ransom (who indeed did feel frightened), "what proof have you that you are being guided or supported by anything except your own individual mind and other people's books?"

"You didn't notice, dear Ransom," said Weston, "that I'd improved a bit since we last met in my knowledge of extraterrestrial language. You are a philologist, they tell me."

Ransom started. "How did you do it?" he blurted out.

"Guidance, you know, guidance," croaked Weston. He was squatting at the roots of his tree with his knees drawn up, and his face, now the colour of putty, wore a fixed and even slightly twisted grin. "Guidance. Guidance," he went on. "Things coming into my head. I'm being prepared all the time. Being made a fit receptacle for it."

"That ought to be fairly easy," said Ransom impatiently. "If this Life-Force is something so ambiguous that God and the Devil are equally good portraits of it, I suppose any receptacle is equally fit, and anything you can do is equally an expression of it."

"There's such a thing as the main current," said Weston. "It's a question of surrendering yourself to that—making yourself the conductor of the live, fiery, central purpose—becoming the very finger with which it reaches forward."

"But I thought that was the Devil aspect of it, a moment ago."

"That is the fundamental paradox. The thing we are reaching forward to is what you would call God. The reaching forward, the dynamism, is what people like you always call the Devil. The people like me, who do the reaching forward, are always martyrs. You revile us, and by us come to your goal."

"Does that mean in plainer language that the things the Force wants you to do are what ordinary people call diabolical?"

"My dear Ransom, I wish you would not keep relapsing on to the popular level. The two things are only moments in the single, unique reality. The world leaps forward through great men and greatness always transcends mere moralism. When the leap has been made our 'diabolism' as you would call it becomes the morality of the next stage; but while we are making it, we are called criminals, heretics, blasphemers. . . ."

"How far does it go? Would you still obey the Life-Force if you found it prompting you to murder me?"

"Yes."

"Or to sell England to the Germans?"

"Yes."

"Or to print lies as serious research in a scientific periodical?"

"Yes."

"God help you!" said Ransom.

"You are still wedded to your conventionalities," said Weston. "Still dealing in abstractions. Can you not even conceive a total commitment—a commitment to something which utterly overrides all our petty ethical pigeon-holes?"

Ransom grasped at the straw. "Wait, Weston," he said abruptly. "That may be a point of contact. You say it's a total commitment. That is, you're giving up yourself. You're not out for your own advantage. No, wait half a second. This *is* the point of contact between your morality and mine. We both acknowledge——"

"Idiot," said Weston. His voice was almost a howl and he had risen to his feet. "Idiot," he repeated. "Can you understand nothing? Will you always try to press everything back into the miserable framework of your old jargon about self and self-sacrifice? That is the old accursed dualism in another form. There is no possible distinction in concrete thought between me and the universe. In so far as I am the conductor of the central forward pressure of the universe, I am it. Do you see, you timid, scruple-mongering fool? I *am* the Universe. I, Weston, am your God and your Devil. I call that Force into me completely. . . ."

Then horrible things began happening. A spasm like that preceding a deadly vomit twisted Weston's face out of recognition. As it passed, for one second something like the old Weston reappeared—the old Weston, staring with eyes of horror and howling, "Ransom, Ransom! For

Christ's sake don't let them——" and instantly his whole body spun round as if he had been hit by a revolver-bullet and he fell to the earth, and was there rolling at Ransom's feet, slavering and chattering and tearing up the moss by handfuls. Gradually the convulsions decreased. He lay still, breathing heavily, his eyes open but without expression. Ransom was kneeling beside him now. It was obvious that the body was alive, and Ransom wondered whether this were a stroke or an epileptic fit, for he had never seen either. He rummaged among the packages and found a bottle of brandy which he uncorked and applied to the patient's mouth. To his consternation the teeth opened, closed on the neck of the bottle and bit it through. No glass was spat out. "O God, I've killed him," said Ransom. But beyond a spurt of blood at the lips there was no change in his appearance. The face suggested that either he was in no pain or in pain beyond all human comprehension. Ransom rose at last, but before doing so he plucked the revolver from Weston's belt, then, walking down to the beach, he threw it as far as he could into the sea.

He stood for some moments gazing out upon the bay and undecided what to do. Presently he turned and climbed up the turfy ridge that bordered the little valley on his left hand. He found himself on a fairly level upland with a good view of the sea, now running high and teased out of its level gold into a continually changing pattern of lights and shadows. For a second or two he could catch no sight of the islands. Then suddenly their tree-tops appeared, hanging high up against the sky, and widely separated. The weather, apparently, was already driving them apart—and even as he thought this they vanished once more into some unseen valley of the waves. What was his chance, he wondered, of ever finding them again? A sense of loneliness smote him, and then a feeling of angry frustration. If Weston were dying, or even if Weston were to live, imprisoned here with him on an island they could not leave, what had been the danger he was sent to avert from Perelandra? And so, having begun to think of himself, he realised that he was hungry. He had seen neither fruit nor gourd on the Fixed Land. Perhaps it was a death trap. He smiled bitterly at the folly which had made him so glad, that morning, to exchange those floating paradises, where every grove dropped sweetness, for this barren rock. But perhaps it was not barren after all. Determined, despite the weariness which was every moment descending upon him, to make a search for food, he was just turning inland when the swift changes of colour that announce the evening of that world overtook him. Uselessly he quickened his pace. Before he had got down into the valley, the grove where he had left Weston was a mere cloud of darkness. Before he had reached it he was in seamless, undimensioned night. An effort or two to grope his way to the place where

Weston's stores had been deposited only served to abolish his sense of direction altogether. He sat down perforce. He called Weston's name aloud once or twice but, as he expected, received no answer. "I'm glad I removed his gun, all the same," thought Ransom; and then, "Well, *qui dort dîne* and I suppose I must make the best of it till the morning." When he lay down he discovered that the solid earth and moss of the Fixed Land was very much less comfortable than the surfaces to which he had lately been accustomed. That, and the thought of the other human being lying, no doubt, close at hand with open eyes and teeth clenched on splintered glass, and the sullen recurring pound of breakers on the beach, all made the night comfortless. "If I lived on Perelandra," he muttered, "Maleldil wouldn't need to *forbid* this island. I wish I'd never set eyes on it."

8

He woke, after a disturbed and dreamful sleep, in full daylight. He had a dry mouth, a crick in his neck, and a soreness in his limbs. It was so unlike all previous wakings in the world of Venus, that for a moment he supposed himself back on Earth: and the dream (for so it seemed to him) of having lived and walked on the oceans of the Morning Star rushed through his memory with a sense of lost sweetness that was well-nigh unbearable. Then he sat up and the facts came back to him. "It's jolly nearly the same as having waked from a dream, though," he thought. Hunger and thirst became at once his dominant sensations, but he conceived it a duty to look first at the sick man—though with very little hope that he could help him. He gazed round. There was the grove of silvery trees all right, but he could not see Weston. Then he glanced at the bay; there was no punt either. Assuming that in the darkness he had blundered into the wrong valley, he rose and approached the stream for a drink. As he lifted his face from the water with a long sigh of satisfaction, his eyes suddenly fell on a little wooden box—and then beyond it on a couple of tins. His brain was working rather slowly and it took him a few seconds to realise that he was in the right valley after all, and a few more to draw conclusions from the fact that the box was open and empty, and that some of the stores had been removed and others left behind. But was it possible that a man in Weston's physical condition could have recovered sufficiently during the night to strike camp and to go away laden with some kind of pack? Was it possible that any man could have faced a sea like that in a collapsible punt? It was true, as he now noticed for the first time, that the storm (which had been a mere squall by Perelandrian standards) appeared to have blown itself out during the night; but there was still a quite formidable swell and it seemed out of the question that the Professor could have left the island. Much more probably he had left the valley on foot and carried the punt with him. Ransom decided that he must find Weston at once: he must keep in touch with his enemy. For if Weston had recovered, there was no doubt he meant mischief of some kind. Ransom was not at all certain that he had understood all his wild talk on the previous day; but what he did understand he disliked very much, and suspected that this vague mysticism about "spirituality" would turn out to be something even nastier than his old and comparatively simple programme of planetary imperialism. It would be unfair to take seriously the things the man had said immediately before his seizure, no doubt; but there was enough without that.

The next few hours Ransom passed in searching the island for food and for Weston. As far as food was concerned, he was rewarded. Some fruit like bilberries could be gathered in handfuls on the upper slopes, and the wooded valleys abounded in a kind of oval nut. The kernel had a toughly soft consistency, rather like cork or kidneys, and the flavour, though somewhat austere and prosaic after the fruit of the floating islands, was not unsatisfactory. The giant mice were as tame as other Perelandrian beasts but seemed stupider. Ransom ascended to the central plateau. The sea was dotted with islands in every direction, rising and falling with the swell, and all separated from one another by wide stretches of water. His eye at once picked out an orange-coloured island, but did not know whether it was that on which he had been living, for he saw at least two others in which the same colour predominated. At one time he counted twenty-three floating islands in all. That, he thought, was more than the temporary archipelago had contained, and allowed him to hope that any one of those he saw might hide the King—or that the King might even at this moment be re-united to the Lady. Without thinking it out very clearly, he had come to rest almost all his hopes on the King.

Of Weston he could find no trace. It really did seem, in spite of all improbabilities, that he had somehow contrived to leave the Fixed Island; and Ransom's anxiety was very great. What Weston, in his new vein, might do, he had no idea. The best to hope for was that he would simply ignore the master and mistress of Perelandra as mere savages or "natives."

Late in the day, being tired, he sat down on the shore. There was very little swell now and the waves, just before they broke, were less than knee-deep. His feet, made soft by the mattress-like surface which one walks on in those floating islands, were hot and sore. Presently he decided to refresh them by a little wading. The delicious quality of the water drew him out till he was waist-deep. As he stood there, deep in thought, he suddenly perceived that what he had taken to be an effect of light on the water was really the back of one of the great silvery fish. "I wonder would it let me ride it?" he thought; and then, watching how the beast nosed towards him and kept itself as near the shallows as it dared, it was borne in upon him that it was trying to attract his attention. Could it have been *sent?* The thought had no sooner darted through his mind than he decided to make the experiment. He laid his hand across the creature's back, and it did not flinch from his touch. Then with some difficulty he scrambled into a sitting position across the narrow part behind its head, and while he was doing this it remained as nearly stationary as it could; but as soon as he was firmly in the saddle it whisked itself about and headed for the sea.

If he had wished to withdraw, it was very soon impossible to do so. Already the green pinnacles of the mountain, as he looked back, had withdrawn their summits from the sky and the coastline of the island had begun to conceal its bays and nesses. The breakers were no longer audible—only the prolonged sibilant or chattering noises of the water about him. Many floating islands were visible, though seen from this level they were mere feathery silhouettes. But the fish seemed to be heading for none of these. Straight on, as if it well knew its way, the beat of the great fins carried him for more than an hour. Then green and purple splashed the whole world, and after that darkness.

Somehow he felt hardly any uneasiness when he found himself swiftly climbing and descending the low hills of water through the black night. And here it was not all black. The heavens had vanished, and the surface of the sea; but far, far below him in the heart of the vacancy through which he appeared to be travelling, strange bursting star shells and writhing streaks of a bluish-green luminosity appeared. At first they were very remote, but soon, as far as he could judge, they were nearer. A whole world of phosphorescent creatures seemed to be at play not far from the surface—coiling eels and darting things in complete armour, and then heraldically fantastic shapes to which the sea-horse of our own waters would be commonplace. They were all round him—twenty or thirty of them often in sight at once. And mixed with all this riot of sea-centaurs and sea-dragons he saw yet stranger forms: fishes, if fishes they were, whose forward part was so nearly human in shape that when he first caught sight of them he thought he had fallen into a dream and shook himself to awake. But it was no dream. There—and there again—it was unmistakable: now a shoulder, now a profile, and then for one second a full face: veritable mermen or mermaids. The resemblance to humanity was indeed greater, not less, than he had first supposed. What had for a moment concealed it from him was the total absence of human expression. Yet the faces were not idiotic; they were not even brutal parodies of humanity like those of our terrestrial apes. They were more like human faces asleep, or faces in which humanity slept while some other life, neither bestial nor diabolic, but merely elvish, out of our orbit, was irrelevantly awake. He remembered his old suspicion that what was myth in one world might always be fact in some other. He wondered also whether the King and Queen of Perelandra, though doubtless the first human pair of this planet, might on the physical side have a marine ancestry. And if so, what then of the man-like things before men in our own world? Must they in truth have been the wistful brutalities whose pictures we see in popular books on evolution? Or were the old myths truer than the modern myths? Had there in truth been a time when satyrs danced in the Italian woods? But he said "Hush" to his mind at this stage, for the mere pleasure of breathing in the fragrance which now began to steal towards him from the blackness ahead. Warm and sweet, and every moment sweeter and purer, and every moment stronger and more filled with all delights, it came to him. He knew well what it was. He would know it henceforward out of the whole universe—the night-breath of a floating island in the star Venus. It was strange to be filled with homesickness for places where his sojourn had been so brief and which were, by any objective standard, so alien to all our race. Or were they? The cord of longing which drew him to the invisible isle seemed to him at that moment to have been fastened long, long before his coming to Perelandra, long before the earliest times that memory could recover in his childhood, before birth, before the birth of man himself, before the origins of time. It was sharp, sweet, wild, and holy, all in one, and in any world where men's nerves have ceased to obey their central desires would doubtless have been aphrodisiac too, but not in Perelandra. The fish was no longer moving. Ransom put out his hand. He found he was touching weed. He crawled forward over the head of the monstrous fish, and levered himself on to the gently moving surface of the island. Short as his absence from such places had been, his earth-trained habits of walking had reasserted themselves, and he fell more than once as he groped his way on the heaving lawn. But it did no harm falling here; good luck to it! There were trees all about him in the dark and when a smooth, cool, rounded object came away in his hand he put it, unfearing, to his lips. It was none of the fruits he had tasted before. It was better than any of them. Well might the Lady say of her world that the fruit you ate at any moment was, at that moment, the best. Wearied with his day's walking and climbing, and, still more, borne down by absolute satisfaction, he sank into dreamless sleep.

He felt that it was several hours later when he awoke and found himself still in darkness. He knew, too, that he had been suddenly waked: and a moment later he was listening to the sound that had waked him. It was the sound of voices—a man's voice and a woman's in earnest conversation. He judged that they were very close to him—for in a Perelandrian night an object is no more visible six inches than six miles away. He perceived at once who the speakers were: but the voices sounded strange, and the emotions of the speakers were obscure to him, with no facial expression to eke them out.

"I am wondering," said the woman's voice, "whether all the people of your world have the habit of talking about the same thing more than once. I have said already that we are forbidden to dwell on the Fixed Land. Why do you not either talk of something else or stop talking?"

"Because this forbidding is such a strange one," said the Man's voice. "And so unlike the ways of Maleldil in my world. And He has not forbidden you to think about dwelling on the Fixed Land."

"That would be a strange thing—to think about what will never happen."

"Nay, in our world we do it all the time. We put words together to mean things that have never happened and places that never were: beautiful words, well put together. And then tell them to one another. We call it stories or poetry. In that old world you spoke of, Malacandra, they did the same. It is for mirth and wonder and wisdom."

"What is the wisdom in it?"

"Because the world is made up not only of what is but of what might be. Maleldil knows both and wants us to know both."

"This is more than I ever thought of. The other—the Piebald one— has already told me things which made me feel like a tree whose branches were growing wider and wider apart. But this goes beyond all. Stepping out of what is into what might be and talking and making things out there . . . alongside the world. I will ask the King what he thinks of it."

"You see, that is what we always come back to. If only you had not been parted from the King."

"Oh, I see. That also is one of the things that might be. The world might be so made that the King and I were never parted."

"The world would not have to be different—only the way you live. In a world where people live on the Fixed Lands they do not become suddenly separated."

"But you remember we are not to live on the Fixed Land."

"No, but He has never forbidden you to think about it. Might not that be one of the reasons why you are forbidden to do it—so that you may have a Might Be to think about, to make Story about as we call it?"

"I will think more of this. I will get the King to make me older about it."

"How greatly I desire to meet this King of yours! But in the matter of Stories he may be no older than you himself."

"That saying of yours is like a tree with no fruit. The King is always older than I, and about all things."

"But Piebald and I have already made you older about certain matters which the King never mentioned to you. That is the new good which you never expected. You thought you would always learn all things from the King; but now Maleldil has sent you other men whom it had never entered your mind to think of and they have told you things the King himself could not know."

"I begin to see now why the King and I were parted at this time. This is a strange and great good He intended for me."

"And if you refused to learn things from me and kept on saying you would wait and ask the King, would that not be like turning away from the fruit you had found to the fruit you had expected?"

"These are deep questions, Stranger. Maleldil is not putting much into my mind about them."

"Do you not see why?"

"No."

"Since Piebald and I have come to your world we have put many things into your mind which Maleldil has not. Do you not see that He is letting go of your hand a little?"

"How could He? He is wherever we go."

"Yes, but in another way. He is making you older—making you to learn things not straight from Him but by your own meetings with other people and your own questions and thoughts."

"He is certainly doing that."

"Yes. He is making you a full woman, for up till now you were only half made—like the beasts who do nothing of themselves. This time, when you meet the King again, it is you who will have things to tell him. It is you who will be older than he and who will make him older."

"Maleldil would not make a thing like that happen. It would be like a fruit with no taste."

"But it would have a taste for *him*. Do you not think the King must sometimes be tired of being the older? Would he not love you more if you were wiser than he?"

"Is this what you call a Poetry or do you mean that it really is?"

"I mean a thing that really is."

"But how could anyone love anything more? It is like saying a thing could be bigger than itself."

"I only meant you could become more like the women of my world."

"What are they like?"

"They are of a great spirit. They always reach out their hands for the new and unexpected good, and see that it is good long before the men understand it. Their minds run ahead of what Maleldil has told them. They do not need to wait for Him to tell them what is good, but know it for themselves as He does. They are, as it were, little Maleldils. And because of their wisdom, their beauty is as much greater than yours as the sweetness of these gourds surpasses the taste of water. And because of their beauty the love which the men have for them is as much greater than the King's love for you as the naked burning of Deep Heaven seen from my world is more wonderful than the golden roof of yours."

"I wish I could see them."

"I wish you could."

"How beautiful is Maleldil and how wonderful are all His works: perhaps He will bring out of me daughters as much greater than I as I am greater than the beasts. It will be better than I thought. I had thought I was to be always Queen and Lady. But I see now that I may be as the eldila. I may be appointed to cherish when they are small and weak children who will grow up and overtop me and at whose feet I shall fall. I see it is not only questions and thoughts that grow out wider and wider like branches. Joy also widens out and comes where we had never thought."

"I will sleep now," said the other voice. As it said this it became, for the first time, unmistakably the voice of Weston—and of Weston disgruntled and snappish. Up till now Ransom, though constantly resolving to join the conversation, had been kept silent in a kind of suspense between two conflicting states of mind. On the one hand he was certain, both from the voice and from many of the things it said, that the male speaker was Weston. On the other hand, the voice, divided from the man's appearance, sounded curiously unlike itself. Still more, the patient persistent manner in which it was used was very unlike the Professor's usual alternation between pompous lecturing and abrupt bullying. And how could a man fresh from such a physical crisis as he had seen Weston undergo have recovered such mastery of himself in a few hours? And how could he have reached the floating island? Ransom had found himself throughout their dialogue confronted with an intolerable contradiction. Something which was and was not Weston was talking: and the sense of this monstrosity, only a few feet away in the darkness, had sent thrills of exquisite horror tingling along his spine, and raised questions in his mind which he tried to dismiss as fantastic. Now that the conversation was over he realised, too, with what intense anxiety he had followed it. At the same moment he was conscious of a sense of triumph. But it was not he who was triumphant. The whole darkness about him rang with victory. He started and half raised himself. Had there been any actual sound? Listening hard he could hear nothing but the low murmurous noise of warm wind and gentle swell. The suggestion of music must have been from within. But as soon as he lay down again he felt assured that it was not. From without, most certainly from without, but not by the sense of hearing, festal revelry and dance and splendour poured into him—no sound, yet in such fashion that it could not be remembered or thought of except as music. It was like having a new sense. It was like being present when the morning stars sang together. It was as if Perelandra had that moment been created—and perhaps in some sense it had. The feeling of a great disaster averted was forced upon his mind, and with it came the hope that there would be no second attempt; and then, sweeter than all, the suggestion that he had been brought there not to do anything but only as a spectator or a witness. A few minutes later he was asleep.

9

The weather had changed during the night. Ransom sat looking out from the edge of the forest in which he had slept, on a flat sea where there were no other islands in view. He had waked a few minutes before and found himself lying alone in a close thicket of stems that were rather reed-like in character but stout as those of birch trees and which carried an almost flat roof of thick foliage. From this there hung fruits as smooth and bright and round as holly-berries, some of which he ate. Then he found his way to open country near the skirts of the island and looked about him. Neither Weston nor the Lady was in sight, and he began walking in a leisurely fashion beside the sea. His bare feet sank a little into a carpet of saffron-coloured vegetation, which covered them with an aromatic dust. As he was looking down at this he suddenly noticed something else. At first he thought it was a creature of more fantastic shape than he had yet seen on Perelandra. Its shape was not only fantastic but hideous. Then he dropped on one knee to examine it. Finally he touched it, with reluctance. A moment later he drew back his hands like a man who had touched a snake.

It was a damaged animal. It was, or had been, one of the brightly coloured frogs. But some accident had happened to it. The whole back had been ripped open in a sort of V-shaped gash, the point of the V being a little behind the head. Something had torn a widening wound backward—as we do in opening an envelope—along the trunk and pulled it out so far behind the animal that the hoppers or hind legs had been almost torn off with it. They were so damaged that the frog could not leap. On earth it would have been merely a nasty sight, but up to this moment Ransom had as yet seen nothing dead or spoiled in Perelandra, and it was like a blow in the face. It was like the first spasm of well-remembered pain warning a man who had thought he was cured that his family have deceived him and he is dying after all. It was like the first lie from the mouth of a friend on whose truth one was willing to stake a thousand pounds. It was irrevocable. The milk-warm wind blowing over the golden sea, the blues and silvers and greens of the floating garden, the sky itself—all these had become, in one instant, merely the illuminated margin of a book whose text was the struggling little horror at his feet, and he himself, in that same instant, had passed into a state of emotion which he could neither control nor understand. He told himself that a creature of that kind probably had very little sensation. But it did not much mend matters. It was not merely pity for pain that had suddenly changed the rhythm of his heart-beats. The thing was an intolerable obscenity which afflicted him with shame. It would have been better, or so he thought at that moment, for the whole universe never to have existed than for this one thing to have happened. Then he decided, in spite of his theoretical belief that it was an organism too low for much pain, that it had better be killed. He had neither boots nor stone nor stick. The frog proved remarkably hard to kill. When it was far too late to desist he saw clearly that he had been a fool to make the attempt. Whatever its sufferings might be he had certainly increased and not diminished them. But he had to go through with it. The job seemed to take nearly an hour. And when at last the mangled result was quite still and he went down to the water's edge to wash, he was sick and shaken. It seems odd to say this of a man who had been on the Somme; but the architects tell us that nothing is great or small save by position.

At last he got up and resumed his walk. Next moment he started and looked at the ground again. He quickened his pace, and then once more stopped and looked. He stood stock-still and covered his face. He called aloud upon heaven to break the nightmare or to let him understand what was happening. A trail of mutilated frogs lay along the edge of the island. Picking his footsteps with care, he followed it. He counted ten, fifteen, twenty: and the twenty-first brought him to a place where the wood came down to the water's edge. He went into the wood and came out on the other side. There he stopped dead and stared. Weston, still clothed but without his pith helmet, was standing about thirty feet away: and as Ransom watched he was tearing a frog—quietly and almost surgically inserting his forefinger, with its long sharp nail, under the skin behind the creature's head and ripping it open. Ransom had not noticed before that Weston had such remarkable nails. Then he finished the operation, threw the bleeding ruin away, and looked up. Their eyes met.

If Ransom said nothing, it was because he could not speak. He saw a man who was certainly not ill, to judge from his easy stance and the powerful use he had just been making of his fingers. He saw a man who was certainly Weston, to judge from his height and build and colouring and features. In that sense he was quite recognisable. But the terror was that he was also unrecognisable. He did not look like a sick man: but he looked very like a dead one. The face which he raised from torturing the frog had that terrible power which the face of a corpse sometimes has of simply rebuffing every conceivable human attitude one can adopt towards it. The expressionless mouth, the unwinking stare of the eyes, something heavy and inorganic in the very folds of the cheek, said clearly: "I have features as you have, but there is nothing in common between you and me." It was this that kept Ransom speechless. What could you say—what appeal or threat could have any meaning—to *that*? And now, forcing its way up into consciousness, thrusting aside every mental habit and every longing not to believe, came the conviction that this, in fact, was not a man: that Weston's body was kept, walking and undecaying, in Perelandra by some wholly different kind of life, and that Weston himself was gone.

It looked at Ransom in silence and at last began to smile. We have all often spoken—Ransom himself had often spoken—of a devilish smile. Now he realised that he had never taken the words seriously. The smile was not bitter, nor raging, nor, in an ordinary sense, sinister; it was not even mocking. It seemed to summon Ransom, with horrible naïveté of welcome, into the world of its own pleasures, as if all men were at one in those pleasures, as if they were the most natural thing in the world and no dispute could ever have occurred about them. It was not furtive, nor ashamed, it had nothing of the conspirator in it. It did not defy goodness, it ignored it to the point of annihilation. Ransom perceived that he had never before seen anything but half-hearted and uneasy attempts at evil. This creature was whole-hearted. The extremity of its evil had passed beyond all struggle into some state which bore a horrible similarity to innocence. It was beyond vice as the Lady was beyond virtue.

The stillness and the smiling lasted for perhaps two whole minutes: certainly not less. Then Ransom made to take a step towards the thing, with no very clear notion of what he would do when he reached it. He stumbled and fell. He had a curious difficulty in getting to his feet again, and when he got to them he overbalanced and fell for the second time. Then there was a moment of darkness with a noise of roaring express trains. After that the golden sky and coloured waves returned and he knew he was alone and recovering from a faint. As he lay there, still unable and perhaps unwilling to rise, it came into his mind that in certain old philosophers and poets he had read that the mere sight of the devils was one of the greatest among the torments of Hell. It had seemed to him till now merely a quaint fancy. And yet (as he now saw) even the children know better: no child would have any difficulty in understanding that there might be a face the mere beholding of which was final calamity. The children, the poets, and the philosophers were right. As there is one Face above all worlds merely to see which is irrevocable joy, so at the bottom of all worlds that face is waiting whose sight alone is the misery from which none who beholds it can recover. And though there seemed to be, and indeed were, a thousand roads by which a man could walk through the world, there was not a single one which did not lead sooner or later either to the Beatific or the Miserific Vision. He himself had, of course, seen only a mask or faint adumbration of it; even so, he was not quite sure that he would live.

When he was able, he got up and set out to search for the thing. He must either try to prevent it from meeting the Lady or at least be present when they met. What he could do, he did not know; but it was clear beyond all evasion that this was what he had been sent for. Weston's body, travelling in a space-ship, had been the bridge by which something else had invaded Perelandra—whether that supreme and original evil whom in Mars they call The Bent One, or one of his lesser followers, made no difference. Ransom was all gooseflesh, and his knees kept getting in each other's way. It surprised him that he could experience so extreme a terror and yet be walking and thinking—as men in war or sickness are surprised to find how much can be borne: "It will drive us mad," "It will kill us outright," we say; and then it happens and we find ourselves neither mad nor dead, still held to the task.

The weather changed. The plain on which he was walking swelled to a wave of land. The sky grew paler: it was soon rather primrose than gold. The sea grew darker, almost the colour of bronze. Soon the island was climbing considerable hills of water. Once or twice he had to sit down and rest. After several hours (for his progress was very slow) he suddenly saw two human figures on what was for the moment a skyline. Next moment they were out of sight as the country heaved up between them and him. It took about half an hour to reach them. Weston's body was standing—swaying and balancing itself to meet each change of the ground in a manner of which the real Weston would have been incapable. It was talking to the Lady. And what surprised Ransom most was that she continued to listen to it without turning to welcome him or even to comment on his arrival when he came and sat down beside her on the soft turf.

"It *is* a great branching out," it was saying. "This making of story or poetry about things that might be but are not. If you shrink back from it, are you not drawing back from the fruit that is offered you?"

"It is not from the making of a story that I shrink back, O Stranger," she answered, "but from this one story that you have put into my head. I can make myself stories about my children or the King. I can make it that the fish fly and the land beasts swim. But if I try to make the story about living on the Fixed Island I do not know how to make it about Maleldil. For if I make it that He has changed His command, that will not go. And if I make it that we are living there against His command, that is like making the sky all black and the water so that we cannot drink it and the air so that we cannot breathe it. But also, I do not see what is the pleasure of trying to make these things."

"To make you wiser, older," said Weston's body.

"Do you know for certain that it will do that?" she asked.

"Yes, for certain," it replied. "That is how the women of my world have become so great and so beautiful."

"Do not listen to him," broke in Ransom; "send him away. Do not hear what he says, do not think of it."

She turned to Ransom for the first time. There had been some very slight change in her face since he had last seen her. It was not sad, nor deeply bewildered, but the hint of something precarious had increased. On the other hand she was clearly pleased to see him, though surprised at his interruption; and her first words revealed that her failure to greet him at his arrival had resulted from her never having envisaged the possibility of a conversation between more than two speakers. And throughout the rest of their talk, her ignorance of the technique of general conversation gave a curious and disquieting quality to the whole scene. She had no notion of how to glance rapidly from one face to another or to disentangle two remarks at once. Sometimes she listened wholly to Ransom, sometimes wholly to the other, but never to both.

"Why do you start speaking before this man has finished, Piebald?" she inquired. "How do they do in your world where you are many and more than two must often be together? Do they not talk in turns; or have you an art to understand even when all speak together? I am not old enough for that."

"I do not want you to hear him at all," said Ransom. "He is——" and then he hesitated. "Bad," "liar," "enemy," none of these words would, as yet, have any meaning for her. Racking his brains he thought of their previous conversation about the great eldil who had held on to the old good and refused the new one. Yes; that would be her only approach to the idea of badness. He was just about to speak but it was too late. Weston's voice anticipated him.

"This Piebald," it said, "does not want you to hear me, because he wants to keep you young. He does not want you to go on to the new fruits that you have never tasted before."

"But how could he want to keep me younger?"

"Have you not seen already," said Weston's body, "that Piebald is one who always shrinks back from the wave that is coming towards us and would like, if he could, to bring back the wave that is past? In the very first hour of his talking with you, did he not betray this? He did not know that all was new since Maleldil became a man and that now all creatures with reason will be men. You had to teach him this. And when he had learned it he did not welcome it. He was sorry that there would be no more of the old furry people. He would bring back that old world if he could. And when you asked him to teach you Death, he would not. He wanted you to remain young, not to learn Death. Was it not he who first put into your mind the very thought that it was possible not to desire the wave that Maleldil was rolling towards us; to shrink so much that you would cut off your arms and legs to prevent it coming?"

"You mean he is so young?"

"He is what in my world we call Bad," said Weston's body. "One who rejects the fruit he is given for the sake of the fruit he expected or the fruit he found last time."

"We must make him older, then," said the Lady, and though she did not look at Ransom, all the Queen and Mother in her were revealed to him and he knew that she wished him, and all things, infinitely well. And he—he could do nothing. His weapon had been knocked out of his hand.

"And will you teach us Death?" said the Lady to Weston's shape, where it stood above her.

"Yes," it said, "it is for this that I came here, that you may have Death in abundance. But you must be very courageous."

"*Courageous*. What is that?"

"It is what makes you to swim on a day when the waves are so great and swift that something inside you bids you to stay on land."

"I know. And those are the best days of all for swimming."

"Yes. But to find Death, and with Death the real oldness and the strong beauty and the uttermost branching out, you must plunge into things greater than waves."

"Go on. Your words are like no other words that I have ever heard.

They are like the bubble breaking on the tree. They make me think of—of—I do not know what they make me think of."

"I will speak greater words than these; but I must wait till you are older."

"Make me older."

"Lady, Lady," broke in Ransom, "will not Maleldil make you older in His own time and His own way, and will not that be far better?"

Weston's face did not turn in his direction either at this point or at any other time during the conversation, but his voice, addressed wholly to the Lady, answered Ransom's interruption.

"You see?" it said. "He himself, though he did not mean nor wish to do so, made you see a few days ago that Maleldil is beginning to teach you to walk by yourself, without holding you by the hand. That was the first branching out. When you came to know that, you were becoming really old. And since then Maleldil has let you learn much—not from His own voice, but from mine. You are becoming your own. That is what Maleldil wants you to do. That is why He has let you be separated from the King and even, in a way, from Himself. His way of making you older is to make you make yourself older. And yet this Piebald would have you sit still and wait for Maleldil to do it all."

"What must we do to Piebald to make him older?" said the Lady.

"I do not think you can help him till you are older yourself," said the voice of Weston. "You cannot help anyone yet. You are as a tree without fruit."

"It is very true," said the Lady. "Go on."

"Then listen," said Weston's body. "Have you understood that to wait for Maleldil's voice when Maleldil wishes you to walk on your own is a kind of disobedience?"

"I think I have."

"The wrong kind of obeying itself can be a disobeying."

The Lady thought for a few moments and then clapped her hands. "I see," she said, "I see! Oh, how old you make me. Before now I have chased a beast for mirth. And it has understood and run away from me. If it had stood still and let me catch it, that would have been a sort of obeying—but not the best sort."

"You understand very well. When you are fully grown you will be even wiser and more beautiful than the women of my own world. And you see that it might be so with Maleldil's biddings."

"I think I do not see quite clearly."

"Are you certain that He really wishes to be always obeyed?"

"How can we not obey what we love?"

"The beast that ran away loved you."

"I wonder," said the Lady, "if that is the same. The beast knows very well when I mean it to run away and when I want it to come to me. But Maleldil has never said to us that any word or work of His was a jest. How could our Beloved need to jest or frolic as we do? He is all a burning joy and a strength. It is like thinking that He needed sleep or food."

"No, it would not be a jest. That is only a thing like it, not the thing itself. But could the taking away of your hand from His—the full growing up—the walking in your own way—could that ever be perfect unless you had, if only once, *seemed* to disobey Him?"

"How could one *seem* to disobey?"

"By doing what He only *seemed* to forbid. There might be a commanding which He wished you to break."

"But if He told us we were to break it, then it would be no command. And if He did not, how should we know?"

"How wise you are growing, beautiful one," said Weston's mouth. "No. If He told you to break what He commanded, it would be no true command, as you have seen. For you are right, He makes no jests. A real disobeying, a real branching out, this is what He secretly longs for: secretly, because to tell you would spoil all."

"I begin to wonder," said the Lady after a pause, "whether you are so much older than I. Surely what you are saying is like fruit with no taste! How can I step out of His will save into something that cannot be wished? Shall I start trying not to love Him—or the King—or the beasts? It would be like trying to walk on water or swim through islands. Shall I try not to sleep or to drink or to laugh? I thought your words had a meaning. But now it seems they have none. To walk out of His will is to walk into nowhere."

"That is true of all His commands except one."

"But can that one be different?"

"Nay, you see of yourself that it is different. These other commands of His—to love, to sleep, to fill this world with your children—you see for yourself that they are good. And they are the same in all worlds. But the command against living on the Fixed Island is not so. You have already learned that He gave no such command to my world. And you cannot see where the goodness of it is. No wonder. If it were really good, must He not have commanded it to all worlds alike? For how could Maleldil not command what was good? There is *no* good in it. Maleldil Himself is showing you that, this moment, through your own reason. It is mere command. It is forbidding for the mere sake of forbidding."

"But why . . . ?"

"In order that you may break it. What other reason can there be? It is not good. It is not the same for other worlds. It stands between you and all settled life, all command of your own days. Is not Maleldil show-ing you as plainly as He can that it was set up as a test—as a great wave you have to go over, that you may become really old, really separate from Him."

"But if this concerns me so deeply, why does He put none of this into my mind? It is all coming from you, Stranger. There is no whisper, even, of the Voice saying Yes to your words."

"But do you not see that there cannot be? He longs—oh, how greatly He longs—to see His creature become fully itself, to stand up in its own reason and its own courage even against Him. But how can He *tell* it to do this? That would spoil all. Whatever it did after that would only be one more step taken *with* Him. This is the one thing of all the things He desires in which He must have no finger. Do you think He is not weary of seeing nothing but Himself in all that He has made? If that contented Him, why should He create at all? To find the Other—the thing whose will is no longer His—that is Maleldil's desire."

"If I could but know this——"

"He must not tell you. He cannot tell you. The nearest He can come to telling you is to let some other creature tell it for Him. And behold, He has done so. Is it for nothing, or without His will, that I have jour-neyed through Deep Heaven to teach you what He would have you know but must not teach you Himself?"

"Lady," said Ransom, "if I speak, will you hear me?"

"Gladly, Piebald."

"This man has said that the law against living on the Fixed Island is different from the other Laws, because it is not the same for all worlds and because we cannot see the goodness in it. And so far he says well. But then he says that it is thus different in order that you may disobey it. But there might be another reason."

"Say it, Piebald."

"I think He made one law of that kind in order that there might be obedience. In all these other matters what you call obeying Him is but doing what seems good in your own eyes also. Is love content with that? You do them, indeed, because they are His will, but not only because they are His will. Where can you taste the joy of obeying unless He bids you do something for which His bidding is the *only* reason? When we spoke last you said that if you told the beasts to walk on their heads, they would delight to do so. So I know that you understand well what I am saying."

"Oh, brave Piebald," said the Green Lady, "this is the best you have said yet. This makes me older far: yet it does not feel like the oldness this other is giving me. Oh, how well I see it! We cannot walk out of

Maleldil's will: but He has given us a way to walk out of *our* will. And there could be no such way except a command like this. Out of our own will. It is like passing out through the world's roof into Deep Heaven. All beyond is Love Himself. I knew there was joy in looking upon the Fixed Island and laying down all thought of ever living there, but I did not till now understand." Her face was radiant as she spoke, but then a shade of bewilderment crossed it. "Piebald," she said, "if you are so young, as this other says, how do you know these things?"

"He says I am young, but I say not."

The voice of Weston's face spoke suddenly, and it was louder and deeper than before and less like Weston's voice.

"I am older than he," it said, "and he dare not deny it. Before the mothers of the mothers of his mother were conceived, I was already older than he could reckon. I have been with Maleldil in Deep Heaven where he never came and heard the eternal councils. And in the order of creation I am greater than he, and before me he is of no account. Is it not so?" The corpse-like face did not even now turn towards him, but the speaker and the Lady both seemed to wait for Ransom to reply. The falsehood which sprang to his mind died on his lips. In that air, even when truth seemed fatal, only truth would serve. Licking his lips and choking down a feeling of nausea, he answered:

"In our world to be older is not always to be wiser."

"Look at him," said Weston's body to the Lady; "consider how white his cheeks have turned and how his forehead is wet. You have not seen such things before: you will see them more often hereafter. It is what happens—it is the beginning of what happens—to little creatures when they set themselves against great ones."

An exquisite thrill of fear travelled along Ransom's spine. What saved him was the face of the Lady. Untouched by the evil so close to her, removed as it were ten years' journey deep within the region of her own innocence, and by that innocence at once protected and so endangered, she looked up at the standing Death above her, puzzled indeed, but not beyond the bounds of cheerful curiosity, and said:

"But he was right, Stranger, about this forbidding. It is you who need to be made older. Can you not see?"

"I have always seen the whole whereof he sees but the half. It is most true that Maleldil has given you a way of walking out of your own will—but out of your deepest will."

"And what is that?"

"Your deepest will, at present, is to obey Him—to be always as you are now, only His beast or His very young child. The way out of that is hard. It was made hard that only the very great, the very wise, the very courageous should dare to walk in it, to go on—on out of this smallness in which you now live—through the dark wave of His forbidding, into the real life, Deep Life, with all its joy and splendour and hardness."

"Listen, Lady," said Ransom. "There is something he is not telling you. All this that we are now talking has been talked before. The thing he wants you to try has been tried before. Long ago, when our world began, there was only one man and one woman in it, as you and the King are in this. And there once before he stood, as he stands now, talking to the woman. He had found her alone as he has found you alone. And she listened, and did the thing Maleldil had forbidden her to do. But no joy and splendour came of it. What came of it I cannot tell you because you have no image of it in your mind. But all love was troubled and made cold, and Maleldil's voice became hard to hear so that wisdom grew little among them; and the woman was against the man and the mother against the child; and when they looked to eat there was no fruit on their trees, and hunting for food took all their time, so that their life became narrower, not wider."

"He has hidden the half of what happened," said Weston's corpse-like mouth. "Hardness came out of it but also splendour. They made with their own hands mountains higher than your Fixed Island. They made for themselves Floating Islands greater than yours which they could move at will through the ocean faster than any bird can fly. Because there was not always food enough, a woman could give the only fruit to her child or her husband and eat death instead—could give them all, as you in your little narrow life of playing and kissing and riding fishes have never done, nor shall do till you break the commandment. Because knowledge was harder to find, those few who found it became more beautiful and excelled their fellows as you excel the beasts; and thousands were striving for their love . . ."

"I think I will go to sleep now," said the Lady quite suddenly. Up to this point she had been listening to Weston's body with open mouth and wide eyes, but as he spoke of the women with the thousands of lovers she yawned, with the unconcealed and unpremeditated yawn of a young cat.

"Not yet," said the other. "There is more. He has not told you that it was this breaking of the commandment which brought Maleldil to our world and because of which He was made man. He dare not deny it."

"Do you say this, Piebald?" asked the Lady.

Ransom was sitting with his fingers locked so tightly that his knuckles were white. The unfairness of it all was wounding him like barbed wire. Unfair . . . unfair. How could Maleldil expect him to fight against this, to fight with every weapon taken from him, forbidden to lie and yet brought to places where truth seemed fatal? It was unfair! A sudden impulse of hot rebellion arose in him. A second later, doubt, like a huge wave, came breaking over him. How if the enemy were right after all? *Felix peccatum Adae.* Even the Church would tell him that good came of disobedience in the end. Yes, and it was true too that he, Ransom, was a timid creature, a man who shrank back from new and hard things. On which side, after all, did the temptation lie? Progress passed before his eyes in a great momentary vision: cities, armies, tall ships, and libraries and fame, and the grandeur of poetry spurting like a fountain out of the labours and ambitions of men. Who could be certain that Creative Evolution was not the deepest truth? From all sorts of secret crannies in his own mind whose very existence he had never before suspected, something wild and heady and delicious began to rise, to pour itself towards the shape of Weston. "It is a spirit, it is a spirit," said this inner voice, "and you are only a man. It goes on from century to century. You are only a man. . . ."

"Do you say this, Piebald?" asked the Lady a second time.

The spell was broken.

"I will tell you what I say," answered Ransom, jumping to his feet. "Of course good came of it. Is Maleldil a beast that we can stop His path, or a leaf that we can twist His shape? Whatever you do, He will make good of it. But not the good He had prepared for you if you had obeyed Him. That is lost for ever. The first King and first Mother of our world did the forbidden thing; and He brought good of it in the end. But what they did was not good; and what they lost we have not seen. And there were some to whom no good came nor ever will come." He turned to the body of Weston. "You," he said, "tell her all. What good came to you? Do *you* rejoice that Maleldil became a man? Tell her of *your* joys, and of what profit you had when you made Maleldil and death acquainted."

In that moment that followed this speech two things happened that were utterly unlike terrestrial experience. The body that had been Weston's threw up its head and opened its mouth and gave a long melancholy howl like a dog; and the Lady lay down, wholly unconcerned, and closed her eyes and was instantly asleep. And while these two things were happening the piece of ground on which the two men stood and the woman lay was rushing down a great hillside of water.

Ransom kept his eyes fixed upon the enemy, but it took no notice of him. Its eyes moved like the eyes of a living man but it was hard to be sure what it was looking at, or whether it really used the eyes as organs of vision at all. One got the impression of a force that cleverly kept the pupils of those eyes fixed in a suitable direction while the mouth talked but which, for its own purpose, used wholly different modes of perception. The thing sat down close to the Lady's head on the far side of her from Ransom. If you could call it sitting down. The body did not reach its squatting position by the normal movements of a man: it was more as if some external force manœuvred it into the right position and then let it drop. It was impossible to point to any particular motion which was definitely non-human. Ransom had the sense of watching an imitation of living motions which had been very well studied and was technically correct: but somehow it lacked the master touch. And he was chilled with an inarticulate, night-nursery horror of the thing he had to deal with—the man-aged corpse, the bogey, the Un-man.

There was nothing to do but to watch: to sit there, for ever if need be, guarding the Lady from the Un-man while their island climbed interminably over the Alps and Andes of burnished water. All three were very still. Beasts and birds came often and looked upon them. Hours later the Un-man began to speak. It did not even look in Ransom's direction; slowly and cumbrously, as if by some machinery that needed oiling, it made its mouth and lips pronounce his name.

"Ransom," it said.

"Well?" said Ransom.

"Nothing," said the Un-man. He shot an inquisitive glance at it. Was the creature mad? But it looked, as before, dead rather than mad, sitting there with the head bowed and the mouth a little open, and some yellow dust from the moss settled in the creases of its cheeks, and the legs crossed tailor-wise, and the hands, with their long metallic-looking nails, pressed flat together on the ground before it. He dismissed the problem from his mind and returned to his own uncomfortable thoughts.

"Ransom," it said again.

"What is it?" said Ransom sharply.

"Nothing," it answered.

Again there was silence; and again, about a minute later, the horrible mouth said:

"Ransom!" This time he made no reply. Another minute and it uttered his name again; and then, like a minute gun, "Ransom . . . Ransom . . . Ransom," perhaps a hundred times.

"What the Hell do you want?" he roared at last.

"Nothing," said the voice. Next time he determined not to answer; but when it had called on him a thousand times he found himself answering whether he would or no, and "Nothing," came the reply. He taught himself to keep silent in the end: not that the torture of resisting his impulse to speak was less than the torture of response but because something within him rose up to combat the tormentor's assurance that he must yield in the end. If the attack had been of some more violent kind it might have been easier to resist. What chilled and almost cowed him was the union of malice with something nearly childish. For temptation, for blasphemy, for a whole battery of horrors, he was in some sort prepared: but hardly for this petty, indefatigable nagging as of a nasty little boy at a preparatory school. Indeed no imagined horror could have surpassed the sense which grew within him as the slow hours passed, that this creature was, by all human standards, inside out—its heart on the surface and its shallowness at the heart. On the surface, great designs and an antagonism to Heaven which involved the fate of worlds: but deep within, when every veil had been pierced, was there, after all, nothing but a black puerility, an aimless empty spitefulness content to sate itself with the tiniest cruelties, as love does not disdain the smallest kindness? What kept him steady, long after all possibility of thinking about something else had disappeared, was the decision that if he must hear either the word Ransom or the word Nothing a million times, he would prefer the word Ransom.

And all the time the little jewel-coloured land went soaring up into the yellow firmament and hung there a moment and tilted its woods and went racing down into the warm lustrous depths between the waves: and the Lady lay sleeping with one arm bent beneath her head and her lips a little parted. Sleeping, assuredly—for her eyes were shut and her breathing regular—yet not looking quite like those who sleep in our world, for her face was full of expression and intelligence, and the limbs looked as if they were ready at any moment to leap up, and altogether she gave the impression that sleep was not a thing that happened to her but an action which she performed.

Then all at once it was night. "Ransom . . . Ransom . . . Ransom . . . Ransom" went on the voice. And suddenly it crossed his mind that though he would some time require sleep, the Un-man might not.

Sleep proved to be indeed the problem. For what seemed a great time, cramped and wearied, and soon hungry and thirsty as well, he sat still in the darkness trying not to attend to the unflagging repetition of "Ransom—Ransom—Ransom." But presently he found himself listening to a conversation of which he knew he had not heard the beginning and realised he had slept. The Lady seemed to be saying very little. Weston's voice was speaking gently and continuously. It was not talking about the Fixed Land nor even about Maleldil. It appeared to be telling, with extreme beauty and pathos, a number of stories, and at first Ransom could not perceive any connecting link between them. They were all about women, but women who had apparently lived at different periods of the world's history and in quite different circumstances. From the Lady's replies it appeared that the stories contained much that she did not understand; but oddly enough the Un-man did not mind. If the questions aroused by any one story proved at all difficult to answer, the speaker simply dropped that story and instantly began another. The heroines of the stories seemed all to have suffered a great deal—they had been oppressed by fathers, cast off by husbands, deserted by lovers. Their children had risen up against them and society had driven them out. But the stories all ended, in a sense, happily: sometimes with honours and praises to a heroine still living, more often with tardy acknowledgment and unavailing tears after her death. As the endless speech proceeded, the Lady's questions grew always fewer; some meaning for the words Death and Sorrow—though what kind of meaning Ransom could not even guess—was apparently being created in her mind by mere repetition. At last it dawned upon him what all these stories were about. Each one of these women had stood forth alone and braved a terrible risk for her child, her lover, or her people. Each had been misunderstood, reviled, and persecuted: but each also magnificently vindicated by the event. The precise details were often not very easy to follow. Ransom had more than a suspicion that many of these noble pioneers had been what in ordinary terrestrial speech we call witches or perverts. But that was all in the background. What emerged from the stories was rather an image than an idea—the picture of the tall, slender form, unbowed though the world's weight rested upon its shoulders, stepping forth fearless and friendless into the dark to do for others what those others forbade it to do yet needed to have done. And all the time, as a sort of background to these goddess shapes, the speaker was building up a picture of the other sex. No word was directly spoken on the subject: but one felt them there as a huge, dim multitude of creatures pitifully childish and complacently arrogant; timid, meticulous, unoriginating; sluggish and ox-like, rooted to the earth almost in their indolence, prepared to try nothing, to risk nothing, to make no exertion, and capable of being raised into full life only by the unthanked and rebellious virtue of their females. It was very well done. Ransom, who had little of the pride of sex, found himself for a few moments all but believing it.

In the midst of this the darkness was suddenly torn by a flash of lightning; a few seconds later came a revel of Perelandrian thunder, like the playing of a heavenly tambourine, and after that warm rain. Ransom did not much regard it. The flash had shown him the Un-man sitting bolt upright, the Lady raised on one elbow, the dragon lying awake at her head, a grove of trees beyond, and great waves against the horizon. He was thinking of what he had seen. He was wondering how the Lady could see that face—those jaws monotonously moving as if they were rather munching than talking—and not know the creature to be evil. He saw, of course, that this was unreasonable of him. He himself was doubtless an uncouth figure in her eyes; she could have no knowledge either about evil or about the normal appearance of terrestrial man to guide her. The expression on her face, revealed in the sudden light, was one that he had not seen there before. Her eyes were not fixed on the narrator: as far as that went, her thoughts might have been a thousand miles away. Her lips were shut and a little pursed. Her eyebrows were slightly raised. He had not yet seen her look so like a woman of our own race; and yet her expression was one he had not very often met on earth—except, as he realised with a shock, on the stage. "Like a tragedy queen" was the disgusting comparison that arose in his mind. Of course it was a gross exaggeration. It was an insult for which he could not forgive himself. And yet . . . and yet . . . the tableau revealed by the lightning had photographed itself on his brain. Do what he would, he found it impossible not to think of that new look in her face. A very *good* tragedy queen, no doubt. The heroine of a very great tragedy, very nobly played by an actress who was a good woman in real life. By earthly standards, an expression to be praised, even to be revered: but remembering all that he had read in her countenance before, the unselfconscious radiance, the frolic sanctity, the depth of stillness that reminded him sometimes of infancy and sometimes of extreme old age while the hard youth and valiancy of face and body denied both, he found this new expression horrifying. The fatal touch of invited grandeur, of enjoyed pathos—the assumption, however slight, of a rôle—seemed a hateful vulgarity. Perhaps she was doing no more—he had good hope that she was doing no more—than responding in a purely imaginative fashion to this new art of Story or Poetry. But by God she'd better not! And for the first time the thought "This can't go on" formulated itself in his mind.

"I will go where the leaves cover us from the rain," said her voice in the darkness. Ransom had hardly noticed that he was getting wet—in a world without clothes it is less important. But he rose when he heard her move and followed her as well as he could by ear. The Un-man seemed to be doing the same. They progressed in total darkness on a surface as variable as that of water. Every now and then there was another flash. One saw the Lady walking erect, the Un-man slouching by her side with Weston's shirt and shorts now sodden and clinging to it, and the dragon puffing and waddling behind. At last they came to a place where the carpet under their feet was dry and there was a drumming noise of rain on firm leaves above their heads. They lay down again. "And another time," began the Un-man at once, "there was a queen in our world who ruled over a little land——"

"Hush!" said the Lady, "let us listen to the rain." Then, after a moment, she added, "What was that? It was some beast I never heard before"—and indeed, there had been something very like a low growl close beside them.

"I do not know," said the voice of Weston.

"I think I do," said Ransom.

"Hush!" said the Lady again, and no more was said that night.

This was the beginning of a series of days and nights which Ransom remembered with loathing for the rest of his life. He had been only too correct in supposing that his enemy required no sleep. Fortunately the Lady did, but she needed a good deal less than Ransom and possibly, as the days passed, came to take less than she needed. It seemed to Ransom that whenever he dozed he awoke to find the Un-man already in conversation with her. He was dead tired. He could hardly have endured it at all but for the fact that their hostess quite frequently dismissed them both from her presence. On such occasions Ransom kept close to the Un-man. It was a rest from the main battle, but it was a very imperfect rest. He did not dare to let the enemy out of his sight for a moment, and every day its society became more unendurable. He had full opportunity to learn the falsity of the maxim that the Prince of Darkness is a gentleman. Again and again he felt that a suave and subtle Mephistopheles with red cloak and rapier and a feather in his cap, or even a sombre tragic Satan out of *Paradise Lost,* would have been a welcome release from the thing he was actually doomed to watch. It was not like dealing with a wicked politician at all: it was much more like being set to guard an imbecile or a monkey or a very nasty child. What had staggered and disgusted him when it first began saying, "Ransom . . . Ransom . . ." continued to disgust him every day and every hour. It showed plenty of subtlety and intelligence when talking to the Lady; but Ransom soon perceived that it regarded intelligence simply and solely as a weapon, which it had no more wish to employ in its off-duty hours than a soldier has to do bayonet practice when he is on leave. Thought was for it a device necessary to certain ends, but thought in itself did not interest it. It assumed reason as externally and inorganically as it had assumed Weston's body. The moment the Lady was out of sight it seemed to relapse. A great deal of his time was spent in protecting the animals from it. Whenever it got out of sight, or even a few yards ahead, it would make a grab at any beast or bird within its reach and pull out some fur or feathers. Ransom tried whenever possible to get between it and its victim. On such occasions there were nasty moments when the two stood facing each other. It never came to a fight, for the Un-man merely grinned and perhaps spat and fell back a little, but before that happened Ransom usually had opportunity to discover how terribly he feared it. For side by side with his disgust, the more childlike terror of living with a ghost or a mechanised corpse never left him for many minutes together. The fact of being *alone* with it sometimes rushed upon his mind with such dismay that it took all his reason to resist his longing for society—his impulse to rush madly over the island until he found the Lady and to beg her protection. When the Un-man could not get animals it was content with plants. It was fond of cutting their outer rinds through with its nails, or grubbing up roots, or pulling off leaves, or even tearing up handfuls of turf. With Ransom himself it had innumerable games to play. It had a whole repertory of obscenities to perform with its own—or rather with Weston's—body: and the mere silliness of them was almost worse than the dirtiness. It would sit making grimaces at him for hours together; and then, for hours more, it would go back to its old repetition of "Ransom . . . Ransom." Often its grimaces achieved a horrible resemblance to people whom Ransom had known and loved in our own world. But worst of all were those moments when it allowed Weston to come back into its countenance. Then its voice, which was always Weston's voice, would begin a pitiful, hesitant mumbling, "You be very careful, Ransom. I'm down in the bottom of a big black hole. No I'm not, though. I'm on Perelandra. I can't think very well now, but that doesn't matter, he does all my thinking for me. It'll get quite easy presently. That boy keeps on shutting the windows. That's all right, they've taken off my head and put someone else's on me. I'll soon be all right now. They won't let me see my press cuttings. So then I went and told him that if they didn't want me in the first Fifteen they could jolly well do without me, see. We'll tell that young whelp it's an insult to the examiners to show up this kind of work. What I want to know is why I should pay for a first-class ticket and then be crowded out like this. It's not fair. Not fair. I never meant any harm. Could you take some of this weight off my chest, I don't want all those clothes. Let me alone. Let me alone. It's not fair. It's not fair. What enormous bluebottles. They say you get used to them"—and then it would end in the canine howl. Ransom never could make up his mind whether it was a trick or whether a decaying psychic energy that had once been Weston were indeed fitfully and miserably alive within the body that sat there beside him. He discovered that any hatred he had once felt for the Professor was dead. He found it natural to pray fervently for his soul. Yet what he felt for Weston was not exactly pity. Up till that moment, whenever he had thought of Hell, he had pictured the lost souls as being still human; now, as the frightful abyss which parts ghosthood from manhood yawned before him, pity was almost swallowed up in horror—in the unconquerable revulsion of the life within him from positive and self-consuming Death. If the remains of Weston were, at such moments, speaking through the lips of the Un-man, then Weston was not now a man at all. The forces which had begun, perhaps years ago, to eat away his humanity had now completed their work. The intoxicated will which had been slowly poisoning the intelligence and the affections had now at last poisoned itself and the whole psychic organism had fallen to pieces. Only a ghost was left—an everlasting unrest, a crumbling, a ruin, an odour of decay. "And this," thought Ransom, "might be my destination; or hers."

But of course the hours spent alone with the Un-man were like hours in a back area. The real business of life was the interminable conversation between the Tempter and the Green Lady. Taken hour by hour the progress was hard to estimate; but as the days passed Ransom could not resist the conviction that the general development was in the enemy's favour. There were, of course, ups and downs. Often the Un-man was unexpectedly repulsed by some simplicity which it seemed not to have anticipated. Often, too, Ransom's own contributions to the terrible debate were for the moment successful. There were times when he thought, "Thank God! We've won at last." But the enemy was never tired, and Ransom grew more weary all the time; and presently he thought he could see signs that the Lady was becoming tired too. In the end he taxed her with it and begged her to send them both away. But she rebuked him, and her rebuke revealed how dangerous the situation had already become. "Shall I go and rest and play," she asked, "while all this lies on our hands? Not till I am certain that there is no great deed to be done by me for the King and for the children of our children."

It was on those lines that the enemy now worked almost exclusively. Though the Lady had no word for Duty he had made it appear to her in the light of a Duty that she should continue to fondle the idea of disobedience, and convinced her that it would be a cowardice if she repulsed him. The ideas of the Great Deed, of the Great Risk, of a kind of martyrdom, were presented to her every day, varied in a thousand forms. The notion of waiting to ask the King before a decision was made had been unobtrusively shuffled aside. Any such "cowardice" was now not to be thought of. The whole point of her action—the whole grandeur— would lie in taking it without the King's knowledge, in leaving him utterly free to repudiate it, so that all the benefits should be his, and all the risks hers; and with the risk, of course, all the magnanimity, the pathos, the tragedy, and the originality. And also, the Tempter hinted, it would be no use asking the King, for he would certainly *not* approve the action: men were like that. The King must be forced to be free. Now, while she was on her own—now or never—the noble thing must be achieved; and with that "Now or never" he began to play on a fear which the Lady apparently shared with the women of earth—the fear that life might be wasted, some great opportunity let slip. "How if I were as a tree that could have born gourds and yet bore none," she said. Ransom tried to convince her that children were fruit enough. But the Un-man asked whether this elaborate division of the human race into two sexes could possibly be meant for no other purpose than offspring?—a matter which might have been more simply provided for, as it was in many of the plants. A moment later it was explaining that men like Ransom in his own world—men of that intensely male and backward-looking type who always shrank away from the new good—had continuously laboured to keep women down to mere childbearing and to ignore the high destiny for which Maleldil had actually created her. It told her that such men had already done incalculable harm. Let her look to it that nothing of the sort happened on Perelandra. It was at this stage that it began to teach her many new words: words like Creative and Intuition and Spiritual. But that was one of its false steps. When she had at last been made to understand what "creative" meant she forgot all about the Great Risk and the tragic loneliness and laughed for a whole minute on end. Finally she told the Un-man that it was younger even than Piebald, and sent them both away.

Ransom gained ground over that; but on the following day he lost it all by losing his temper. The enemy had been pressing on her with more than usual ardour the nobility of self-sacrifice and self-dedication, and the enchantment seemed to be deepening in her mind every moment, when Ransom, goaded beyond all patience, had leaped to his feet and really turned upon her, talking far too quickly and almost shouting, and even forgetting his Old Solar and intermixing English words. He tried to tell her that he'd seen this kind of "unselfishness" in action: to tell her of women making themselves sick with hunger rather than begin the meal before the man of the house returned, though they knew perfectly well that there was nothing he disliked more; of mothers wearing themselves to a ravelling to marry some daughter to a man whom she detested; of Agrippina and of Lady Macbeth. "Can you not see," he shouted, "that he is making you say words that mean nothing? What is the good of saying you would do this for the King's sake when you know it is what the King would hate most? Are you Maleldil that you should determine what is good for the King?" But she understood only a very small part of what he said and was bewildered by his manner. The Un-man made capital out of this speech.

But through all these ups and downs, all changes of the front line, all counter-attacks and stands and withdrawals, Ransom came to see more and more clearly the strategy of the whole affair. The Lady's response to the suggestion of becoming a risk-bearer, a tragic pioneer, was still a response made chiefly out of her love for the King and for her unborn children, and even, in a sense, of Maleldil Himself. The idea that He might not really wish to be obeyed to the letter was the sluice through which the whole flood of suggestion had been admitted to her mind. But mixed with this response, from the moment when the Un-man began its tragic stories, there was the faintest touch of theatricality, the first hint of a self-admiring inclination to seize a grand rôle in the drama of her world. It was clear that the Un-man's whole effort was to increase this element. As long as this was but one drop, so to speak, in the sea of her mind, he would not really succeed. Perhaps, while it remained so, she was protected from actual disobedience: perhaps no rational creature, until such a motive became dominant, could really throw away happiness for anything quite so vague as the Tempter's chatter about Deeper Life and the Upward Path. The veiled egoism in the conception of noble revolt must be increased. And Ransom thought, despite many rallies on her part and many setbacks suffered by the enemy, that it was, very slowly and yet perceptibly, increasing. The matter was, of course, cruelly, cruelly complicated. What the Un-man said was always very nearly true. Certainly it must be part of the Divine plan that this happy creature should mature, should become more and more a creature of free choice, should become, in a sense, more distinct from God and from her husband in order thereby to be at one with them in a richer fashion. In fact, he had seen this very process going on from the moment at which he met her, and had, unconsciously, assisted it. This present temptation, if conquered, would itself be the next, and greatest, step in the same direction: an obedience freer, more reasoned, more conscious than any she had known before, was being put in her power. But for that very reason the fatal false step which, once taken, would thrust her down into the terrible slavery of appetite and hate and economics and government which our race knows so well, could be made to sound so like the true one. What made him feel sure that the dangerous element in her interest was growing was her progressive disregard of the plain intellectual bones of the problem. It became harder to recall her mind to the *data*—a command from Maleldil, a complete uncertainty about the results of breaking it, and a present happiness so great that hardly any change could be for the better. The turgid swell of indistinctly splendid images which the Un-man aroused, and the transcendent importance of the central image, carried all this away. She was still in her innocence. No evil intention had been formed in her mind. But if her will was uncorrupted, half her imagination was already filled with bright, poisonous shapes. "This can't go on," thought Ransom for the second time. But all his arguments proved in the long run unavailing, and it did go on.

There came a night when he was so tired that towards morning he fell into a leaden sleep and slept far into the following day. He woke to find himself alone. A great horror came over him. "What could I have done? What could I have done?" he cried out, for he thought that all was lost. With sick heart and sore head he staggered to the edge of the island: his idea was to find a fish and to pursue the truants to the Fixed Land where he felt little doubt that they had gone. In the bitterness and confusion of his mind he forgot that he had no notion in which direction that land now lay nor how far it was distant. Hurrying through the woods, he emerged into an open place and suddenly found that he was not alone. Two human figures, robed to their feet, stood before him, silent under the yellow sky. Their clothes were of purple and blue, their heads wore chaplets of silver leaves, and their feet were bare. They seemed to him to be, the one the ugliest, and the other the most beautiful, of the children of men. Then one of them spoke and he realised that they were none other than the Green Lady herself and the haunted body of Weston. The robes were of feathers, and he knew well the Perelandrian birds from which they had been derived; the art of the weaving it could be called, was beyond his comprehension.

"Welcome, Piebald," said the Lady. "You have slept long. What do you think of us in our leaves?"

"The birds," said Ransom. "The poor birds! What has he done to them?"

"He has found the feathers somewhere," said the Lady carelessly. "They drop them."

"Why have you done this, Lady?"

"He has been making me older again. Why did you never tell me, Piebald?"

"Tell you what?"

"We never knew. This one showed me that the trees have leaves and the beasts have fur, and said that in your world the men and women also hung beautiful things about them. Why do you not tell us how we look? Oh, Piebald, Piebald, I hope this is not going to be another of the new goods from which you draw back your hand. It cannot be new to you if they all do it in your world."

"Ah," said Ransom, "but it is different there. It is cold."

"So the Stranger said," she answered. "But not in all parts of your world. He says they do it even where it is warm."

"Has he said why they do it?"

"To be beautiful. Why else?" said the Lady, with some wonder in her face.

"Thank Heaven," thought Ransom, "he is only teaching her vanity"; for he had feared something worse. Yet could it be possible, in the long run, to wear clothes without learning modesty, and through modesty lasciviousness?

"Do you think we are more beautiful?" said the Lady, interrupting his thoughts.

"No," said Ransom; and then, correcting himself, "I don't know." It was, indeed, not easy to reply. The Un-man, now that Weston's prosaic shirt and shorts were concealed, looked a more exotic and therefore a more imaginatively, less squalidly, hideous figure. As for the Lady—that she looked in some way worse was not doubtful. Yet there is a plainness in nudity—as we speak of "plain" bread. A sort of richness, a flamboyancy, a concession, as it were, to lower conceptions of the beautiful, had come with the purple robe. For the first (and last) time she appeared to him at that moment as a woman whom an earth-born man might conceivably love. And this was intolerable. The ghastly inappropriateness of the idea had, all in one moment, stolen something from the colours of the landscape and the scent of the flowers.

"Do you think we are more beautiful?" repeated the Lady.

"What does it matter?" said Ransom dully.

"Everyone should wish to be as beautiful as they can," she answered. "And we cannot see ourselves."

"We can," said Weston's body.

"How can this be?" said the Lady, turning to it. "Even if you could roll your eyes right round to look inside they would see only blackness."

"Not that way," it answered. "I will show you." It walked a few paces away to where Weston's pack lay in the yellow turf. With that curious distinctness which often falls upon us when we are anxious and preoccupied Ransom noticed the exact make and pattern of the pack. It must have been from the same shop in London where he had bought his own: and that little fact, suddenly reminding him that Weston had once been a man, that he too had once had pleasures and pains and a human mind, almost brought the tears into his eyes. The horrible fingers which Weston would never use again worked at the buckles and brought out a small bright object—an English pocket mirror that might have cost three-and-six. He handed it to the Green Lady. She turned it over in her hands.

"What is it? What am I to do with it?" she said.

"Look in it," said the Un-man.

"How?"

"Look!" he said. Then taking it from her he held it up to her face. She stared for quite an appreciable time without apparently making anything of it. Then she started back with a cry and covered her face. Ransom started too. It was the first time he had seen her the mere passive recipient of any emotion. The world about him was big with change.

"Oh—oh," she cried. "What is it? I saw a face."

"Only your own face, beautiful one," said the Un-man.

"I know," said the Lady, still averting her eyes from the mirror. "My face—out there—looking at me. Am I growing older or is it something else? I feel . . . I feel . . . my heart is beating too hard. I am not warm. What is it?" She glanced from one of them to the other. The mysteries had all vanished from her face. It was as easy to read as that of a man in a shelter when a bomb is coming.

"What is it?" she repeated.

"It is called Fear," said Weston's mouth. Then the creature turned its face full on Ransom and grinned.

"Fear," she said. "This is Fear," pondering the discovery; then, with abrupt finality, "I do not like it."

"It will go away," said the Un-man, when Ransom interrupted.

"It will never go away if you do what he wishes. It is into more and more fear that he is leading you."

"It is," said the Un-man, "into the great waves and through them and beyond. Now that you know Fear, you see that it must be you who shall taste it on behalf of your race. You know the King will not. You do not wish him to. But there is no cause for fear in this little thing: rather of joy. What is fearful in it?"

"Things being two when they are one," replied the Lady decisively. "That thing" (she pointed at the mirror) "is me and not me."

"But if you do not look you will never know how beautiful you are."

"It comes into my mind, Stranger," she answered, "that a fruit does not eat itself, and a man cannot be together with himself."

"A fruit cannot do that because it is only a fruit," said the Un-man. "But we can do it. We call this thing a mirror. A man can love himself, and be together with himself. That is what it means to be a man or a woman—to walk alongside oneself as if one were a second person and to delight in one's own beauty. Mirrors were made to teach this art."

"Is it a good?" said the Lady.

"No," said Ransom.

"How can you find out without trying?" said the Un-man.

"If you try it and it is not good," said Ransom, "how do you know whether you will be able to stop doing it?"

"I am walking alongside myself already," said the Lady. "But I do not yet know what I look like. If I have become two I had better know what the other is. As for you, Piebald, one look will show me this woman's face and why should I look more than once?"

She took the mirror, timidly but firmly, from the Un-man and looked into it in silence for the better part of a minute. Then she let it sink and stood holding it at her side.

"It is very strange," she said at last.

"It is very beautiful," said the Un-man. "Do you not think so?"

"Yes."

"But you have not yet found what you set out to find."

"What was that? I have forgotten."

"Whether the robe of feathers made you more beautiful or less."

"I saw only a face."

"Hold it further away and you will see the whole of the alongside woman—the other who is yourself. Or no—I will hold it."

The commonplace suggestions of the scene became grotesque at this stage. She looked at herself first with the robe, then without it, then with it again; finally she decided against it and threw it away. The Un-man picked it up.

"Will you not keep it?" he said: "you might wish to carry it on some days even if you do not wish for it on all days."

"*Keep* it?" she asked, not clearly understanding.

"I had forgotten," said the Un-man. "I had forgotten that you would not live on the Fixed Land nor build a house nor in any way become mistress of your own days. *Keeping* means putting a thing where you know you can always find it again, and where rain, and beasts, and other people cannot reach it. I would give you this mirror to keep. It would be the Queen's mirror, a gift brought into the world from Deep Heaven: the other women would not have it. But you have reminded me. There can be no gifts, no keeping, no foresight while you live as you do—from day to day, like the beasts."

But the Lady did not appear to be listening to him. She stood like one almost dazed with the richness of a day-dream. She did not look in the least like a woman who is thinking about a new dress. The expression of her face was noble. It was a great deal too noble. Greatness, tragedy, high sentiment—these were obviously what occupied her thoughts. Ransom perceived that the affair of the robes and the mirror had been only superficially concerned with what is commonly called female vanity. The image of her beautiful body had been offered to her only as a means to awake the far more perilous image of her great soul. The external and, as it were, dramatic conception of the self was the enemy's true aim. He was making her mind a theatre in which that phantom self should hold the stage. He had already written the play.

I I

Because he had slept so late that morning Ransom found it easy to keep awake the following night. The sea had become calm and there was no rain. He sat upright in the darkness with his back against a tree. The others were close beside him—the Lady, to judge by her breathing, asleep and the Un-man doubtless waiting to arouse her and resume its solicitations the moment Ransom should doze. For the third time, more strongly than ever before, it came into his head, "This can't go on."

The Enemy was using Third Degree methods. It seemed to Ransom that, but for a miracle, the Lady's resistance was bound to be worn away in the end. Why did no miracle come? Or rather, why no miracle on the right side? For the presence of the Enemy was in itself a kind of Miracle. Had Hell a prerogative to work wonders? Why did Heaven work none? Not for the first time he found himself questioning Divine Justice. He could not understand why Maleldil should remain absent when the Enemy was there in person.

But while he was thinking this, as suddenly and sharply as if the solid darkness about him had spoken with articulate voice, he knew that Maleldil was not absent. That sense—so very welcome yet never welcomed without the overcoming of a certain resistance—that sense of the Presence which he had once or twice before experienced on Perelandra, returned to him. The darkness was packed quite full. It seemed to press upon his trunk so that he could hardly use his lungs: it seemed to close in on his skull like a crown of intolerable weight so that for a space he could hardly think. Moreover, he became aware in some indefinable fashion that it had never been absent, that only some unconscious activity of his own had succeeded in ignoring it for the past few days.

Inner silence is for our race a difficult achievement. There is a chattering part of the mind which continues, until it is corrected, to chatter on even in the holiest places. Thus, while one part of Ransom remained, as it were, prostrated in a hush of fear and love that resembled a kind of death, something else inside him, wholly unaffected by reverence, continued to pour queries and objections into his brain. "It's all very well," said this voluble critic, "a presence of *that* sort! But the Enemy is really here, really saying and doing things. Where is Maleldil's representative?"

The answer which came back to him, quick as a fencer's or a tennis player's *riposte,* out of the silence and the darkness, almost took his breath away. It seemed Blasphemous. "Anyway, what can I do?" babbled the voluble self. "I've done all I can. I've talked till I'm sick of it. It's no good, I tell you." He tried to persuade himself that he, Ransom, could not possibly be Maleldil's representative as the Un-man was the representative of Hell. The suggestion was, he argued, itself diabolical—a temptation to fatuous pride, to megalomania. He was horrified when the darkness simply flung back this argument in his face, almost impatiently. And then—he wondered how it had escaped him till now—he was forced to perceive that his own coming to Perelandra was at least as much of a marvel as the Enemy's. That miracle on the right side, which he had demanded, had in fact occurred. He himself was the miracle.

"Oh, but this is nonsense," said the voluble self. He, Ransom, with his ridiculous piebald body and his ten times defeated arguments—what sort of a miracle was that? His mind darted hopefully down a side-alley that seemed to promise escape. Very well then. He *had* been brought here miraculously. He was in God's hands. As long as he did his best—and he *had* done his best—God would see to the final issue. He had not succeeded. But he had done his best. No one could do more. "'Tis not in mortals to command success." He must not be worried about the final result. Maleldil would see to that. And Maleldil would bring him safe back to earth after his very real, though unsuccessful, efforts. Probably Maleldil's real intention was that he should publish to the human race the truths he had learned on the planet Venus. As for the fate of Venus, that could not really rest upon his shoulders. It was in God's hands. One must be content to leave it there. One must have Faith. . . .

It snapped like a violin string. Not one rag of all this evasion was left. Relentlessly, unmistakably, the Darkness pressed down upon him the knowledge that this picture of the situation was utterly false. His journey to Perelandra was not a moral exercise, nor a sham fight. If the issue lay in Maleldil's hands, Ransom and the Lady *were* those hands. The fate of a world really depended on how they behaved in the next few hours. The thing was irreducibly, nakedly real. They could, if they chose, decline to save the innocence of this new race, and if they declined its innocence would not be saved. It rested with no other creature in all time or all space. This he saw clearly, though as yet he had no inkling of what he could do.

The voluble self protested, wildly, swiftly, like the propeller of a ship racing when it is out of the water. The imprudence, the unfairness, the absurdity of it! Did Maleldil *want* to lose worlds? What was the sense of so arranging things that anything really important should finally and absolutely depend on such a man of straw as himself? And at that moment, far away on Earth, as he now could not help remembering, men were at war, and white-faced subalterns and freckled corporals who had but lately begun to shave, stood in horrible gaps or crawled forward in deadly darkness, awaking, like him, to the preposterous truth that all really depended on their actions; and far away in time Horatius stood on the bridge, and Constantine settled in his mind whether he would or would not embrace the new religion, and Eve herself stood looking upon the forbidden fruit and the Heaven of Heavens waited for her decision. He writhed and ground his teeth, but could not help seeing. Thus, and not otherwise, the world was made. Either something or nothing must depend on individual choices. And if something, who could set bounds to it? A stone may determine the course of a river. He was that stone at this horrible moment which had become the centre of the whole universe. The eldila of all worlds, the sinless organisms of everlasting light, were silent in Deep Heaven to see what Elwin Ransom of Cambridge would do.

Then came blessed relief. He suddenly realised that he did not know what he *could* do. He almost laughed with joy. All this horror had been premature. No definite task was before him. All that was being demanded of him was a general and preliminary resolution to oppose the Enemy in any mode which circumstances might show to be desirable: in fact—and he flew back to the comforting words as a child flies back to its mother's arms—"to do his best"—or rather, to go on doing his best, for he had really been doing it all along. "What bug-bears we make of things unnecessarily!" he murmured, settling himself in a slightly more comfortable position. A mild flood of what appeared to him to be cheerful and rational piety rose and engulfed him.

Hullo! What was this? He sat straight upright again, his heart beating wildly against his side. His thoughts had stumbled on an idea from which they started back as a man starts back when he has touched a hot poker. But this time the idea was really too childish to entertain. This time it *must* be a deception, risen from his own mind. It stood to reason that a struggle with the Devil meant a *spiritual* struggle . . . the notion of a physical combat was only fit for a savage. If only it *were* as simple as that . . . but here the voluble self had made a fatal mistake. The habit of imaginative honesty was too deeply engrained in Ransom to let him toy for more than a second with the pretence that he feared bodily strife with the Un-man less than he feared anything else. Vivid pictures crowded upon him . . . the deadly cold of those hands (he had touched the creature accidentally some hours before) . . . the long metallic nails . . . ripping off narrow strips of flesh, pulling out tendons. One would die slowly. Up to the very end that cruel idiocy would smile into one's face. One would give way long before one died—beg for mercy, promise it help, worship, anything.

It was fortunate that something so horrible should be so obviously out of the question. Almost, but not quite, Ransom decreed that whatever the Silence and the Darkness seemed to be saying about this, no such crude, materialistic struggle could possibly be what Maleldil really intended. Any suggestion to the contrary must be only his own morbid fancy. It would degrade the spiritual warfare to the condition of mere mythology. But here he got another check. Long since on Mars, and more strongly since he came to Perelandra, Ransom had been perceiving that the triple distinction of truth from myth and of both from fact was purely terrestrial—was part and parcel of that unhappy division between soul and body which resulted from the Fall. Even on earth the sacraments existed as a permanent reminder that the division was neither wholesome nor final. The Incarnation had been the beginning of its disappearance. In Perelandra it would have no meaning at all. Whatever happened here would be of such a nature that earth-men would call it mythological. All this he had thought before. Now he knew it. The Presence in the darkness, never before so formidable, was putting these truths into his hands, like terrible jewels.

The voluble self was almost thrown out of its argumentative stride— became for some seconds as the voice of a mere whimpering child begging to be let off, to be allowed to go home. Then it rallied. It explained precisely where the absurdity of a physical battle with the Un-man lay. It would be quite irrelevant to the spiritual issue. If the Lady were to be kept in obedience only by the forcible removal of the Tempter, what was the use of that? What would it prove? And if the temptation were not a proving or testing, why was it allowed to happen at all? Did Maleldil suggest that our own world might have been saved if the elephant had accidentally trodden on the serpent a moment before Eve was about to yield? Was it as easy and as un-moral as that? The thing was patently absurd!

The terrible silence went on. It became more and more like a face, a face not without sadness, that looks upon you while you are telling lies, and never interrupts, but gradually you know that it knows, and falter, and contradict yourself, and lapse into silence. The voluble self petered out in the end. Almost the Darkness said to Ransom, "You know you are only wasting time." Every minute it became clearer to him that the parallel he had tried to draw between Eden and Perelandra was crude and imperfect. What had happened on Earth, when Maleldil was born a man at Bethlehem, had altered the universe for ever. The new world of Perelandra was not a mere repetition of the old world Tellus. Maleldil never repeated Himself. As the Lady had said, the same wave never came twice. When Eve fell, God was not Man. He had not yet made men members of His body: since then He had, and through them henceforward He would save and suffer. One of the purposes for which He had done all this was to save Perelandra not through Himself but through Himself in Ransom. If Ransom refused, the plan, so far, miscarried. For that point in the story, a story far more complicated than he had conceived, it was he who had been selected. With a strange sense of "fallings from him, vanishings," he perceived that you might just as well call Perelandra, not Tellus, the centre. You might look upon the Perelandrian story as merely an indirect consequence of the Incarnation on earth: or you might look on the Earth story as mere preparation for the new worlds of which Perelandra was the first. The one was neither more nor less true than the other. Nothing was more or less important than anything else, nothing was a copy or model of anything else.

At the same time he also perceived that his voluble self had begged the question. Up to this point the Lady had repelled her assailant. She was shaken and weary, and there were some stains perhaps in her imagination, but she had stood. In that respect the story already differed from anything that he certainly knew about the mother of our own race. He did not know whether Eve had resisted at all, or if so, for how long. Still less did he know how the story would have ended if she had. If the "serpent" had been foiled, and returned the next day, and the next . . . what then? Would the trial have lasted for ever? How would Maleldil have stopped it? Here on Perelandra his own intuition had been not that no temptation must occur but that "This can't go on." This stopping of a third-degree solicitation, already more than once refused, was a problem to which the terrestrial Fall offered no clue—a new task, and for that new task a new character in the drama, who appeared (most unfortunately) to be himself. In vain did his mind hark back, time after time, to the Book of Genesis, asking "What would have happened?" But to this the Darkness gave him no answer. Patiently and inexorably it brought him back to the here and the now, and to the growing certainty of what was here and now demanded. Almost he felt that the words "would have happened" were meaningless—mere invitations to wander in what the Lady would have called an "alongside world" which had no reality. Only the actual was real: and every actual situation was new. Here in Perelandra the temptation would be stopped by Ransom, or it would not be stopped at all. The Voice—for it was almost with a Voice that he was now contending—seemed to create around this alternative an infinite vacancy. This chapter, this page, this very sentence, in the cosmic story was utterly and eternally itself; no other passage that had occurred or ever would occur could be substituted for it.

He fell back on a different line of defence. How *could* he fight the immortal enemy? Even if he were a fighting man—instead of a sedentary scholar with weak eyes and a baddish wound from the last war—what use was there in fighting it? It couldn't be killed, could it? But the answer was almost immediately plain. Weston's body could be destroyed; and presumably that body was the Enemy's only foothold in Perelandra. By that body, when that body still obeyed a human will, it had entered the new world: expelled from it, it would doubtless have no other habitation. It had entered that body at Weston's own invitation, and without such invitation could enter no other. Ransom remembered that the unclean spirits, in the Bible, had a horror of being cast out into the "deep." And thinking of these things he perceived at last, with a sinking of heart, that if physical action were indeed demanded of him, it was an action, by ordinary standards, neither impossible nor hopeless. On the physical plane it was one middle-aged, sedentary body against another, and both unarmed save for fists and teeth and nails. At the thought of these details, terror and disgust overcame him. To kill the thing with such weapons (he remembered his killing of the frog) would be a nightmare; to be killed—who knew how slowly?—was more than he could face. That he would be killed he felt certain. "When," he asked, "did I ever win a fight in all my life?"

He was no longer making efforts to resist the conviction of what he must do. He had exhausted all his efforts. The answer was plain beyond all subterfuge. The Voice out of the night spoke it to him in such unanswerable fashion that, though there was no noise, he almost felt it must wake the woman who slept close by. He was faced with the impossible. This he must do: this he could not do. In vain he reminded himself of the things that unbelieving boys might at this moment be doing on Earth for a lesser cause. His will was in that valley where the appeal to shame becomes useless—nay, makes the valley darker and deeper. He believed he could face the Un-man with firearms: even that he could stand up unarmed and face certain death if the creature had retained Weston's revolver. But to come to grips with it, to go voluntarily into those dead yet living arms, to grapple with it, naked chest to naked chest. . . . Terrible follies came into his mind. He would fail to obey the Voice, but it would be all right because he would repent later on, when he was back on Earth. He would lose his nerve as St. Peter had done, and be, like St. Peter, forgiven. Intellectually, of course, he knew the answer to these temptations perfectly well; but he was at one of those moments when all the utterances of intellect sound like twice-told tales. Then some crosswind of the mind changed his mood. Perhaps he would fight and win, perhaps not even be badly mauled. But no faintest hint of a guarantee in that direction came to him from the darkness. The future was black as the night itself.

"It is not for nothing that you are named Ransom," said the Voice.

And he knew that this was no fancy of his own. He knew it for a very curious reason—because he had known for many years that his surname was derived not from *ransom* but from *Ranolf's son*. It would never have occurred to him thus to associate the two words. To connect the name Ransom with the act of ransoming would have been for him a mere pun. But even his voluble self did not now dare to suggest that the Voice was making a play upon words. All in a moment of time he perceived that what was, to human philologists, a merely accidental resemblance of two sounds, was in truth no accident. The whole distinction between things accidental and things designed, like the distinction between fact and myth, was purely terrestrial. The pattern is so large that within the little frame of earthly experience there appear pieces of it between which we can see no connection, and other pieces between which we can. Hence we rightly, for our use, distinguish the accidental from the essential. But step outside that frame and the distinction drops down into the void, fluttering useless wings. He had been forced out of the frame, caught up into the larger pattern. He knew now why the old philosophers had said that there is no such thing as chance or fortune beyond the Moon. Before his Mother had born him, before his ancestors had been called Ransoms, before *ransom* had been the name for a payment that delivers, before the world was made, all these things had so stood together in eternity that the very significance of the pattern at this point lay in their coming together in just this fashion. And he bowed his head and groaned and repined against his fate—to be still a man and yet to be forced up into the metaphysical world, to enact what philosophy only thinks.

"My name also is Ransom," said the Voice.

It was some time before the purport of this saying dawned upon him. He whom the other worlds call Maleldil, was the world's ransom, his own ransom, well he knew. But to what purpose was it said now? Before the answer came to him he felt its insufferable approach and held out his arms before him as if he could keep it from forcing open the door of his mind. But it came. So *that* was the real issue. If he now failed, this world also would hereafter be redeemed. If he were not the ransom, Another would be. Yet nothing was ever repeated. Not a second crucifixion: perhaps—who knows—not even a second Incarnation . . . some act of even more appalling love, some glory of yet deeper humility. For he had seen already how the pattern grows and how from each world it sprouts into the next through some other dimension. The small external evil which Satan had done in Malacandra was only as a line: the deeper evil he had done in Earth was as a square: if Venus fell, her evil would be a cube—her Redemption beyond conceiving. Yet redeemed she would be. He had long known that great issues hung on his choice; but as he now realised the true width of the frightful freedom that was being put into his hands—a width to which all merely spatial infinity seemed narrow—he felt like a man brought out under naked heaven, on the edge of a precipice, into the teeth of a wind that came howling from the Pole. He had pictured himself, till now, standing before the Lord, like Peter. But it was worse. He sat before Him like Pilate. It lay with him to save or to spill. His hands had been reddened, as all men's hands have been, in the slaying before the foundation of the world; now, if he chose, he could dip them again in the same blood. "Mercy," he groaned; and then, "Lord, why me?" But there was no answer.

The thing still seemed impossible. But gradually something happened to him which had happened to him only twice before in his life. It had happened once while he was trying to make up his mind to do a very dangerous job in the last war. It had happened again while he was screwing his resolution to go and see a certain man in London and make to him an excessively embarrassing confession which justice demanded. In both cases the thing had seemed a sheer impossibility: he had not thought but known that, being what he was, he was psychologically incapable of doing it; and then, without any apparent movement of the will, as objective and unemotional as the reading on a dial, there had arisen before him, with perfect certitude, the knowledge "about this time tomorrow you will have done the impossible." The same thing happened now. His fear, his shame, his love, all his arguments, were not altered in the least. The thing was neither more nor less dreadful than it had been before. The only difference was that he knew—almost as a historical proposition—that it was going to be done. He might beg, weep, or rebel—might curse or adore—sing like a martyr or blaspheme like a devil. It made not the slightest difference. The thing was going to be done. There was going to arrive, in the course of time, a moment at which he would have done it. The future act stood there, fixed and unaltered as if he had already performed it. It was a mere irrelevant detail that it happened to occupy the position we call future instead of that which we call past. The whole struggle was over, and yet there seemed to have been no moment of victory. You might say, if you liked, that the power of choice had been simply set aside and an inflexible destiny substituted for it. On the other hand, you might say that he had delivered from the rhetoric of his passions and had emerged into unassailable freedom. Ransom could not, for the life of him, see any difference between these two statements. Predestination and freedom were apparently identical. He could no longer see any meaning in the many arguments he had heard on this subject.

No sooner had he discovered that he would certainly try to kill the Un-man to-morrow than the doing of it appeared to him a smaller matter than he had supposed. He could hardly remember why he had accused himself of megalomania when the idea first occurred to him. It was true that if he left it undone, Maleldil Himself would do some greater thing instead. In that sense, he stood for Maleldil: but no more than Eve would have stood for Him by simply not eating the apple, or than any man stands for Him in doing any good action. As there was no comparison in person, so there was none in suffering—or only such comparison as may be between a man who burns his finger putting out a spark and a fireman who loses his life in fighting a conflagration because that spark was not put out. He asked no longer "Why me?" It might as well be he as another. It might as well be any other choice as this. The fierce light which he had seen resting on this moment of decision rested in reality on all.

"I have cast your Enemy into sleep," said the Voice. "He will not wake till morning. Get up. Walk twenty paces back into the wood; there sleep. Your sister sleeps also."

12

When some dreaded morning comes we usually wake fully to it at once. Ransom passed with no intermediate stages from dreamless sleep to a full consciousness of his task. He found himself alone—the island gently rocking on a sea that was neither calm nor stormy. The golden light, glinting through indigo trunks of trees, told him in which direction the water lay. He went to it and bathed. Then, having landed again, he lay down and drank. He stood for a few minutes running his hands through his wet hair and stroking his limbs. Looking down at his own body he noticed how greatly the sunburn on one side and the pallor on the other had decreased. He would hardly be christened Piebald if the Lady were now to meet him for the first time. His colour had become more like ivory: and his toes, after so many days of nakedness, had begun to lose the cramped, squalid shape imposed by boots. Altogether he thought better of himself as a human animal than he had done before. He felt pretty certain that he would never again wield an un-maimed body until a greater morning came for the whole universe, and he was glad that the instrument had been thus tuned up to concert pitch before he had to surrender it. "When I wake up after Thy image, I shall be satisfied," he said to himself.

Presently he walked into the woods. Accidentally—for he was at the moment intent on food—he blundered through a whole cloud of the arboreal bubbles. The pleasure was as sharp as when he had first experienced it, and his very stride was different as he emerged from them. Although this was to be his last meal, he did not even now feel it proper to look for any favorite fruit. But what met him was gourds. "A good breakfast on the morning you're hanged," he thought whimsically as he let the empty shell drop from his hand—filled for the moment with such pleasure as seemed to make the whole world a dance. "All said and done," he thought, "it's been worth it. I have had a time. I have lived in Paradise."

He went a little farther in the wood, which grew thickly hereabout, and almost tripped over the sleeping form of the Lady. It was unusual for her to be sleeping at this time of the day, and he assumed it was Maleldil's doing. "I shall never see her again," he thought; and then, "I shall never again look on a female body in quite the same way as I look on this." As he stood looking down on her, what was most with him was an intense and orphaned longing that he might, if only for once, have seen the great Mother of his own race thus, in her innocence and splendour. "Other things, other blessings, other glories," he murmured. "But never that. Never in all worlds, that. God can make good use of all that happens. But the loss is real." He looked at her once again and then walked abruptly past the place where she lay. "I was right," he thought, "it couldn't have gone on. It was time to stop it."

It took him a long time, wandering like this, in and out of the dark yet coloured thickets, before he found his Enemy. He came on his old friend the dragon, just as he had first seen it, coiled about the trunk of a tree, but it also was asleep; and now he noticed that ever since he awoke he had perceived no chattering of birds, no rustling of sleek bodies or peering of brown eyes through the leafage, nor heard any noise but that of water. It seemed that the Lord God had cast that whole island or perhaps that whole world into deep sleep. For a moment this gave him a sense of desolation, but almost at once he rejoiced that no memory of blood and rage should be left imprinted in these happy minds.

After about an hour, suddenly rounding a little clump of bubble-trees he found himself face to face with the Un-man. "Is it wounded already?" he thought as the first vision of a blood-stained chest broke on him. Then he saw that of course it was not its own blood. A bird, already half plucked and with beak wide open in the soundless yell of strangulation, was feebly struggling in its long clever hands. Ransom found himself acting before he knew what he had done. Some memory of boxing at his preparatory school must have awaked, for he found he had delivered a straight left with all his might on the Un-man's jaw. But he had forgotten that he was not fighting with gloves; what recalled him to himself was the pain as his fist crashed against the jaw-bone—it seemed almost to have broken his knuckles—and the sickening jar all up his arm. He stood still for a second under the shock of it and this gave the Un-man time to fall back about six paces. It too had not liked the first taste of the encounter. It had apparently bitten its tongue, for blood came bubbling out of the mouth when it tried to speak. It was still holding the bird.

"So you mean to try strength," it said in English, speaking thick.

"Put down that bird," said Ransom.

"But this is very foolish," said the Un-man. "Do you not know who I am?"

"I know *what* you are," said Ransom. "Which of them doesn't matter."

"And you think, little one," it answered, "that you can fight with me? You think He will help you, perhaps? Many thought that. I've known Him longer than you, little one. They all think He's going to help them—till they come to their senses screaming recantations too late in the middle of the fire, mouldering in concentration camps, writhing under saws, jibbering in mad-houses, or nailed on to crosses. Could He help Himself?"—and the creature suddenly threw back its head and cried in a voice so loud that it seemed the golden sky-roof must break, *"Eloi, Eloi, lama sabachthani."*

And the moment it had done so, Ransom felt certain that the sounds it had made were perfect Aramaic of the First Century. The Un-man was not quoting; it was remembering. These were the very words spoken from the Cross, treasured through all those years in the burning memory of the outcast creature which had heard them, and now brought forward in hideous parody; the horror made him momentarily sick. Befor he had recovered the Un-man was upon him, howling like a gale, with eyes so wide opened that they seemed to have no lids, and with all its hair rising on its scalp. It had him caught tightly to its chest, with its arms about him, and its nails were ripping great strips off his back. His own arms were inside its embrace and, pummelling wildly, he could get no blow at it. He turned his head and bit deeply into the muscle of its right arm, at first without success, then deeper. It gave a howl, tried to hold on, and then suddenly he was free. Its defence was for an instant unready and he found himself raining punches about the region of its heart, faster and harder than he had supposed possible. He could hear through its open mouth the great gusts of breath that he was knocking out of it. Then its hands came up again, fingers arched like claws. It was not trying to box. It wanted to grapple. He knocked its right arm aside with a horrible shock of bone against bone and caught it a jab on the fleshy part of the chin: at the same moment its nails tore his right. He grabbed at its arms. More by luck than by skill he got it held by both wrists.

What followed for the next minute or so would hardly have looked like a fight at all to any spectator. The Un-man was trying with every ounce of power it could find in Weston's body to wrench its arms free from Ransom's hands, and he, with every ounce of his power, was trying to retain his manacle hold round its wrists. But this effort, which sent streams of sweat down the backs of both combatants, resulted in a slow and seemingly leisurely, and even aimless, movement of both pairs of arms. Neither could for the moment hurt the other. The Un-man bent forward its head and tried to bite, but Ransom straightened his arms and kept it at arm's length. There seemed no reason why this should ever end.

Then suddenly it shot out its leg and crooked it behind his knee. He was nearly taken off his feet. Movements became quick and flurried on both sides. Ransom in his turn tried to trip, and failed. He started bending the enemy's left arm back by main force with some idea of breaking or at least spraining it. But in the effort to do so he must have weakened his hold on the other wrist. It got its right free. He had just time to close his eyes before the nails tore fiercely down his cheek and the pain put an end to the blows his left was already raining on its ribs. A second later—he did not know how it happened—they were standing apart, their chests heaving in great gasps, each staring at the other.

Both were doubtless sorry spectacles. Ransom could not see his own wounds but he seemed to be covered with blood. The enemy's eyes were nearly closed and the body, wherever the remains of Weston's shirt did not conceal it, was a mass of what would soon be bruises. This, and its laboured breathing, and the very taste of its strength in their grapples, had altered Ransom's state of mind completely. He had been astonished to find it no stronger. He had all along, despite what reason told him, expected that the strength of its body would be superhuman, diabolical. He had reckoned on arms that could no more be caught and stopped than the blades of an aeroplane's propeller. But now he knew, by actual experience, that its bodily strength was merely that of Weston. On the physical plane it was one middle-aged scholar against another. Weston had been the more powerfully built of the two men, but he was fat; his body would not take punishment well. Ransom was nimbler and better breathed. His former certainty of death now seemed to him ridiculous. It was a very fair match. There was no reason why he should not win—and live.

This time it was Ransom who attacked, and the second bout was much the same as the first. What it came to was that whenever he could box Ransom was superior; whenever he came under tooth and claw he was beaten. His mind, even in the thick of it, was now quite clear. He saw that the issue of the day hung on a very simple question—whether loss of blood would undo him before heavy blows on heart and kidneys undid the other.

All that rich world was asleep about them. There were no rules, no umpire, no spectators; but mere exhaustion, constantly compelling them to fall apart, divided the grotesque duel into rounds as accurately as could be wished. Ransom could never remember how many of these rounds were fought. The thing became like the frantic repetitions of delirium, and thirst a greater pain than any the adversary could inflict. Sometimes they were both on the ground together. Once he was actually astride the enemy's chest, squeezing its throat with both hands and—he found to his surprise—shouting a line out of *The Battle of Maldon*: but it tore his arms so with its nails and so pounded his back with its knees that he was thrown off.

Then he remembers—as one remembers an island of consciousness preceded and followed by long anæsthesia—going forward to meet the Un-man for what seemed the thousandth time and knowing clearly that he could not fight much more. He remembers seeing the Enemy for a moment looking not like Weston but like a mandrill, and realising almost at once that this was delirium. He wavered. Then an experience that perhaps no good man can ever have in our world came over him— a torrent of perfectly unmixed and lawful hatred. The energy of hating, never before felt without some guilt, without some dim knowledge that he was failing fully to distinguish the sinner from the sin, rose into his arms and legs till he felt that they were pillars of burning blood. What was before him appeared no longer a creature of corrupted will. It was corruption itself to which will was attached only as an instrument. Ages ago it had been a Person: but the ruins of personality now survived in it only as weapons at the disposal of a furious self-exiled negation. It is perhaps difficult to understand why this filled Ransom not with horror but with a kind of joy. The joy came from finding at last what hatred was made for. As a boy with an axe rejoices on finding a tree, or a boy with a box of coloured chalks rejoices on finding a pile of perfectly white paper, so he rejoiced in the perfect congruity between his emotion and its object. Bleeding and trembling with weariness as he was, he felt that nothing was beyond his power, and when he flung himself upon the living Death, the eternal Surd in the universal mathematic, he was astonished, and yet (on a deeper level) not astonished at all, at his own strength. His arms seemed to move quicker than his thought. His hands taught him terrible things. He felt its ribs break, he heard its jaw-bone crack. The whole creature seemed to be cracking and splitting under his blows. His own pains, where it tore him, somehow failed to matter. He felt that he could so fight, so hate with a perfect hatred, for a whole year.

All at once he found he was beating the air. He was in such a state that at first he could not understand what was happening—could not believe that the Un-man had fled. His momentary stupidity gave it a start; and when he came to his senses he was just in time to see it vanishing into the wood, with a limping uneven stride, with one arm hanging useless, and with its dog-like howl. He dashed after it. For a second or so it was concealed from him by the tree trunks. Then it was once more in sight. He began running with all his power, but it kept its lead.

It was a fantastic chase, in and out of the lights and shadows and up and down the slowly moving ridges and valleys. They passed the dragon where it slept. They passed the Lady, sleeping with a smile on her face. The Un-man stooped low as it passed her with the fingers of its left hand crooked for scratching. It would have torn her if it dared, but Ransom was close behind and it could not risk the delay. They passed through a flock of large orange-coloured birds all fast asleep, each on one leg, each with its head beneath its wing, so that they looked like a grove of formal and flowery shrubs. They picked their steps where pairs and families of the yellow wallabies lay on their backs with eyes fast shut and their small forepaws folded on their breasts as if they were crusaders carved on tombs. They stooped beneath branches which were bowed down because on them lay the tree-pigs, making a comfortable noise like a child's snore. They crashed through thickets of bubble-trees and forgot, for the moment, their weariness. It was a large island. They came out of the woods and rushed across wide fields of saffron or of silver, sometimes deep to their ankles and sometimes to their waists in the cool or poignant scents. They rushed down into yet other woods which lay, as they approached them, at the bottom of secret valleys, but rose before they reached them to crown the summits of lonely hills. Ransom could not gain on his quarry. It was a wonder that any creature so maimed as its uneven strides showed it to be, could maintain that pace. If the ankle were really sprained, as he suspected, it must suffer indescribably at every step. Then the horrible thought came into his mind that perhaps it could somehow hand over the pain to be borne by whatever remnants of Weston's consciousness yet survived in its body. The idea that something which had once been of his own kind and fed at a human breast might even now be imprisoned in the thing he was pursuing redoubled his hatred, which was unlike nearly all other hatreds he had ever known, for it increased his strength.

As they emerged from about the fourth wood he saw the sea before them not thirty yards away. The Un-man rushed on as if it made no distinction between land and water and plunged in with a great splash. He could see its head, dark against the coppery sea, as it swam. Ransom rejoiced, for swimming was the only sport in which he had ever approached excellence. As he took the water he lost sight of the Un-man for a moment; then, looking up and shaking the wet hair from his face as he struck out in pursuit (his hair was very long by now), he saw its whole body upright and above the surface as though it were sitting on the sea. A second glance and he realised that it had mounted a fish. Apparently the charm'd slumber extended only to the island, for the Un-man on his mount was making good speed. It was stooping down doing something to its fish, Ransom could not see what. Doubtless it would have many ways of urging the animal to quicken its pace.

For a moment he was in despair: but he had forgotten the man-loving nature of these sea-horses. He found almost at once that he was in a complete shoal of the creatures, leaping and frisking to attract his attention. In spite of their good will it was no easy matter to get himself on to the slippery surface of the fine specimen which his grabbing hands first reached: while he was struggling to mount, the distance widened between him and the fugitive. But at last it was done. Settling himself behind the great goggle-eyed head he nudged the animal with his knees, kicked it with his heels, whispered words of praise and encouragement, and in general did all he could to awake its mettle. It began threshing its way forward. But looking ahead Ransom could no longer see any sign of the Un-man, but only the long empty ridge of the next wave coming towards him. Doubtless the quarry was beyond the ridge. Then he noticed that he had no cause to be bothered about the direction. The slope of water was dotted all over with the great fish, each marked by a heap of yellow foam and some of them spouting as well. The Un-man possibly had not reckoned on the instinct which made them follow as leader any of their company on whom a human being sat. They were all forging straight ahead, no more uncertain of their course than homing rooks or bloodhounds on a scent. As Ransom and his fish rose to the top of the wave, he found himself looking down on a wide shallow trough shaped much like a valley in the home counties. Far away and now approaching the opposite slope was the little, dark puppet-like silhouette of the Un-man: and between it and him the whole school of fish was spread out in three or four lines. Clearly there was no danger of losing touch. Ransom was hunting him with the fish and they would not cease to follow. He laughed aloud. "My hounds are bred out of the Spartan kind, so flew'd so sanded," he roared.

Now for the first time the blessed fact that he was no longer fighting nor even standing thrust itself upon his attention. He made to assume a more relaxed position and was pulled up sharp by a grinding pain across his back. He foolishly put back his hand to explore his shoulders, and almost screamed at the pain of his own touch. His back seemed to be in shreds and the shreds seemed to be all stuck together. At the same time he noticed that he had lost a tooth and that nearly all the skin was gone from his knuckles; and underneath the smarting surface pains, deeper and more ominous aches racked him from head to foot. He had not known he was so knocked up.

Then he remembered that he was thirsty. Now that he had begun to cool and stiffen he found the task of getting a drink from the water that raced by him extremely difficult. His first idea had been to stoop low till his head was almost upside down and bury his face in the water: but a single attempt cured him of that. He was reduced to putting down his cupped hands, and even this, as his stiffness grew upon him, had to be done with infinite caution and with many groans and gasps. It took many minutes to get a tiny sip which merely mocked his thirst. The quenching of that thirst kept him employed for what seemed to be half an hour—a half-hour of sharp pains and insane pleasures. Nothing had ever tasted so good. Even when he had done drinking he went on taking up water and splashing it over himself. This would have been among the happiest moments of his life—if only the smarting of his back did not seem to be getting worse and if only he were not afraid that there was poison in the cuts. His legs kept on getting stuck to the fish and having to be unstuck with pain and care. Every now and then blackness threatened to come over him. He could easily have fainted, but he thought "This will never do" and fixed his eyes on objects close at hand and thought plain thoughts and so retained his consciousness.

All this time the Un-man rode on before him, up-wave and down-wave, and the fishes followed and Ransom followed the fishes. There seemed to be more of them now, as if the chase had met other shoals and gathered them up into itself in snowball fashion: and soon there were creatures other than fish. Birds with long necks like swans—he could not tell their colour for they looked black against the sky—came, wheeling at first, overhead, but afterwards they settled in long straight files—all following the Un-man. The crying of these birds was often audible, and it was the wildest sound that Ransom had ever heard, the loneliest, and the one that had least to do with Man. No land was in sight, nor had been for many hours. He was on the high seas, the waste places of Perelandra, as he had not been since his first arrival. The sea-noises continuously filled his ear: the sea-smell, unmistakable and stirring as that of our Tellurian oceans, but quite different in its warmth and golden sweetness, entered into his brain. It also was wild and strange. It was not hostile: if it had been, its wildness and strangeness would have been the less, for hostility is a relation and an enemy is not a total stranger. It came into his head that he knew nothing at all about this world. Some day, no doubt, it would be peopled by the descendants of the King and Queen. But all its millions of years in the unpeopled past, all its uncounted miles of laughing water in the lonely present . . . did they exist solely for that? It was strange that he to whom a wood or a morning sky on earth had sometimes been a kind of meal, should have had to come to another planet in order to realise Nature as a thing in her own right. The diffused meaning, the inscrutable character, which had been both in Tellus and Perelandra since they split off from the Sun, and which would be, in one sense, displaced by the advent of imperial man, yet, in some other sense, not displaced at all, enfolded him on every side and caught him into itself.

13

Darkness fell upon the waves as suddenly as if it had been poured out of a bottle. As soon as the colours and the distances were thus taken away, sound and pain became more emphatic. The world was reduced to a dull ache, and sudden stabs, and the beating of the fish's fins, and the monotonous yet infinitely varied noises of the water. Then he found himself almost falling off the fish, recovered his seat with difficulty, and realised that he had been asleep, perhaps for hours. He foresaw that this danger would continually recur. After some consideration he levered himself painfully out of the narrow saddle behind its head and stretched his body at full length along the fish's back. He parted his legs and wound them about the creature as far as he could and did the same with his arms, hoping that thus he could retain his mount even while sleeping. It was the best he could do. A strange thrilling sensation crept over him, communicated doubtless from the movement of its muscles. It gave him the illusion of sharing in its strong bestial life, as if he were himself becoming a fish.

Long after this he found himself staring into something like a human face. It ought to have terrified him but, as sometimes happens to us in a dream, it did not. It was a bluish-greenish face shining apparently by its own light. The eyes were much larger than those of a man and gave it a goblin appearance. A fringe of corrugated membranes at the sides suggested whiskers. With a shock he realised that he was not dreaming, but awake. The thing was real. He was still lying, sore and wearied, on the body of the fish and this face belonged to something that was swimming alongside him. He remembered the swimming submen or mermen whom he had seen before. He was not at all frightened, and he guessed that the creature's reaction to him was the very same as his to it—an uneasy, though not hostile, bewilderment. Each was wholly irrelevant to the other. They met as the branches of different trees meet when the wind brings them together.

Ransom now raised himself once more to a sitting position. He found that the darkness was not complete. His own fish swam in a bath of phosphorescence and so did the stranger at his side. All about him were other blobs and daggers of blue light and he could dimly make out from the shapes which were fish and which were the water-people. Their movements faintly indicated the contours of the waves and introduced some hint of perspective into the night. He noticed presently that several of the water-people in his immediate neighbourhood seemed to be feeding. They were picking dark masses of something off the water with their webbed frog-like hands and devouring it. As they munched, it hung out of their mouths in bushy and shredded bundles and looked like moustaches. It is significant that it never occurred to him to try to establish any contact with these beings, as he had done with every other animal on Perelandra, nor did they try to establish any with him. They did not seem to be the natural subjects of man as the other creatures were. He got the impression that they simply shared a planet with him as sheep and horses share a field, each species ignoring the other. Later, this came to be a trouble in his mind: but for the moment he was occupied with a more practical problem. The sight of their eating had reminded him that he was hungry, and he was wondering whether the stuff they ate were eatable by him. It took him a long time, scooping the water with his fingers, to catch any of it. When at last he did it turned out to be of the same general structure as one of our smaller sea-weeds, and to have little bladders that popped when one pressed them. It was tough and slippery, but not salt like the weed of a Tellurian sea. What it tasted like, he could never properly describe. It is to be noted all through this story that while Ransom was on Perelandra his sense of taste had become something more than it was on Earth: it gave knowledge as well as pleasure, though not a knowledge that can be reduced to words. As soon as he had eaten a few mouthfuls of the seaweed he felt his mind oddly changed. He felt the surface of the sea to be the top of the world. He thought of the floating islands as we think of clouds; he saw them in imagination as they would appear from below—mats of fibre with long streamers hanging down from them, and became startlingly conscious of his own experience in walking on the topside of them as a miracle or a myth. He felt his memory of the Green Lady and all her promised descendants and all the issues which had occupied him ever since he came to Perelandra rapidly fading from his mind, as a dream fades when we wake, or as if it were shouldered aside by a whole world of interests and emotions to which he could give no name. It terrified him. In spite of his hunger he threw the rest of the weed away.

He must have slept again, for the next scene that he remembers was in daylight. The Un-man was still visible ahead, and the shoal of fishes was still spread out between it and him. The birds had abandoned the chase. And now at last a full and prosaic sense of his position descended upon him. It is a curious flaw in the reason, to judge from Ransom's experience, that when a man comes to a strange planet he at first quite forgets its size. That whole world is so small in comparison with his journey through space that he forgets the distances within it: any two places in Mars, or in Venus, appear to him like places in the same town. But now, as Ransom looked round once more and saw nothing in every direction but golden sky and tumbling waves, the full absurdity of this delusion was borne in upon him. Even if there were continents in Perelandra, he might well be divided from the nearest of them by the breadth of the Pacific or more. But he had no reason to suppose that there were any. He had no reason to suppose that even the floating islands were very numerous, or that they were equally distributed over the surface of the planet. Even if their loose archipelago spread over a thousand square miles, what would that be but a negligible freckling in a landless ocean that rolled for ever round a globe not much smaller than the World of Men? Soon his fish would be tired. Already, he fancied, it was not swimming at its original speed. The Un-man would doubtless torture its mount to swim till it died. But he could not do that. As he was thinking of these things and staring ahead, he saw something that turned his heart cold. One of the other fish deliberately turned out of line, spurted a little column of foam, dived, and reappeared some yards away, apparently drifting. In a few minutes it was out of sight. It had had enough.

And now the experiences of the past day and night began to make a direct assault upon his faith. The solitude of the seas and, still more, the experiences which had followed his taste of the seaweed, had insinuated a doubt as to whether this world in any real sense belonged to those who called themselves its King and Queen. How could it be made for them when most of it, in fact, was uninhabitable by them? Was not the very idea naïve and anthropomorphic in the highest degree? As for the great prohibition, on which so much had seemed to hang—was it really so important? What did these roarers with the yellow foam, and these strange people who lived in them, care whether two little creatures, now far away, lived or did not live on one particular rock? The parallelism between the scenes he had lately witnessed and those recorded in the

Book of Genesis, and which had hitherto given him the feeling of knowing by experience what other men only believe, now began to shrink in importance. Need it prove anything more than that similar irrational *taboos* had accompanied the dawn of reason in two different worlds? It was all very well to talk of Maleldil: but where was Maleldil now? If this illimitable ocean said anything, it said something very different. Like all solitudes it was, indeed, haunted: but not by an anthropomorphic Deity, rather by the wholly inscrutable to which man and his life remained eternally irrelevant. And beyond this ocean was space itself. In vain did Ransom try to remember that he had been in "space" and found it Heaven, tingling with a fulness of life for which infinity itself was not one cubic inch too large. All that seemed like a dream. That opposite mode of thought which he had often mocked and called in mockery The Empirical Bogey, came surging into his mind—the great myth of our century with its gases and galaxies, its light years and evolutions, its nightmare perspectives of simple arithmetic in which everything that can possibly hold significance for the mind becomes the mere by-product of essential disorder. Always till now he had belittled it, had treated with a certain disdain its flat superlatives, its clownish amazement that different things should be of different sizes, its glib munificence of ciphers. Even now, his reason was not quite subdued, though his heart would not listen to his reason. Part of him still knew that the size of a thing is its least important characteristic, that the material universe derived from the comparing and mythopœic power within him that very majesty before which he was now asked to abase himself, and that mere numbers could not overawe us unless we lent them, from our own resources, that awfulness which they themselves could no more supply than a banker's ledger. But this knowledge remained an abstraction. Mere bigness and loneliness overbore him.

These thoughts must have taken several hours and absorbed all his attention. He was aroused by what he least expected—the sound of a human voice. Emerging from his reverie he saw that all the fishes had deserted him. His own was swimming feebly: and there a few yards away, no longer fleeing him but moving slowly towards him, was the Unman. It sat hugging itself, its eyes almost shut up with bruises, its flesh the colour of liver, its leg apparently broken, its mouth twisted with pain.

"Ransom," it said feebly.

Ransom held his tongue. He was not going to encourage it to start that game again.

"Ransom," it said again in a broken voice, "for God's sake speak to me."

He glanced at it in surprise. Tears were on its cheeks.

"Ransom, don't cold-shoulder me," it said. "Tell me what has happened. What have they done to us? You—you're all bleeding. My leg's broken . . ." its voice died away in a whimper.

"Who are you?" he asked sharply.

"Oh, don't pretend you don't know me," mumbled Weston's voice. "I'm Weston. You're Ransom—Elwin Ransom of Leicester, Cambridge, the philologist. We've had our quarrels, I know. I'm sorry. I dare say I've been in the wrong. Ransom, you'll not leave me to die in this horrible place, will you?"

"Where did you learn Aramaic?" asked Ransom, keeping his eyes on the other.

"Aramaic?" said Weston's voice. "I don't know what you're talking about. It's not much of a game to make fun of a dying man."

"But are you really Weston?" said Ransom, for he began to think that Weston had actually come back.

"Who else should I be?" came the answer, with a burst of weak temper, on the verge of tears.

"Where have you been?" asked Ransom.

Weston—if it was Weston—shuddered. "Where are we now?" he asked presently.

"In Perelandra—Venus, you know," answered Ransom.

"Have you found the space-ship?" asked Weston.

"I never saw it except at a distance," said Ransom. "And I've no idea where it is now—a couple of hundred miles away for all I know."

"You mean we're trapped?" said Weston, almost in a scream. Ransom said nothing and the other bowed his head and cried like a baby.

"Come," said Ransom at last, "there's no good taking it like that. Hang it all, you'd not be much better off if you were on Earth. You remember they're having a war there. The Germans may be bombing London to bits at this moment!" Then seeing the creature still crying, he added, "Buck up, Weston. It's only death, all said and done. We should have to die some day, you know. We shan't lack water, and hunger—without thirst—isn't too bad. As for drowning—well, a bayonet wound, or cancer, would be worse."

"You mean to say you're going to leave me," said Weston.

"I can't, even if I wanted to," said Ransom. "Don't you see I'm in the same position as yourself?"

"You'll promise not to go off and leave me in the lurch?" said Weston.

"All right, I'll promise if you like. Where could I go to?"

Weston looked very slowly all round and then urged his fish a little nearer to Ransom's.

"Where is ... *it?*" he asked in a whisper. "You know," and he made meaningless gestures.

"I might ask you the same question," said Ransom.

"Me?" said Weston. His face was, in one way and another, so disfigured that it was hard to be sure of its expression.

"Have you any idea of what's been happening to you for the last few days?" said Ransom.

Weston once more looked all round him uneasily.

"It's all true, you know," he said at last.

"What's all true?" said Ransom.

Suddenly Weston turned on him with a snarl of rage. "It's all very well for *you*," he said. "Drowning doesn't hurt and death is bound to come anyway, and all that nonsense. What do *you* know about death? It's all true, I tell you."

"What are you talking about?"

"I've been stuffing myself up with a lot of nonsense all my life," said Weston. "Trying to persuade myself that it matters what happens to the human race ... trying to believe that anything you can do will make the universe bearable. It's all rot, do you see?"

"And something else is truer!"

"Yes," said Weston, and then was silent for a long time.

"We'd better turn our fishes head on to this," said Ransom presently, his eyes on the seas, "or we'll be driven apart." Weston obeyed without seeming to notice what he did, and for a time the two men were riding very slowly side by side.

"I'll tell you what's truer," said Weston presently.

"What?"

"A little child that creeps upstairs when nobody's looking and very slowly turns the handle to take one peep into the room where its grandmother's dead body is laid out—and then runs away and has bad dreams. An enormous grandmother, you understand."

"What do you mean by saying that's truer?"

"I mean that child knows something about the universe which all science and all religion is trying to hide."

Ransom said nothing.

"Lots of things," said Weston presently. "Children are afraid to go through a churchyard at night, and the grown-ups tell them not to be silly: but the children know better than the grown-ups. People in Central Africa doing beastly things with masks on in the middle of the night—and missionaries and civil servants say it's all superstition. Well, the blacks know more about the universe than the white people. Dirty priests in back streets in Dublin frightening half-witted children to death with stories about it. You'd say they are unenlightened. They're not: except that they think there is a way of escape. There isn't. That is the real universe, always will be. That's what it all *means.*"

"I'm not quite clear——" began Ransom, when Weston interrupted him.

"That's why it's so important to live as long as you can. All the good things are now—a thin little rind of what we call life, put on for show, and then—the *real* universe for ever and ever. To thicken the rind by one centimetre—to live one week, one day, one half-hour longer—that's the only thing that matters. Of course you don't know it: but every man who is waiting to be hanged knows it. You say, 'What difference does a short reprieve make?' What difference!!"

"But nobody need go there," said Ransom.

"I know that's what you believe," said Weston. "But you're wrong. It's only a small parcel of civilised people who think that. Humanity as a whole knows better. It knows—Homer knew—that *all* the dead have sunk down into the inner darkness: under the rind. All witless, all twittering, gibbering, decaying. Bogeymen. Every savage knows that *all* ghosts hate the living who are still enjoying the rind: just as old women hate girls who still have their good looks. It's quite right to be afraid of the ghosts. You're going to be one all the same."

"You don't believe in God," said Ransom.

"Well, now, that's another point," said Weston. "I've been to church as well as you when I was a boy. There's more sense in parts of the Bible than you religious people know. Doesn't it say He's the God of the living, not of the dead? That's just it. Perhaps your God does exist—but it makes no difference whether He does or not. No, of course you wouldn't see it; but one day you will. I don't think you've got the idea of the rind—the thin outer skin which we call life—really clear. Picture the universe as an infinite globe with this very thin crust on the outside. But remember its thickness is a thickness of *time.* It's about seventy years thick in the best places. We are born on the surface of it and all our lives we are sinking through it. When we've got all the way through then we are what's called Dead: we've got into the dark part inside, the real globe. If your God exists, He's not in the globe—He's outside, like a moon. As we pass into the interior we pass out of His ken. He doesn't follow us in. You would express it by saying He's not in time—which you think comforting! In other words He stays put: out in the light and air, outside. But we are in time. We 'move with the times.' That is, from His point of view, we move *away,* into what He regards as nonentity, where He never follows. That is all there is to us, all there ever was. He may be there in what you call 'Life,' or He may not. What difference does it make? *We're* not going to be there for long!"

"That could hardly be the whole story," said Ransom. "If the whole universe were like that, then we, being parts of it, would feel at home in such a universe. The very fact that it strikes us as monstrous————"

"Yes," interrupted Weston, "that would be all very well if it wasn't that reasoning itself is only valid as long as you stay in the rind. It has nothing to do with the real universe. Even the ordinary scientists—like what I used to be myself—are beginning to find that out. Haven't you seen the real meaning of all this modern stuff about the dangers of extrapolation and bent space and the indeterminacy of the atom? They don't say in so many words, of course, but what they're getting to, even before they die nowadays, is what all men get to when they're dead—the knowledge that reality is neither rational nor consistent nor anything else. In a sense you might say it isn't there. 'Real' and 'Unreal,' 'true' and 'false'—they're all only on the surface. They give way the moment you press them."

"If all this were true," said Ransom, "what would be the point of saying it?"

"Or of anything else?" replied Weston. "The only point in anything is that there isn't any point. Why do ghosts want to frighten? Because they *are* ghosts. What else is there to do?"

"I get the idea," said Ransom. "That the account a man gives of the universe, or of any other building, depends very much on where he is standing."

"But specially," said Weston, "on whether he's inside or out. All the things you like to dwell upon are outsides. A planet like our own, or like Perelandra, for instance. Or a beautiful human body. All the colours and pleasant shapes are merely where it ends, where it ceases to be. Inside, what do you get? Darkness, worms, heat, pressure, salt, suffocation, stink."

They ploughed forward for a few minutes in silence over waves which were now growing larger. The fish seemed to be making little headway.

"Of course you don't care," said Weston. "What do you people in the rind care about us? You haven't been pulled down yet. It's like a dream I once had, though I didn't know then how true it was. I dreamed I was lying dead—you know, nicely laid out in the ward in a nursing home with my face settled by the undertaker and big lilies in the room. And then a sort of a person who was all falling to bits—like a tramp, you know, only it was himself not his clothes that was coming to pieces—

came and stood at the foot of the bed, just hating me. 'All right,' he said, 'all right. You think you're mighty fine with your clean sheet and your shiny coffin being got ready. I began like that. We all did. Just wait and see what you come down to in the end.' "

"Really," said Ransom, "I think you might just as well shut up."

"Then there's Spiritualism," said Weston, ignoring this suggestion. "I used to think it all nonsense. But it isn't. It's all true. You've noticed that all *pleasant* accounts of the dead are traditional or philosophical? What actual experiment discovers is quite different. Ectoplasm—slimy films coming out of a medium's belly and making great, chaotic, tumbledown faces. Automatic writing producing reams of rubbish."

"*Are* you Weston?" said Ransom, suddenly turning upon his companion. The persistent mumbling voice, so articulate that you had to listen to it and yet so inarticulate that you had to strain your ears to follow what it said, was beginning to madden him.

"Don't be angry," said the voice. "There's no good being angry with me. I thought you might be sorry. My God, Ransom, it's awful. You don't understand. Right down under layers and layers. Buried alive. You try to connect things and can't. They take your head off . . . and you can't even look back on what life was like in the rind, because you know it never did mean anything even from the beginning."

"What are you?" cried Ransom. "How do you know what death is like? God knows, I'd help you if I could. But give me the facts. Where have you been these few days?"

"Hush," said the other suddenly, "what's that?"

Ransom listened. Certainly there did seem to be a new element in the great concourse of noises with which they were surrounded. At first he could not define it. The seas were very big now and the wind was strong. All at once his companion reached out his hand and clutched Ransom's arm.

"Oh, my God!" he cried. "Oh, Ransom, Ransom! We shall be killed. Killed and put back under the rind. Ransom, you promised to help me. Don't let them get me again."

"Shut up," said Ransom in disgust, for the creature was wailing and blubbering so that he could hear nothing else: and he wanted very much to identify the deeper note that had mingled with the piping wind and roar of water.

"Breakers," said Weston, "breakers, you fool! Can't you hear? There's a country over there! There's a rocky coast. Look there—no, to your right. We shall be smashed into a jelly. Look—O God, here comes the dark!"

And the dark came. Horror of death such as he had never known, horror of the terrified creature at his side, descended upon Ransom: finally, horror with no definite object. In a few minutes he could see through the jet-black night the luminous cloud of foam. From the way in which it shot steeply upward he judged it was breaking on cliffs. Invisible birds, with a shriek and flurry, passed low overhead.

"Are you there, Weston?" he shouted. "What cheer? Pull yourself together. All that stuff you've been talking is lunacy. Say a child's prayer if you can't say a man's. Repent your sins. Take my hand. There are hundreds of mere boys on Earth facing death this moment. We'll do very well."

His hand was clutched in the darkness, rather more firmly than he wished. "I can't bear it, I can't bear it," came Weston's voice.

"Steady now. None of that," he shouted back, for Weston had suddenly gripped his arm with both hands.

"I can't bear it," came the voice again.

"Hi!" said Ransom. "Let go. What the devil are you doing?"—and as he spoke strong arms had plucked him from the saddle, had wrapped him round in a terrible embrace just below his thighs, and, clutching uselessly at the smooth surface of the fish's body, he was dragged down. The waters closed over his head: and still his enemy pulled him down into the warm depth, and down farther yet to where it was no longer warm.

14

I can't hold my breath any longer," thought Ransom. "I can't. I can't."
Cold slimy things slid upwards over his agonised body. He decided to
stop holding his breath, to open his mouth and die, but his will did not
obey this decision. Not only his chest but his temples felt as if they were
going to burst. It was idle to struggle. His arms met no adversary and his
legs were pinioned. He became aware that they were moving upwards.
But this gave him no hope. The surface was too far away, he could not
hold out till they reached it. In the immediate presence of death all ideas
of the after life were withdrawn from his mind. The mere abstract
proposition, "This is a man dying," floated before him in an unemotional way. Suddenly a roar of sound rushed back upon his ears—intolerable boomings and clangings. His mouth opened automatically. He
was breathing again. In a pitch darkness full of echoes he was clutching
what seemed to be gravel and kicking wildly to throw off the grip that
still held his legs. Then he was free and fighting once more: a blind
struggle half in and half out of the water on what seemed to be a pebbly
beach, with sharper rocks here and there that cut his feet and elbows.
The blackness was filled with gasping curses, now in his own voice, now
in Weston's, with yelps of pain, thudding concussions, and the noise of
laboured breath. In the end he was astride of the enemy. He pressed its
sides between his knees till its ribs cracked and clasped his hands round
its throat. Somehow he was able to resist its fierce tearing at his arms—
to keep on pressing. Once before he had had to press like this, but that
had been on an artery, to save life, not to kill. It seemed to last for ages.
Long after the creature's struggles had ceased he did not dare to relax his

grip. Even when he was quite sure that it breathed no longer he retained his seat on its chest and kept his tired hands, though now loosely, on its throat. He was nearly fainting himself, but he counted a thousand before he would shift his posture. Even then he continued to sit on its body. He did not know whether in the last few hours the spirit which had spoken to him was really Weston's or whether he had been the victim of a ruse. Indeed, it made little difference. There was, no doubt, a confusion of persons in damnation: what Pantheists falsely hoped of Heaven bad men really received in Hell. They were melted down into their Master, as a lead soldier slips down and loses his shape in the ladle held over the gas ring. The question whether Satan, or one whom Satan has digested, is acting on any given occasion, has in the long run no clear significance. In the meantime, the great thing was not to be tricked again.

There was nothing to be done, then, except to wait for the morning. From the roar of echoes all about him he concluded that they were in a very narrow bay between cliffs. How they had ever made it was a mystery. The morning must be many hours distant. This was a considerable nuisance. He determined not to leave the body till he had examined it by daylight and perhaps taken further steps to make sure that it could not be re-animated. Till then he must pass the time as best he could. The pebbly beach was not very comfortable, and when he tried to lean back he found a jagged wall. Fortunately he was so tired that for a time the mere fact of sitting still contented him. But this phase passed.

He tried to make the best of it. He determined to give up guessing how the time was going. "The only safe answer," he told himself, "is to think of the earliest hour you can suppose possible, and then assume the real time is two hours earlier than that." He beguiled himself by recapitulating the whole story of his adventure in Perelandra. He recited all that he could remember of the *Iliad*, the *Odyssey*, the *Æneid*, the *Chanson de Roland*, *Paradise Lost*, the *Kalevala*, the *Hunting of the Snark*, and a rhyme about Germanic sound-laws which he had composed as a freshman. He tried to spend as long as he could hunting for the lines he could not remember. He set himself a chess problem. He tried to rough out a chapter for a book he was writing. But it was all rather a failure.

These things went on, alternating with periods of dogged inactivity, until it seemed to him that he could hardly remember a time before that night. He could scarcely believe that even to a bored and wakeful man twelve hours could appear so long. And the noise—the gritty, slippery discomfort! It was very odd, now he came to think it, that this country should have none of those sweet night breezes which he had met everywhere else in Perelandra. It was odd too (but this thought came to him what seemed hours later) that he had not even the phosphorescent wave-crests to feed his eyes on. Very slowly a possible explanation of both facts dawned upon him: and it would also explain why the darkness lasted so long. The idea was too terrible for any indulgence of fear. Controlling himself, he rose stiffly to his feet and began picking his steps along the beach. His progress was very slow: but presently his outstretched arms touched perpendicular rock. He stood on tiptoe and stretched his hands up as far as he could. They found nothing but rock. "Don't get the wind up," he said to himself. He started groping his way back. He came to the Un-man's body, passed it, and went beyond it round the opposite beach. It curved rapidly, and here, before he had gone twenty steps his hands—which he was holding above his head—met not a wall, but a roof, of rock. A few paces farther and it was lower. Then he had to stoop. A little later and he had to go on his hands and knees. It was obvious that the roof came down and finally met the beach.

Sick with despair he felt his way back to the body and sat down. The truth was now beyond doubt. There was no good waiting for the morning. There would be no morning here till the end of the world, and perhaps he had already waited a night and a day. The clanging echoes, the dead air, the very smell of the place, all confirmed this. He and his enemy when they sank had clearly, by some hundredth chance, been carried through a hole in the cliffs well below water-level and come up on the beach of a cavern. Was it possible to reverse the process? He went down to the water's edge—or rather as he groped his way down to where the shingle was wet, the water came to meet him. It thundered over his head far up behind him, and then receded with a tug which he only resisted by spread-eagling himself on the beach and gripping the stones. It would be useless to plunge into *that*—he would merely have his ribs broken against the opposite wall of the cave. If one had light, and a high place to dive from, it was conceivable one might get down to the bottom and strike the exit . . . but very doubtful. And anyway, one had no light.

Although the air was not very good he supposed that this prison must be supplied with air from somewhere—but whether from any aperture that he could possibly reach was another matter. He turned at once and began exploring the rock behind the beach. At first it seemed hopeless, but the conviction that caves may lead you anywhere dies hard, and after some time his groping hands found a shelf about three feet high. He stepped up on it. He had expected it to be only a few inches deep but his hands could find no wall before him. Very cautiously he took some paces forward. His right foot touched something sharp. He whistled with the pain and went on even more cautiously. Then he found vertical rock—smooth as high as he could reach. He turned to his right and presently lost it. He turned left and began to go forward again and almost at once stubbed his toe. After nursing it for a moment he went down on hands and knees. He seemed to be among boulders, but the way was practicable. For ten minutes or so he made fairly good going, pretty steeply upward, sometimes on slippery shingle, sometimes over the tops of the big stones. Then he came to another cliff. There appeared to be a shelf on this about four feet up, but this time a really shallow one. He got on to it somehow and glued himself to the face, feeling out to left and right for further grips.

When he found one and realised that he was now about to attempt some real climbing, he hesitated. He remembered that what was above him might be a cliff which even in daylight and properly clothed he would never dare to attempt: but hope whispered that it might equally well be only seven feet high and that a few minutes of coolness might bring him into those gently winding passages up into the heart of the mountain which had, by now, won such a firm place in his imagination. He decided to go on. What worried him was not, in fact, the fear of falling, but the fear of cutting himself off from the water. Starvation he thought he could face: not thirst. But he went on. For some minutes he did things which he had never done on Earth. Doubtless he was in one way helped by the darkness: he had no real sensation of height and no giddiness. On the other hand, to work by touch alone made crazy climbing. Doubtless if anyone had seen him he would have appeared at one moment to take mad risks and at another to indulge in excessive caution. He tried to keep out of his mind the possibility that he might be climbing merely towards a roof.

After about quarter of an hour he found himself on a wide horizontal surface—either a much deeper shelf or the top of the precipice. He rested here for a while and licked his cuts. Then he got up and felt his way forwards, expecting every moment to meet another rock wall. When, after about thirty paces, he had not done so, he tried shouting and judged from the sound that he was in a fairly open place. Then he continued. The floor was of small pebble and ascended fairly steeply. There were some larger stones but he had learned to curl up his toes as his foot felt for the next pace and he seldom stubbed them now. One minor trouble was that even in this perfect blackness he could not help straining his eyes to see. It gave him a headache and created phantom lights and colours.

This slow uphill trek through darkness lasted so long that he began to fear he was going round in a circle, or that he had blundered into some gallery which ran on for ever beneath the surface of the planet. The steady ascent in some degree reassured him. The starvation for light became very painful. He found himself thinking about light as a hungry man thinks about food—picturing April hillsides with milky clouds racing over them in blue skies or quiet circles of lamp-light on tables pleasantly littered with books and pipes. By a curious confusion of mind he found it impossible not to imagine that the slope he walked on was not merely dark, but black in its own right, as if with soot. He felt that his feet and hands must be blackened by touching it. Whenever he pictured himself arriving at any light, he also pictured that light revealing a world of soot all around him.

He struck his head sharply against something and sat down half stunned. When he had collected himself he found by groping that the shingle slope had run up into a roof of smooth rock. His heart was very low as he sat there digesting this discovery. The sound of the waves came up faint and melancholy from below and told him that he was now at a great height. At last, though with very little hope, he began walking to his right, keeping contact with the roof by raising his arms. Presently it receded beyond his reach. A long time after that he heard a sound of water. He went on more slowly in great fear of encountering a waterfall. The shingle began to be wet and finally he stood in a little pool. Turning to his left he found, indeed, a waterfall, but it was a tiny stream with no force of water that could endanger him. He knelt in the rippling pool and drank from the fall and put his aching head and weary shoulders under it. Then, greatly refreshed, he tried to work his way up it.

Though the stones were slippery with some kind of moss and many of the pools were deep, it presented no serious difficulties. In about twenty minutes he had reached the top, and as far as he could judge by shouting and noticing the echoes he was now in a very large cave indeed. He took the stream for guidance and proceeded to follow it up. In that featureless dark it was some sort of company. Some real hope—distinct from that mere convention of hope which supports men in desperate situations—began to enter his mind.

It was shortly after this that he began to be worried by the noises. The last faint booming of the sea in the little hole whence he had set out so many hours ago had now died away and the predominant sound was the gentle tinkling of the stream. But he now began to think that he heard other noises mixed with it. Sometimes it would be a dull plump as if something had slipped into one of the pools behind him: sometimes, more mysteriously, a dry rattling sound as if metal were being dragged over the stones. At first he put it down to imagination. Then he stopped once or twice to listen and heard nothing; but each time when he went on it began again. At last, stopping once more, he heard it quite unmistakably. Could it be that the Un-man had after all come to life and was still following him? But that seemed improbable, for its whole plan had been to escape. It was not so easy to dispose of the other possibility—that these caverns might have inhabitants. All this experience, indeed, assured him that if there were such inhabitants they would probably be harmless, but somehow he could not quite believe that anything which lived in such a place would be agreeable, and a little echo of the Un-man's—or was it Weston's—talk came back to him. "All beautiful on the surface, but down inside—darkness, heat, horror, and stink." Then it occurred to him that if some creature were following him up the stream it might be well for him to leave its banks and wait till the creature had gone past. But if it were hunting him it would presumably hunt by scent; and in any case he would not risk losing the stream. In the end he went on.

Whether through weakness—for he was now very hungry indeed—or because the noises behind made him involuntarily quicken his pace, he found himself unpleasantly hot, and even the stream did not appear very refreshing when he put his feet in it. He began to think that whether he were pursued or not he must have a short rest—but just at that moment he saw the light. His eyes had been mocked so often before that he would not at first believe it. He shut them while he counted a hundred and looked again. He turned round and sat down for several minutes, praying that it might not be a delusion, and looked again. "Well," said Ransom, "if it is a delusion, it's a pretty stubborn one." A very dim, tiny, quivering luminosity, slightly red in colour, was before him. It was too weak to illuminate anything else and in that world of blackness he could not tell whether it was five feet or five miles away. He set out at once, with beating heart. Thank Heaven, the stream appeared to be leading him towards it.

While he thought it was still a long way off he found himself almost stepping into it. It was a circle of light lying on the surface of the water, which thereabouts formed a deepish trembling pool. It came from above. Stepping into the pool he looked up. An irregularly shaped patch of light, now quite distinctly red, was immediately above him. This time it was strong enough to show him the objects immediately around it, and when his eyes had mastered them he perceived that he was looking up a funnel or fissure. Its lower aperture lay in the roof of his own cavern which must here be only a few feet above his head: its upper aperture was obviously in the floor of a separate and higher chamber whence the light came. He could see the uneven side of the funnel, dimly illuminated, and clothed with pads and streamers of a jelly-like and rather unpleasing vegetation. Down this water was trickling and falling on his head and shoulders in a warm rain. This warmth, together with the red colour of the light, suggested that the upper cave was illuminated by subterranean fire. It will not be clear to the reader, and it was not clear to Ransom when he thought about it afterwards, why he immediately decided to get into the upper cave if he possibly could. What really moved him, he thinks, was the mere hunger for light. The very first glance at the funnel restored dimensions and perspective to his world, and this in itself was like delivery from prison. It seemed to tell him far more than it actually did of his surroundings: it gave him back that whole frame of spatial directions without which a man seems hardly able to call his body his own. After this, any return to the horrible black vacancy, the world of soot and grime, the world without size or distance, in which he had been wandering, was out of the question. Perhaps also he had some idea that whatever was following him would cease to follow if he could get into the lighted cave.

But it was not easy to do. He could not reach the opening of the funnel. Even when he jumped he only just touched the fringe of its vegetation. At last he hit upon an unlikely plan which was the best he could think of. There was just enough light here for him to see a number of larger stones among the gravel, and he set to work to build up a pile in the centre of the pool. He worked rather feverishly and often had to undo what he had done: and he tried it several times before it was really high enough. When at last it was completed and he stood sweating and shaky on the summit the real hazard was still to be run. He had to grip the vegetation on each side above his head, trusting to luck that it would hold, and half jump, half pull himself up as quickly as he could, since if it held at all it would, he felt sure, not hold for long. Somehow or other he managed it. He got himself wedged into the fissure with his back against one side and his feet against the other, like a mountaineer in what is called a chimney. The thick squashy growth protected his skin, and after a few upward struggles he found the walls of the passage so irregular that it could be climbed in the ordinary way. The heat increased rapidly. "I'm a fool to have come up here," said Ransom: but even as he said so, he was at the top.

At first he was blinded by the light. When at last he could take in his surroundings he found himself in a vast hall so filled with firelight that it gave him the impression of being hollowed out of red clay. He was looking along the length of it. The floor sloped down to the left side. On his right it sloped upward to what appeared a cliff edge, beyond which was an abyss of blinding brightness. A broad shallow river was flowing down the middle of the cavern. The roof was so high as to be invisible, but the walls soared up into darkness with broad curves like the roots of a beech tree.

He staggered to his feet, splashed across the river (which was hot to the touch) and approached the cliff edge. The fire appeared to be thousands of feet below him and he could not see the other side of the pit in which it swelled and roared and writhed. His eyes could only bear it for a second or so, and when he turned away the rest of the cavern seemed dark. The heat of his body was painful. He drew away from the cliff edge and sat down with his back to the fire to collect his thoughts.

They were collected in an unlooked-for way. Suddenly and irresistibly, like an attack by tanks, that whole view of the universe which Weston (if it were Weston) had so lately preached to him, took all but complete possession of his mind. He seemed to see that he had been living all his life in a world of illusion. The ghosts, the damned ghosts, were right. The beauty of Perelandra, the innocence of the Lady, the sufferings of saints, and the kindly affections of men, were all only an appearance and outward show. What he had called the worlds were but the skins of the worlds: a quarter of a mile beneath the surface, and from thence through thousands of miles of dark and silence and infernal fire, to the very heart of each, Reality lived—the meaningless, the un-made, the omnipotent idiocy to which all spirits were irrelevant and before which all efforts were vain. Whatever was following him would come up that wet, dark hole, would presently be excreted by that hideous duct, and then he would die. He fixed his eyes upon the dark opening from which he had himself just emerged. And then—"I thought as much," said Ransom.

Slowly, shakily, with unnatural and inhuman movements a human form, scarlet in the firelight, crawled out on to the floor of the cave. It was Un-man, of course: dragging its broken leg and with its lower jaw sagging open like that of a corpse, it raised itself to a standing position. And then, close behind it, something else came up out of the hole. First came what looked like branches of trees, and then seven or eight spots of light, irregularly grouped like a constellation. Then a tubular mass which reflected the red glow as if it were polished. His heart gave a great leap as the branches suddenly resolved themselves into long wiry feelers and the dotted lights became the many eyes of a shell-helmeted head and the mass that followed it was revealed as a large roughly cylindrical body. Horrible things followed—angular, many jointed legs, and presently, when he thought the whole body was in sight, a second body came following it and after that a third. The thing was in three parts, united only by a kind of wasp's waist structure—three parts that did not seem to be truly aligned and made it look as if it had been trodden on—a huge, many legged, quivering deformity, standing just behind the Un-man so that the horrible shadows of both danced in enormous and united menace on the wall of rock behind them.

"They want to frighten me," said something in Ransom's brain, and at the same moment he became convinced both that the Un-man had summoned this great crawler and also that the evil thoughts which had preceded the appearance of the enemy had been **poured** into his own mind by the enemy's will. The knowledge that his **thoughts** could be thus managed from without did not awake terror but rage. Ransom found that he had risen, that he was approaching the Un-man, that he was saying things, perhaps foolish things, in English. "Do you think I'm going to stand *this?*" he yelled. "Get out of my brain. It isn't yours, I tell you! Get out of it." As he shouted he had picked up a big, jagged stone from beside the stream. "Ransom," croaked the Un-man, "wait! We're both trapped . . ." but Ransom was already upon it.

"In the name of the Father and of the Son and of the Holy Ghost, here goes—I mean Amen," said Ransom, and hurled the stone as hard as he could into the Un-man's face. The Un-man fell as a pencil falls, the face smashed out of all recognition. Ransom did not give it a glance but turned to face the other horror. But where had the horror gone? The creature was there, a curiously shaped creature no doubt, but all loathing had vanished clean out of his mind, so that neither then nor at any other time could he remember it, nor ever understand again why one should quarrel with an animal for having more legs or eyes than oneself. All that he had felt from childhood about insects and reptiles died that moment: died utterly, as hideous music does when you switch off the wireless. Apparently it had all, even from the beginning, been a dark enchantment of the enemy's. Once, as he had sat writing near an open window in Cambridge, he had looked up and shuddered to see, as he supposed, a many coloured beetle of unusually hideous shape crawling across his paper. A second glance showed him that it was a dead leaf, moved by the breeze; and instantly the very curves and re-entrants which had made its ugliness turned into its beauties. At this moment he had almost the same sensation. He saw at once that the creature intended him no harm—had indeed no intentions at all. It had been drawn thither by the Un-man, and now stood still, tentatively moving its antennæ. Then, apparently not liking its surroundings, it turned laboriously round and began descending into the hole by which it had come. As he saw the last section of its tripartite body wobble on the edge of the aperture, and then finally tip upward with its torpedo-shaped tail in the air, Ransom almost laughed. "Like an animated corridor train" was his comment.

He turned to the Un-man. It had hardly anything left that you could call a head, but he thought it better to take no risks. He took it by its ankles and lugged it up to the edge of the cliff: then, after resting a few seconds, he shoved it over. He saw its shape black, for a second, against the sea of fire: and then that was the end of it.

He rolled rather than crawled back to the stream and drank deeply. "This may be the end of me or it may not," thought Ransom. "There may be a way out of these caves or there may not. But I won't go another step further to-day. Not if it was to save my life—not to save my life. That's flat. Glory be to God, I'm tired." A second later he was asleep.

15

For the rest of the subterranean journey after his long sleep in the firelit cave, Ransom was somewhat light-headed with hunger and fatigue. He remembers lying still after he woke for what seemed many hours and even debating with himself whether it was worth going on. The actual moment of decision has vanished from his mind. Pictures come back in a chaotic, disjointed fashion. There was a long gallery open to the fire-pit on one side and a terrible place where clouds of steam went up for ever and ever. Doubtless one of the many torrents that roared in the neighbourhood here fell into the depth of the fire. Beyond that were great halls still dimly illuminated and full of unknown mineral wealth that sparkled and danced in the light and mocked his eyes as if he were exploring a hall of mirrors by the help of a pocket torch. It seemed to him also, though this may have been delirium, that he came through a vast cathedral space which was more like the work of art than that of Nature, with two great thrones at one end and chairs on either hand too large for human occupants. If the things were real, he never found any explanation of them. There was a dark tunnel in which a wind from Heaven knows where was blowing and drove sand in his face. There was also a place where he himself walked in darkness and looked down through fathom below fathom of shafts and natural arches and winding gulfs on to a smooth floor lit with a cold green light. And as he stood and looked it seemed to him that four of the great earth-beetles, dwarfed by distance to the size of gnats, and crawling two by two, came slowly into sight. And they were drawing behind them a flat car, and on the car, upright, unshaken, stood a mantled form, huge and still and slender.

And driving its strange team it passed on with insufferable majesty and went out of sight. Assuredly the inside of this world was not for man. But it was for something. And it appeared to Ransom that there might, if a man could find it, be some way to renew the old Pagan practice of propitiating the local gods of unknown places in such fashion that it was no offence to God Himself but only a prudent and courteous apology for trespass. That thing, that swathed form in its chariot, was no doubt his fellow creature. It did not follow that they were equals or had an equal right in the under-land. A long time after this came the drumming—the *boom-ba-ba-ba-boom-boom* out of pitch darkness, distant at first, then all around him, then dying away after endless prolongation of echoes in the black labyrinth. Then came the fountain of cold light—a column, as of water, shining with some radiance of its own, and pulsating, and never any nearer however long he travelled and at last suddenly eclipsed. He did not find what it was. And so, after more strangeness and grandeur and labour than I can tell, there came a moment when his feet slid without warning on clay—a wild grasp—a spasm of terror—and he was spluttering and struggling in deep, swift-flowing water. He thought that even if he escaped being battered to death against the walls of the channel he would presently plunge along with the stream into the pit of fire. But the channel must have been very straight and the current perhaps was less violent than he had supposed. At all events he never touched the sides. He lay helpless, in the end, rushing forward through echoing darkness. It lasted a long time.

You will understand that what with expectation of death, and weariness, and the great noise, he was confused in mind. Looking back on the adventure afterwards it seemed to him that he floated out of blackness into greyness and then into an inexplicable chaos of semi-transparent blues and greens and whites. There was a hint of arches above his head and faintly shining columns, but all vague and all obliterating one another as soon as seen. It looked like a cave of ice, but it was too warm for that. And the roof above him seemed to be itself rippling like water, but this was doubtless a reflection. A moment later and he was rushed out into broad daylight and air and warmth, and rolled head over heels, and deposited, dazzled and breathless, in the shallows of a great pool.

He was now almost too weak to move. Something in the air, and the wide silence which made a background to the lonely crying of birds, told him that he was on a high mountain top. He rolled rather than crawled out of the pool on to sweet blue turf. Looking back whence he had come he saw a river pouring from the mouth of a cave, a cave that seemed indeed to be made of ice. Under it the water was spectral blue, but near where he lay it was warm amber. There was mist and freshness and dew all about him. At his side rose a cliff mantled with streamers of bright vegetation, but gleaming like glass where its own surface showed through. But this he heeded little. There were rich clusters of a grape-like fruit glowing under the little pointed leaves, and he could reach them without getting up. Eating passed into sleeping by a transition he could never remember.

At this point it becomes increasingly difficult to give Ransom's experiences in any certain order. How long he lay beside the river at the cavern mouth eating and sleeping and waking only to eat and sleep again, he has no idea. He thinks it was only a day or two, but from the state of his body when this period of convalescence ended I should imagine it must have been more like a fortnight or three weeks. It was a time to be remembered only in dreams as we remember infancy. Indeed it was a second infancy, in which he was breast-fed by the planet Venus herself: unweaned till he moved from that place. Three impressions of this long Sabbath remain. One is the endless sound of rejoicing water. Another is the delicious life that he sucked from the clusters which almost seemed to bow themselves unasked into his upstretched hands. The third is the song. Now high in air above him, now welling up as if from glens and valleys far below, it floated through his sleep and was the first sound at every waking. It was formless as the song of a bird, yet it was not a bird's voice. As a bird's voice is to a flute, so this was to a cello: low and ripe and tender, full-bellied, rich and golden-brown: passionate too, but not with the passions of men.

Because he was weaned so gradually from this state of rest I cannot give his impressions of the place he lay in, bit by bit, as he came to take it in. But when he was cured and his mind was clear again, this was what he saw. The cliffs out of which his river had broken through the cave were not of ice, but of some kind of translucent rock. Any little splinter broken off them was as transparent as glass, but the cliffs themselves, when you looked at them close, seemed to become opaque about six inches from the surface. If you waded up-stream into the cave and then turned back and looked towards the light, the edges of the arch which formed the cave's mouth were distinctly transparent: and everything looked blue inside the cave. He did not know what happened at the top of these cliffs.

Before him the lawn of blue turf continued level for about thirty paces, and then dropped with a steep slope, leading the river down in a series of cataracts. The slope was covered with flowers which shook continually in a light breeze. It went down a long way and ended in a winding and wooded valley which curled out of sight on his right hand round a majestic slope: but beyond that, lower down—so much lower down as to be almost incredible—one caught the point of mountain tops, and beyond that, fainter yet, the hint of still lower valleys, and then a vanishing of everything in golden haze. On the opposite side of this valley the earth leaped up in great sweeps and folds of almost Himalayan height to the red rocks. They were not red like Devonshire cliffs: they were true rose-red, as if they had been painted. Their brightness astonished him, and so did the needle-like sharpness of their spires, until it occurred to him that he was in a young world and that these mountains might, geologically speaking, be in their infancy. Also, they might be farther off than they looked.

To his left and behind him the crystal cliffs shut off his view. To his right they soon ended and beyond them the ground rose to another and nearer peak—a much lower one than those he saw across the valley. The fantastic steepness of all the slopes confirmed his idea that he was on a very young mountain.

Except for the song it was all very still. When he saw birds flying they were usually a long way below him. On the slopes to his right and, less distinctly, on the slope of the great *massif* which faced him, there was a continual rippling effect which he could not account for. It was like water flowing: but since, if it were a stream on the remoter mountain, it would have to be a stream two or three miles wide, this seemed improbable.

In trying to put the completed picture together I have omitted something which, in fact, made it a long job for Ransom to get that picture. The whole place was subject to mists. It kept on vanishing in a veil of saffron or very pale gold and reappearing again—almost as if the golden sky-roof, which indeed looked only a few feet above the mountain-tops, were opening and pouring down riches upon the world.

Day by day as he came to know more of the place, Ransom also came to know more of the state of his own body. For a long time he was too stiff almost to move and even an incautious breath made him wince. It healed, however, surprisingly quickly. But just as a man who has had a fall only discovers the real hurt when the minor bruises and cuts are less painful, so Ransom was nearly well before he detected his most serious injury. It was a wound in his heel. The shape made it quite clear that the wound had been inflicted by human teeth—the nasty, blunt teeth of our own species which crush and grind more than they cut. Oddly enough, he had no recollection of this particular bite in any of his innumerable tussles with the Un-man. It did not look unhealthy, but it was still bleeding. It was not bleeding at all fast, but nothing he could do would stop it. But he worried very little about this. Neither the future nor the past really concerned him at this period. Wishing and fearing were modes of consciousness for which he seemed to have lost the faculty.

Nevertheless there came a day when he felt the need of some activity and yet did not feel ready to leave the little lair between the pool and the cliff which had become like a home. He employed that day in doing something which may appear rather foolish and yet at the time it seemed to him that he could hardly omit it. He had discovered that the substance of the translucent cliffs was not very hard. Now he took a sharp stone of a different kind, and cleared a wide space on the cliff wall of vegetation. Then he made measurements and spaced it all out carefully and after a few hours had produced the following. The language was Old Solar but the letters were Roman.

WITHIN THESE CAVES WAS BURNED

THE BODY

OF

EDWARD ROLLES WESTON

A LEARNED HNAU OF THE WORLD WHICH THOSE WHO INHABIT IT

CALL TELLUS

BUT THE ELDILA

THULCANDRA

HE WAS BORN WHEN TELLUS HAD COMPLETED

ONE THOUSAND EIGHT HUNDRED AND NINETY-SIX REVOLUTIONS

ABOUT ARBOL

SINCE THE TIME WHEN

MALELDIL

BLESSED BE HE

WAS BORN AS A HNAU IN THULCANDRA

HE STUDIED THE PROPERTIES OF BODIES

AND FIRST OF THE TELLURIANS TRAVELLED THROUGH DEEP

HEAVEN TO MALACANDRA

AND TO PERELANDRA

WHERE HE GAVE UP HIS WILL AND REASON

TO THE BENT ELDIL

WHEN TELLUS WAS MAKING

THE ONE THOUSANDTH NINE HUNDREDTH AND FORTY-SECOND

REVOLUTION AFTER THE BIRTH OF MALELDIL

BLESSED BE HE

"That was a tomfool thing to do," said Ransom to himself contentedly as he lay down again. "No one will ever read it. But there ought to be some record. He was a great physicist after all. Anyway, it has given me some exercise." He yawned prodigiously and settled down to yet another twelve hours of sleep.

The next day he was better and began taking little walks, not going down but strolling to and fro on the hillside on each side of the cave. The following day he was better still. But on the third day he was well, and ready for adventures.

He set out very early in the morning and began to follow the watercourse down the hill. The slope was very steep but there were no outcroppings of rock and the turf was soft and springy and to his surprise he found that the descent brought no weariness to his knees. When he had been going about half an hour and the peaks of the opposite mountain were now too high to see and the crystal cliffs behind him were only a distant glare, he came to a new kind of vegetation. He was approaching a forest of little trees whose trunks were only about two and a half feet high; but from the top of each trunk there grew long streamers which did not rise in the air but flowed in the wind downhill and parallel to the ground. Thus, when he went in among them, he found himself wading knee deep and more in a continually rippling sea of them—a sea which presently tossed all about him as far as his eye could reach. It was blue in colour, but far lighter than the blue of the turf—almost a Cambridge blue at the centre of each streamer, but dying away at their tasselled and feathery edges into a delicacy of bluish grey which it would take the subtlest effects of smoke and cloud to rival in our world. The soft, almost impalpable, caresses of the long thin leaves on his flesh, the low, singing, rustling, whispering music, and the frolic movement all about him, began to set his heart beating with that almost formidable sense of delight which he had felt before in Perelandra. He realised that these dwarf forests—these ripple-trees as he now christened them—were the explanation of that water-like movement he had seen on the farther slopes.

When he was tired he sat down and found himself at once in a new world. The streamers now flowed above his head. He was in a forest made for dwarfs, a forest with a blue transparent roof, continually moving and casting an endless dance of lights and shades upon its mossy floor. And presently he saw that it was indeed made for dwarfs. Through the moss, which here was of extraordinary fineness, he saw the hithering and thithering of what at first he took for insects but what proved, on closer inspection, to be tiny mammals. They were many mountain mice, exquisite scale models of those he had seen on the Forbidden Island, each about the size of a bumble bee. There were little miracles of grace which looked more like horses than anything he had yet seen on this world, though they resembled proto-hippos rather than his modern representative.

"How can I avoid treading on thousands of these?" he wondered. But they were not really very numerous and the main crowd of them seemed to be all moving away on his left. When he made to rise he noticed that there were already very few of them in sight.

He continued to wade down through the rippling streamers (it was like a sort of vegetable surf-bathing) for about an hour longer. Then he came into woods and presently to a river with a rocky course flowing across his path to the right. He had, in fact, reached the wooded valley, and knew that the ground which sloped upwards through trees on the far side of the water was the beginning of the great ascent. Here was amber shade and solemn height under the forest roof, and rocks wet with cataracts, and, over all, the noise of that deep singing. It was so loud now and so full of melody that he went downstream, a little out of his way, to look for its origin. This brought him almost at once out of stately aisles and open glades into a different kind of wood. Soon he was pressing his way through thornless thickets, all in bloom. His head was covered with the petals that showered on it, his sides gilded with pollen. Much that his fingers touched was gummy and at each pace his contact with soil and bush appeared to wake new odours that darted into his brain and there begot wild and enormous pleasures. The noise was very loud now and the thicket very dense so that he could not see a yard ahead, when the music stopped suddenly. There was a sound of rustling and broken twigs and he made hastily in that direction, but found nothing. He had almost decided to give up the search when the song began again a little farther away. Once more he made after it; once more the creature stopped singing and evaded him. He must have played thus at hide-and-seek with it for the best part of an hour before his search was rewarded.

Treading delicately during one of the loudest bursts of music he at last saw through the flowery branches a black something. Standing still whenever it stopped singing, and advancing with great caution whenever it began again, he stalked it for ten minutes. At last it was in full view, and singing, and ignorant that it was watched. It sat upright like a dog, black and sleek and shiny, but its shoulders were high above Ransom's head, and the forelegs on which they were pillared were like young trees and the wide soft pads on which they rested were large as those of a camel. The enormous rounded belly was white, and far up above the shoulders the neck rose like that of a horse. The head was in profile from where Ransom stood—the mouth wide open as it sang of joy in thick-coming trills, and the music almost visibly rippled in its glossy throat. He stared in wonder at the wide liquid eyes and the quivering, sensitive nostrils. Then the creature stopped, saw him, and darted away, and stood, now a few paces distant, on all four legs, not much smaller than a young elephant, swaying a long bushy tail. It was the first thing in Perelandra which seemed to show any fear of man. Yet it was not fear. When he called to it it came nearer. It put its velvet nose into his hand and endured his touch; but almost at once it darted back and, bending its long neck, buried its head in its paws. He could make no headway with it, and when at length it retreated out of sight he did not follow it. To do so would have seemed an injury to its fawn-like shyness, to the yielding softness of its expression, its evident wish to be for ever a sound and only a sound in the thickest centre of untravelled woods. He resumed his journey: a few seconds later the song broke out behind him, louder and lovelier than before, as if in a paean of rejoicing at its recovered privacy.

Ransom now addressed himself seriously to the ascent of the great mountain and in a few minutes emerged from the woods on to its lower slopes. He continued ascending so steeply that he used hands as well as feet for about half an hour and was puzzled to find himself doing it with almost no fatigue. Then he came once more into a region of ripple-trees. This time the wind was blowing the streamers not down the mountain-side but up it, so that his course had to the eye the astonishing appearance of lying through a wide blue waterfall which flowed the wrong way, curving and foaming towards the heights. Whenever the wind failed for a second or two the extreme ends of the streamers began to curl back under the influence of gravitation, so that it looked as if the heads of the waves were being flung back by a high wind. He continued going up through this for a long time, never feeling any real need for rest but resting occasionally none the less. He was now so high that the crystal cliffs from which he had set out appeared on a level with him as he looked across the valley. He now saw that the land leaped up beyond them into a whole waste of the same translucent formation which ended in a kind of glassy table-land. Under the naked sun of our own planet this would have been too bright to look at: here, it was a tremulous dazzle changing every moment under the undulations which the Perelandrian sky receives from the ocean. To the left of this table-land were some peaks of greenish rock. He went on. Little by little the peaks and the table-land sank and grew smaller, and presently there arose beyond them an exquisite haze like vaporised amethyst and emerald and gold, and the edge of this haze rose as he rose, and became at last the horizon of the sea, high lifted above the hills. And the sea grew ever larger and the mountains less, and the horizon of the sea rose and rose till all the lower mountains behind him seemed to be lying at the bottom of a great bowl of sea; but ahead, the interminable slope, now blue, now violet, now flickering with the smoke-like upward movement of the ripple-trees, soared up and up to the sky. And now the wooded valley in which he had met the singing beast was invisible and the mountain from which he had set out looked no more than a little swell on the slope of the great mountain, and there was not a bird in the air, nor any creature underneath the streamers, and still he went on unwearied, but always bleeding a little from his heel. He was not lonely nor afraid. He had no desires and did not even think about reaching the top nor why he should reach it. To be always climbing this was not, in his present mood, a process but a state, and in that state of life he was content. It did once cross his mind that he had died and felt no weariness because he had no body. The wound in his heel convinced him that this was not so; but if it had been so indeed, and these had been trans-mortal mountains, his journey could hardly have been more great and strange.

That night he lay on the slopes between the stems of the ripple-trees with the sweet-scented, wind-proof, delicately-whispering roof above his head, and when morning came he resumed his journey. At first he climbed through dense mists. When these parted, he found himself so high that the concave of the sea seemed to close him in on every side but one: and on that one he saw the rose-red peaks, no longer very distant, and a pass between the two nearest ones through which he caught a glimpse of something soft and flushed. And now he began to feel a strange mixture of sensations—a sense of perfect duty to enter that secret place which the peaks were guarding combined with an equal sense of trespass. He dared not go up that pass: he dared not do otherwise. He looked to see an angel with a flaming sword: he knew that Maleldil bade him go on. "This is the holiest and the most unholy thing I have ever done," he thought; but he went on. And now he was right in the pass. The peaks on either hand were not of red rock. Cores of rock they must have had; but what he saw were great matterhorns clothed in flowers—a flower shaped something like a lily but tinted like a rose. And soon the ground on which he trod was carpeted with the same flowers and he must crush them as he walked; and here at last his bleeding left no visible trace.

From the neck between the two peaks he looked a little down, for the top of the mountain was a shallow cup. He saw a valley, a few acres in size, as secret as a valley in the top of a cloud: a valley pure rose-red, with ten or twelve of the glowing peaks about it, and in the centre a pool, married in pure unrippled clearness to the gold of the sky. The lilies came down to its very edge and lined all its bays and headlands. Yielding without resistance to the awe which was gaining upon him, he walked forward with slow paces and bowed head. There was something white near the water's edge. An altar? A patch of white lilies among the red? A tomb? But whose tomb? No, it was not a tomb but a coffin, open and empty, and its lid lying beside it.

Then of course he understood. This thing was his own brother to the coffin-like chariot in which the strength of angels had brought him from Earth to Venus. It was prepared for his return. If he had said, "It is for my burial," his feelings would not have been very different. And while he thought of this he became gradually aware that there was something odd about the flowers at two places in his immediate neighbourhood. Next, he perceived that the oddity was an oddity in the light; thirdly, that it was in the air as well as on the ground. Then, as the blood pricked his veins and a familiar, yet strange, sense of diminished being possessed him, he knew that he was in the presence of two eldila. He stood still. It was not for him to speak.

16

A clear voice like a chime of remote bells, a voice with no blood in it, spoke out of the air and sent a tingling through his frame.

"They have already set foot on the sand and are beginning to ascend," it said.

"The small one from Thulcandra is already here," said a second voice.

"Look on him, beloved, and love him," said the first. "He is indeed but breathing dust and a careless touch would unmake him. And in his best thoughts there are such things mingled as, if we thought them, our light would perish. But he is in the body of Maleldil and his sins are forgiven. His very name in his own tongue is Elwin, the friend of the eldila."

"How great is your knowledge!" said the second voice.

"I have been down into the air of Thulcandra," said the first, "which the small ones call Tellus. A thickened air is full of the Darkened as Deep Heaven is of the Light Ones. I have heard the prisoners there talking in their divided tongues and Elwin has taught me how it is with them."

From these words Ransom knew the speaker was the Oyarsa of Malacandra, the great archon of Mars. He did not, of course, recognise the voice, for there is no difference between one eldil's voice and another's. It is by art, not nature, that they affect human ear-drums and their words owe nothing to lungs or lips.

"If it is good, Oyarsa," said Ransom, "tell me who is this other."

"It is Oyarsa," said Oyarsa, "and here that is not my name. In my own sphere I am Oyarsa. Here I am only Malacandra."

"I am Perelandra," said the other voice.

"I do not understand," said Ransom. "The Woman told me there were no eldila in this world."

"They have not seen my face till to-day," said the second voice, "except as they see it in the water and the roof-heaven, the islands, the caves, and the trees. I was not set to rule them, but while they were young I ruled all else. I rounded this ball when it first arose from Arbol. I spun the air about it and wove the roof. I built the Fixed Island and this, the holy mountain, as Maleldil taught me. The beasts that sing and the beasts that fly and all that swims on my breast and all that creeps and tunnels within me down to the centre has been mine. And to-day all this is taken from me. Blessed be He."

"The small one will not understand you," said the Lord of Malacandra. "He will think that this is a grievous thing in your eyes."

"He does not say this, Malacandra."

"No. That is another strange thing about the children of Adam."

There was a moment's silence and then Malacandra addressed Ransom. "You will think of this best if you think of it in the likeness of certain things from your own world."

"I think I understand," said Ransom, "for one of Maleldil's sayers has told us. It is like when the children of a great house come to their full age. Then those who administered all their riches, and whom perhaps they have never seen, come and put all in their hands and give up their keys."

"You understand well," said Perelandra. "Or like when the singing beast leaves the dumb dam who suckled him."

"The singing beast?" said Ransom. "I would gladly hear more of this."

"The beasts of that kind have no milk and always what they bring forth is suckled by the she-beast of another kind. She is great and beautiful and dumb, and till the young singing beast is weaned it is among her whelps and is subject to her. But when it is grown it becomes the most delicate and glorious of all beasts and goes from her. And she wonders at its song."

"Why has Maleldil made such a thing?" said Ransom.

"That is to ask why Maleldil has made me," said Perelandra. "But now it is enough to say that from the habits of these two beasts much wisdom will come into the minds of my King and my Queen and their children. But the hour is upon us, and this is enough."

"What hour?" asked Ransom.

"Today is the morning day," said one or other or both the voices.

But there was something much more than sound about Ransom and his heart began beating fast.

"The morning . . . do you mean . . . ?" he asked. "Is all well? Has the Queen found the King?"

"The world is born to-day," said Malacandra. "To-day for the first time two creatures of the low worlds, two images of Maleldil that breathe and breed like the beasts, step up that step at which your parents fell, and sit in the throne of what they were meant to be. It was never seen before. Because it did not happen in your world a greater thing happened, but not this. Because the greater thing happened in Thulcandra, this and not the greater thing happens here."

"Elwin is falling to the ground," said the other voice.

"Be comforted," said Malacandra. "It is no doing of yours. You are not great, though you could have prevented a thing so great that Deep Heaven sees it with amazement. Be comforted, small one, in your smallness. He lays no merit on you. Receive and be glad. Have no fear, lest your shoulders be bearing this world. Look! it is beneath your head and carries you."

"Will they come here?" asked Ransom some time later.

"They are already well up the mountain's side," said Perelandra. "And our hour is upon us. Let us prepare our shapes. We are hard for them to see while we remain in ourselves."

"It is very well said," answered Malacandra. "But in what form shall we show ourselves to do them honour?"

"Let us appear to the small one here," said the other. "For he is a man and can tell us what is pleasing to their senses."

"I can see—I can see *something* even now," said Ransom.

"Would you have the King strain his eyes to see those who come to do him honour?" said the archon of Perelandra. "But look on this and tell us how it deals with you."

The very faint light—the almost imperceptible alteration in the visual field—which betokens an eldil vanished suddenly. The rosy peaks and the calm pool vanished also. A tornado of sheer monstrosities seemed to be pouring over Ransom. Darting pillars filled with eyes, lightning pulsations of flame, talons and beaks and billowy masses of what suggested snow, volleyed through cubes and heptagons into an infinite black void. "Stop it . . . stop it," he yelled, and the scene cleared. He gazed round blinking on the field of lilies, and presently gave the eldila to understand that this kind of appearance was not suited to human sensations. "Look then on this," said the voices again. And he looked with some reluctance, and far off between the peaks on the other side of the little valley there came rolling wheels. There was nothing but that—concentric wheels moving with a rather sickening slowness one inside the other. There was nothing terrible about them if you could get used to their appalling size, but there was also nothing significant. He bade them to try yet a third time. And suddenly two human figures stood before him on the opposite side of the lake.

They were taller than the Sorns, the giants whom he had met in Mars. They were perhaps thirty feet high. They were burning white like white-hot iron. The outline of their bodies when he looked at it steadily against the red landscape seemed to be faintly, swiftly undulating as though the permanence of their shape, like that of waterfalls or flames, co-existed with a rushing movement of the matter it contained. For a fraction of an inch inward from this outline the landscape was just visible through them: beyond that they were opaque.

Whenever he looked straight at them they appeared to be rushing towards him with enormous speed: whenever his eyes took in their surroundings he realised that they were stationary. This may have been due in part to the fact that their long and sparkling hair stood out straight behind them as if in a great wind. But if there were a wind it was not made of air, for no petal of the flowers was shaken. They were not standing quite vertically in relation to the floor of the valley: but to Ransom it appeared (as it had appeared to me on Earth when I saw one) that the eldils were vertical. It was the valley—it was the whole world of Perelandra—which was aslant. He remembered the words of Oyarsa long ago in Mars, "I am not *here* in the same way you are *here.*" It was borne in upon him that the creatures were really moving, though not moving in relation to him. This planet which inevitably seemed to him while he was in it an unmoving world—*the* world, in fact—was to them a thing moving through the heavens. In relation to their own celestial frame of reference they were rushing forward to keep abreast of the mountain valley. Had they stood still, they would have flashed past him too quickly for him to see, doubly dropped behind by the planet's spin on its own axis and by its onward march around the Sun.

Their bodies, he said, were white. But a flush of diverse colours began at about the shoulders and streamed up the necks and flickered over face and head and stood out around the head like plumage or a halo. He told me he could in a sense remember these colours—that is, he would know them if he saw them again—but that he cannot by any effort call up a visual image of them nor give them any name. The very few people with whom he and I can discuss these matters all give the same explanation. We think that when creatures of the hypersomatic kind choose to "appear" to us, they are not in fact affecting our retina at all, but directly manipulating the relevant parts of our brain. If so, it is quite possible that they can produce there the sensations we *should* have if our eyes were capable of receiving those colours in the spectrum which are actually beyond their range. The "plumage" or halo of the one eldil was extremely different from that of the other. The Oyarsa of Mars shone with cold and morning colours, a little metallic—pure, hard, and bracing. The Oyarsa of Venus glowed with a warm splendour, full of the suggestion of teeming vegetable life.

The faces surprised him very much. Nothing less like the "angel" of popular art could well be imagined. The rich variety, the hint of undeveloped possibilities, which make the interest of human faces, were entirely absent. One single, changeless expression—so clear that it hurt and dazzled him—was stamped on each and there was nothing else there at all. In that sense their faces were as "primitive," as unnatural, if you like, as those of archaic statues from Ægina. What this one thing was he could not be certain. He concluded in the end that it was charity. But it was terrifyingly different from the expression of human charity, which we always see either blossoming out of, or hastening to descend into, natural affection. Here there was no affection at all: no least lingering memory of it even at ten million years' distance, no germ from which it could spring in any future, however remote. Pure, spiritual, intellectual love shot from their faces like barbed lightning. It was so unlike the love we experience that its expression could easily be mistaken for ferocity.

Both the bodies were naked, and both were free from any sexual characteristics, either primary or secondary. That, one would have expected. But whence came this curious difference between them? He found that he could point to no single feature wherein the difference resided, yet it was impossible to ignore. One could try—Ransom has tried a hundred times—to put it into words. He has said that Malacandra was like rhythm and Perelandra like melody. He has said that Malacandra affected him like a quantitative, Perelandra like an accentual, metre. He thinks that the first held in his hand something like a spear, but the hands of the other were open, with the palms towards him. But I don't know that any of these attempts has helped me much. At all events what Ransom saw at that moment was the real meaning of gender. Everyone must sometimes have wondered why in nearly all tongues certain inanimate objects are masculine and others feminine. What is masculine about a mountain or feminine about certain trees? Ransom has cured me of believing that this is a purely morphological phenomenon, depending on the form of the word. Still less is gender an imaginative extension of sex. Our ancestors did not make mountains masculine because they projected male characteristics into them. The real process is the reverse. Gender is a reality, and a more fundamental reality than sex. Sex is, in fact, merely the adaptation to organic life of a fundamental polarity which divides all created beings. Female sex is simply one of the things that have feminine gender; there are many others, and Masculine and Feminine meet us on planes of reality where male and female would be simply meaningless. Masculine is not attenuated male, nor feminine attenuated female. On the contrary, the male and female of organic creatures are rather faint and blurred reflections of masculine and feminine. Their reproductive functions, their differences in strength and size, partly exhibit, but partly also confuse and misrepresent, the real polarity. All this Ransom saw, as it were, with his own eyes. The two white creatures were sexless. But he of Malacandra was masculine (not male); she of Perelandra was feminine (not female). Malacandra seemed to him to have the look of one standing armed, at the ramparts of his own remote archaic world, in ceaseless vigilance, his eyes ever roaming the earth-ward horizon whence his danger came long ago. "A sailor's look," Ransom once said to me; "you know . . . eyes that are impregnated with distance." But the eyes of Perelandra opened, as it were, inward, as if they were the curtained gateway to a world of waves and murmurings and wandering airs, of life that rocked in winds and splashed on mossy stones and descended as the dew and arose sunward in thin-spun delicacy of mist. On Mars the very forests are of stone; in Venus the lands swim. For now he thought of them no more as Malacandra and Perelandra. He called them by their Tellurian names. With deep wonder he thought to himself, "My eyes have seen Mars and Venus. I have seen Ares and Aphrodite." He asked them how they were known to the old poets of Tellus. When and from whom had the children of Adam learned that Ares was a man of war and that Aphrodite rose from the sea foam? Earth has been besieged, an enemy-occupied territory, since before history began. The gods have had no commerce there. How then do we know of them? It comes, they told him, a long way round and through many stages. There is an environment of minds as well as of space. The universe is one—a spider's web wherein each mind lives along every line, a vast whispering gallery where (save for the direct action of Maleldil) though no news travels unchanged yet no secret can be rigorously kept. In the mind of the fallen Archon under whom our planet groans, the memory of Deep Heaven and the gods with whom he once consorted is still alive. Nay, in the very matter of our world, the traces of the celestial commonwealth are not quite lost. Memory passes through the womb and hovers in the air. The Muse is a real thing. A faint breath, as Virgil says, reaches even the late generations. Our mythology is based on a solider reality than we dream: but it is also at an almost infinite distance from that base. And when they told him this, Ransom at last understood why mythology was what it was— gleams of celestial strength and beauty falling on a jungle of filth and imbecility. His cheeks burned on behalf of our race when he looked on the true Mars and Venus and remembered the follies that have been talked of them on Earth. Then a doubt struck him.

"But do I see you as you really are?" he asked.

"Only Maleldil sees any creature as it really is," said Mars.

"How do you see one another?" asked Ransom.

"There are no holding places in your mind for an answer to that."

"Am I then seeing only an appearance? Is it not real at all?"

"You see only an appearance, small one. You have never seen more than an appearance of anything—not of Arbol, nor of a stone, nor of your own body. This appearance is as true as what you see of those."

"But . . . there were those other appearances."

"No. There was only the failure of appearance."

I don't understand," said Ransom. "Were all those other things—the wheels and the eyes—more real than this or less?"

"There is no meaning in your question," said Mars. "You can see a stone, if it is a fit distance from you and if you and it are moving at speeds not too different. But if one throws the stone at your eye, what then is the appearance?"

"I should feel pain and perhaps see splintered light," said Ransom. "But I don't know that I should call that an appearance of the stone."

"Yet it would be the true operation of the stone. And there is your question answered. We are now at the right distance from you."

"And were you nearer in what I first saw?"

"I do not mean that kind of distance."

"And then," said Ransom, still pondering, "there is what I had thought was your wonted appearance—the very faint light, Oyarsa, as I used to see it in your own world. What of that?"

"That is enough appearance for us to speak to you by. No more was needed between us: no more is needed now. It is to honour the King that we would now appear more. That light is the overflow or echo into the world of your senses of vehicles made for appearance to one another and to the greater eldila."

At this moment Ransom suddenly noticed an increasing disturbance of sound behind his back—of unco-ordinated sound, husky and patter-ing noises which broke in on the mountain silence and the crystal voices of the gods with a delicious note of warm animality. He glanced round. Romping, prancing, fluttering, gliding, crawling, waddling, with every kind of movement—in every kind of shape and colour and size—a whole zoo of beasts and birds was pouring into a flowery valley through the passes between the peaks at his back. They came mostly in their pairs, male and female together, fawning upon one another, climbing over one another, diving under one another's bellies, perching upon one another's backs. Flaming plumage, gilded beaks, glossy flanks, liquid eyes, great red caverns of whinneying or of bleating mouths, and thickets of switching tails, surrounded him on every side. "A regular Noah's Ark!" thought Ransom, and then, with sudden seriousness, "But there will be no ark needed in this world."

The song of four singing beasts rose in almost deafening triumph above the restless multitude. The great eldil of Perelandra kept back the creatures to the hither side of the pool, leaving the opposite side of the valley empty except for the coffin-like object. Ransom was not clear whether Venus spoke to the beasts or even whether they were conscious of her presence. Her connection with them was perhaps of some subtler kind—quite different from the relations he had observed between them and the Green Lady. Both the eldila were now on the same side of the pool with Ransom. He and they and all the beasts were facing in the same direction. The thing began to arrange itself. First, on the very brink of the pool, were the eldila, standing: between them, and a little back, was Ransom, still sitting among the lilies. Behind him the four singing beasts, sitting up on their haunches like fire-dogs, and proclaiming joy to all ears. Behind these again, the other animals. The sense of ceremony deepened. The expectation became intense. In our foolish human fashion he asked a question merely for the purpose of breaking it. "How can they climb to here and go down again and yet be off this island before nightfall?" Nobody answered him. He did not need an answer, for somehow he knew perfectly well that *this* island had never been forbidden them, and that one purpose in forbidding the other had been to lead them to this their destined throne. Instead of answering, the gods said, "Be still."

Ransom's eyes had grown so used to the tinted softness of Perelandrian daylight—and specially since his journey in the dark guts of the mountain—that he had quite ceased to notice its difference from the daylight of our own world. It was, therefore, with a shock of double amazement that he now suddenly saw the peaks on the far side of the valley showing really dark against what seemed a terrestrial dawn. A moment later sharp, well-defined shadows—long, like the shadows at early morning—were streaming back from every beast and every unevenness of the ground and each lily had its light and its dark side. Up and up came the light from the mountain slope. It filled the whole valley. The shadows disappeared again. All was in a pure daylight that seemed to come from nowhere in particular. He knew ever afterwards what is meant by a light "resting on" or "overshadowing" a holy thing, but not emanating from it. For as the light reached its perfection and settled itself, as it were, like a lord upon his throne or like wine in a bowl, and filled the whole flowery cup of the mountain top, every cranny, with its purity, the holy thing, Paradise itself in its two Persons, Paradise walking hand in hand, its two bodies shining in the light like emeralds yet not themselves too bright to look at, came in sight in the cleft between two peaks, and stood a moment with its male right hand lifted in regal and pontifical benediction, and they walked down and stood on the far side of the water. And the gods knelt and bowed their huge bodies before the small forms of that young King and Queen.

17

There was great silence on the mountain top and Ransom also had fallen down before the human pair. When at last he raised his eyes from the four blessed feet, he found himself involuntarily speaking though his voice was broken and his eyes dimmed. "Do not move away, do not raise me up," he said. "I have never before seen a man or a woman. I have lived all my life among shadows and broken images. Oh, my Father and my Mother, my Lord and my Lady, do not move, do not answer me yet. My own father and mother I have never seen. Take me for your son. We have been alone in my world for a great time."

The eyes of the Queen looked upon him with love and recognition, but it was not of the Queen that he thought most. It was hard to think of anything but the King. And how shall I—I who have not seen him—tell you what he was like? It was hard even for Ransom to tell me of the King's face. But we dare not withhold the truth. It was that face which no man can say he does not know. You might ask how it was possible to look upon it and not to commit idolatry, not to mistake it for that of which it was the likeness. For the resemblance was, in its own fashion, infinite, so that almost you could wonder at finding no sorrows in his brow and no wounds in his hands and feet. Yet there was no danger of mistaking, not one moment of confusion, no least sally of the will towards forbidden reverence. Where likeness was greatest, mistake was least possible. Perhaps this is always so. A clever wax-work can be made so like a man that for a moment it deceives us: the great portrait which is far more deeply like him does not. Plaster images of the Holy One may before now have drawn to themselves the adoration they were meant to arouse for the reality. But here, where His live image, like Him within and without, made by His own bare hands out of the depth of divine artistry, His masterpiece of self-portraiture coming forth from His workshop to delight all worlds, walked and spoke before Ransom's eyes, it could never be taken for more than an image. Nay, the very beauty of it lay in the certainty that it was a copy, like and not the same, an echo, a rhyme, an exquisite reverberation of the uncreated music prolonged in a created medium.

Ransom was lost for a while in the wonder of these things, so that when he came to himself he found that Perelandra was speaking, and what he heard seemed to be the end of a long oration. "The floating lands and the firm lands," she was saying, "the air and the curtains at the gates of Deep Heaven, the seas and the Holy Mountain, the rivers above and the rivers of underland, the fire, the fish, the birds, the beasts, and the others of the waves whom yet you know not; all these Maleldil puts into your hand from this day forth as far as you live in time and farther. My word henceforth is nothing: your word is law unchangeable and the very daughter of the Voice. In all that circle which this world runs about Arbol, you are Oyarsa. Enjoy it well. Give names to all creatures, guide all natures to perfection. Strengthen the feebler, lighten the darker, love all. Hail and be glad, oh man and woman, Oyarsa-Perelendri, the Adam, the Crown, Tor and Tinidril, Baru and Baru'ah, Ask and Embla, Yatsur and Yatsurah, dear to Maleldil. Blessed be He!"

When the King spoke in answer, Ransom looked up at him again. He saw that the human pair were now seated on a low bank that rose near the margin of the pool. So great was the light, that they cast clear reflections in the water as they might have done in our own world.

"We give you thanks, fair foster mother," said the King, "and specially for this world in which you have laboured for long ages as Maleldil's very hand that all might be ready for us when we woke. We have not known you till to-day. We have often wondered whose hand it was that we saw in the long waves and the bright islands and whose breath delighted us in the wind at morning. For though we were young then, we saw dimly that to say 'It is Maleldil' was true, but not all the truth. This world we receive: our joy is the greater because we take it by your gift as well as by His. But what does He put into your mind to do henceforward?"

"It lies in your bidding, Tor-Oyarsa," said Perelandra, "whether I now converse in Deep Heaven only or also in that part of Deep Heaven which is to you a World."

"It is very much our will," said the King, "that you remain with us, both for the love we bear you and also that you may strengthen us with counsel and even with your operations. Not till we have gone many times about Arbol shall we grow up to the full management of the dominion which Maleldil puts into our hands: nor are we yet ripe to steer the world through Heaven nor to make rain and fair weather upon us. If it seems good to you, remain."

"I am content," said Perelandra.

While this dialogue proceeded, it was a wonder that the contrast between the Adam and the eldils was not a discord. On the one side, the crystal, bloodless voice, and the immutable expression of the snow-white face; on the other the blood coursing in the veins, the feeling trembling on the lips and sparkling in the eyes, the might of the man's shoulders, the wonder of the woman's breasts, a splendour of virility and richness of womanhood unknown on earth, a living torrent of perfect animality—yet when these met, the one did not seem rank nor the other spectral. *Animal rationale*—an animal, yet also a reasonable soul: such, he remembered, was the old definition of Man. But he had never till now seen the reality. For now he saw this living Paradise, the Lord and Lady, as the resolution of discords, the bridge that spans what would else be a chasm in creation, the keystone of the whole arch. By entering that mountain valley they had suddenly united the warm multitude of the brutes behind him with the transcorporeal intelligences at his side. They closed the circle, and with their coming all the separate notes of strength or beauty which that assembly had hitherto struck became one music. But now the King was speaking again.

"And as it is not Maleldil's gift simply," he said, "but also Maleldil's gift through you, and thereby the richer, so it is not through you only, but through a third, and thereby the richer again. And this is the first word I speak as Tor-Oyarsa-Perelendri; that in our world, as long as it is a world, neither shall morning come nor night but that we and all our children shall speak to Maleldil of Ransom the man of Thulcandra and praise him to one another. And to you, Ransom, I say this, that you have called us Lord and Father, Lady and Mother. And rightly, for this is our name. But in another fashion we call you Lord and Father. For it seems to us that Maleldil sent you into our world at that day when the time of our being young drew to its end, and from it we must now go up or go down, into corruption or into perfection. Maleldil has taken us where He meant us to be: but of Maleldil's instruments in this, you were the chief."

They made him go across the water to them, wading, for it came only to his knees. He would have fallen at their feet but they would not let him. They rose to meet him and both kissed him, mouth to mouth and heart to heart as equals embrace. They would have made him sit between them, but when they saw that this troubled him they let it be. He went and sat down on the level ground, below them, and a little to the left. From there he faced the assembly—the huge shapes of the gods and the concourse of beasts. And then the Queen spoke.

"As soon as you had taken away the Evil One," she said, "and I awoke from sleep, my mind was cleared. It is a wonder to me, Piebald, that for all those days you and I could have been so young. The reason for not yet living on the Fixed Land is now so plain. How could I wish to live there except because it was Fixed? And why should I desire the Fixed except to make sure—to be able on one day to command where I should be the next and what should happen to me? It was to reject the wave—to draw my hands out of Maleldil's, to say to Him, 'Not thus, but thus'—to put in our own power what times should roll towards us . . . as if you gathered fruits together to-day for to-morrow's eating instead of taking what came. That would have been cold love and feeble trust. And out of it how could we ever have climbed back into love and trust again?"

"I see it well," said Ransom. "Though in my world it would pass for folly. We have been evil so long"—and then he stopped, doubtful of being understood and surprised that he had used a word for *evil* which he had not hitherto known that he knew, and which he had not heard either in Mars or in Venus.

"We know these things now," said the King, seeing Ransom's hesitation. "All this, all that happened in your world, Maleldil has put into our mind. We have learned of evil, though not as the Evil One wished us to learn. We have learned better than that, and know it more, for it is waking that understands sleep and not sleep that understands waking. There is an ignorance of evil that comes from being young: there is a darker ignorance that comes from doing it, as men by sleeping lose the knowledge of sleep. You are more ignorant of evil in Thulcandra now than in the days before your Lord and Lady began to do it. But Maleldil has brought us out of the one ignorance, and we have not entered the other. It was by the Evil One himself that he brought us out of the first. Little did that dark mind know the errand on which he really came to Perelandra!"

"Forgive me, my Father, if I speak foolishly," said Ransom. "I see how evil has been made known to the Queen, but not how it was made known to you."

Then unexpectedly the King laughed. His body was very big and his laugh was like an earthquake in it, loud and deep and long, till in the end Ransom laughed too, though he had not seen the joke, and the Queen laughed as well. And the birds began clapping their wings and the beasts wagging their tails, and the light seemed brighter and the pulse of the whole assembly quickened, and new modes of joy that had nothing to do with mirth as we understand it passed into them all, as if it were from the very air, or as if there were dancing in Deep Heaven. Some say there always is.

"I know what he is thinking," said the King, looking upon the Queen. "He is thinking that you suffered and strove and I have a world for my reward." Then he turned to Ransom and continued. "You are right," he said, "I know now what they say in your world about justice. And perhaps they say well, for in that world things always fall below justice. But Maleldil always goes above it. All is gift. I am Oyarsa not by His gift alone but by our foster mother's, not by hers alone but by yours, not by yours alone but my wife's—nay, in some sort, by gift of the very beasts and birds. Through many hands, enriched with many different kinds of love and labour, the gift comes to me. It is the Law. The best fruits are plucked for each by some hand that is not his own."

"That is not the whole of what happened, Piebald," said the Queen. "The King has not told you all. Maleldil drove him far away into a green sea where forests grow up from the bottom through the waves. . . ."

"Its name is Lur," said the King.

"Its name is Lur," repeated the eldila. And Ransom realised that the King had uttered not an observation but an enactment.

"And there in Lur (it is far hence)," said the Queen, "strange things befell him."

"Is it good to ask about these things?" said Ransom.

"There were many things," said Tor the King. "For many hours I learned the properties of shapes by drawing lines in the turf of a little island on which I rode. For many hours I learned new things about Maleldil and about His Father and the Third One. We knew little of this while we were young. But after that He showed me in a darkness what was happening to the Queen. And I knew it was possible for her to be undone. And then I saw what had happened in your world, and how your Mother fell and how your Father went with her, doing her no good thereby and bringing the darkness upon all their children. And then it was before me like a thing coming towards my hand . . . what I should do in like case. There I learned of evil and good, of anguish and joy."

Ransom had expected the King to relate his decision, but when the King's voice died away into thoughtful silence he had not the assurance to question him.

"Yes . . ." said the King, musing. "Though a man were to be torn in two halves . . . though half of him turned into earth. . . . The living half must still follow Maleldil. For if it also lay down and became earth, what hope would there be for the whole? But while one half lived, through it He might send life back into the other." Here he paused for a long time, and then spoke again somewhat quickly. "He gave me no assurance. No fixed land. Always one must throw oneself into the wave." Then he cleared his brow and turned to the eldila and spoke in a new voice.

"Certainly, O foster mother," he said. "We have much need of counsel for already we feel that growing up within our bodies which our young wisdom can hardly overtake. They will not always be bodies bound to the low worlds. Hear the second word that I speak as Tor-Oyarsa-Perelendri. While this World goes about Arbol ten thousand times, we shall judge and hearten our people from this throne. Its name is Tai Harendrimar, The Hill of Life."

"Its name is Tai Harendrimar," said the eldila.

"On the Fixed Land which once was forbidden," said Tor the King, "we will make a great place to the splendour of Maleldil. Our sons shall bend the pillars of rock into arches——"

"What are arches?" said Tinidril the Queen.

"Arches," said Tor the King, "are when pillars of stone throw out branches like trees and knit their branches together and bear up a great dome as of leafage, but the leaves shall be shaped stones. And there our sons will make images."

"What are images?" said Tinidril.

"Splendour of Deep Heaven!" cried the King with a great laugh. "It seems there are too many new words in the air. I had thought these things were coming out of your mind into mine, and lo! you have not thought them at all. Yet I think Maleldil passed them to me through you, none the less. I will show you images, I will show you houses. It may be that in this matter our natures are reversed and it is you who beget and I who bear. But let us speak of plainer matters. We will fill this world with our children. We will know this world to the centre. We will make the nobler of the beasts so wise that they will become *hnau* and speak: their lives shall awake to a new life in us as we awake in Maleldil. When the time is ripe for it and the ten thousand circlings are nearly at an end, we will tear the sky curtain and Deep Heaven shall become familiar to the eyes of our sons as the trees and the waves to ours."

"And what after this, Tor-Oyarsa?" said Malacandra.

"Then it is Maleldil's purpose to make us free of Deep Heaven. Our bodies will be changed, but not all changed. We shall be as the eldila, but not all as eldila. And so will all our sons and daughters be changed in the time of this ripeness, until the number is made up which Maleldil read in His Father's mind before times flowed."

"And that," said Ransom, "will be the end?"

Tor the King stared at him.

"The end?" he said. "Who spoke of an end?"

"The end of your world, I mean," said Ransom.

"Splendour of Heaven!" said Tor. "Your thoughts are unlike ours. About that time we shall be not far from the beginning of all things. But there will be one matter to settle before the beginning rightly begins."

"What is that?" asked Ransom.

"Your own world," said Tor, "Thulcandra. The siege of your world shall be raised, the black spot cleared away, before the real beginning. In those days Maleldil will go to war—in us, and in many who once were *hnau* on your world, and in many from far off and in many eldila, and, last of all, in Himself unveiled, He will go down to Thulcandra. Some of us will go before. It is in my mind, Malacandra, that thou and I will be among those. We shall fall upon your moon, wherein there is a secret evil, and which is as the shield of the Dark Lord of Thulcandra—scarred with many a blow. We shall break her. Her light shall be put out. Her fragments shall fall into your world and the seas and the smoke shall arise so that the dwellers in Thulcandra will no longer see the light of Arbol. And as Maleldil Himself draws near, the evil things in your world shall show themselves stripped of disguise so that plagues and horrors shall cover your lands and seas. But in the end all shall be cleansed, and even the memory of your Black Oyarsa blotted out, and your world shall be fair and sweet and reunited to the field of Arbol and its true name shall be heard again. But can it be, Friend, that no rumour of all this is heard in Thulcandra? Do your people think that their Dark Lord will hold his prey forever?"

"Most of them," said Ransom, "have ceased to think of such things at all. Some of us still have the knowledge: but I did not at once see what you were talking of, because what you call the beginning we are accustomed to call the Last Things."

"I do not call it the beginning," said Tor the King. "It is but the wiping out of a false start in order that the world may *then* begin. As when a man lies down to sleep, if he finds a twisted root under his shoulder he will change his place—and after that his real sleep begins. Or as a man setting foot on an island, may make a false step. He steadies himself and after that his journey begins. You would not call that steadying of himself a last thing?"

"And is the whole story of my race no more than this?" said Ransom.

"I see no more than beginnings in the history of the Low Worlds," said Tor the King. "And in yours a failure to begin. You talk of evenings before the day has dawned. I set forth even now on ten thousand years of preparation—I, the first of my race, my race the first of races, to begin. I tell you that when the last of my children has ripened and ripeness has spread from them to all the Low Worlds, it will be whispered that the morning is at hand."

"I am full of doubts and ignorance," said Ransom. "In our world those who know Maleldil at all believe that His coming down to us and being a man is the central happening of all that happens. If you take that from me, Father, whither will you lead me? Surely not to the enemy's talk which thrusts my world and my race into a remote corner and gives me a universe, with no centre at all, but millions of worlds that lead nowhere or (what is worse) to more and more worlds for ever, and comes over me with numbers and empty spaces and repetitions and asks me to bow down before bigness. Or do you make your world the centre? But I am troubled. What of the people on Malacandra? Would they also think that their world was the centre? I do not even see how your world can rightly be called yours. You were made yesterday and it is from of old. The most of it is water where you cannot live. And what of the things beneath its crust? And of the great spaces with no world at all? Is the enemy easily answered when He says that all is without plan or meaning? As soon as we think we see one it melts away into nothing, or into some other plan that we never dreamed of, and what was the centre becomes the rim, till we doubt if any shape or plan or pattern was ever more than a trick of our own eyes, cheated with hope, or tired with too much looking. To what is all driving? What is the morning you speak of? What is it the beginning of?"

"The beginning of the Great Game, of the Great Dance," said Tor. "I know little of it as yet. Let the eldila speak."

The voice that spoke next seemed to be that of Mars, but Ransom was not certain. And who spoke after that, he does not know at all. For in the conversation that followed—if it can be called a conversation—though he believes that he himself was sometimes the speaker, he never knew which words were his or another's, or even whether a man or an eldil was talking. The speeches followed one another—if, indeed, they did not all take place at the same time—like the parts of a music into which all five of them had entered as instruments or like a wind blowing through five trees that stand together on a hilltop.

"We would not talk of it like that," said the first voice. "The Great Dance does not wait to be perfect until the peoples of the Low Worlds are gathered into it. We speak not of when it will begin. It has begun from before always. There was no time when we did not rejoice before His face as now. The dance which we dance is at the centre and for the dance all things were made. Blessed be He!"

Another said, "Never did He make two things the same; never did He utter one word twice. After earths, not better earths but beasts; after beasts, not better beasts, but spirits. After a falling, not a recovery but a new creation. Out of the new creation, not a third but the mode of change itself is changed for ever. Blessed is He!"

And another said, "It is loaded with justice as a tree bows down with fruit. All is righteousness and there is no equality. Not as when stones lie side by side, but as when stones support and are supported in an arch, such is His order; rule and obedience, begetting and bearing, heat glancing down, life growing up. Blessed be He!"

One said, "They who add years to years in lumpish aggregation, or miles to miles and galaxies to galaxies, shall not come near His greatness. The day of the fields of Arbol will fade and the days of Deep Heaven itself are numbered. Not thus is He great. He dwells (all of Him dwells) within the seed of the smallest flower and is not cramped: Deep Heaven is inside Him who is inside the seed and does not distend Him. Blessed be He!"

"The edge of each nature borders on that whereof it contains no shadow or similitude. Of many points one line; of many lines one shape; of many shapes one solid body; of many senses and thoughts one person; of three persons, Himself. As is the circle to the sphere, so are the ancient worlds that needed no redemption to that world wherein He was born and died. As is a point to a line, so is that world to the far-off fruits of its redeeming. Blessed be He!"

"Yet the circle is not less round than the sphere, and the sphere is the home and fatherland of circles. Infinite multitudes of circles lie enclosed in every sphere, and if they spoke they would say, For us were spheres created. Let no mouth open to gainsay them. Blessed be He!"

"The peoples of the ancient worlds who never sinned, for whom He never came down, are the peoples for whose sake the Low Worlds were made. For though the healing what was wounded and the straightening what was bent is a new dimension of glory, yet the straight was not made that it might be bent nor the whole that it might be wounded. The ancient peoples are at the centre. Blessed be He!"

"All which is not itself the Great Dance was made in order that He might come down into it. In the Fallen World He prepared for Himself a body and was united with the Dust and made it glorious for ever. This is the end and final cause of all creating, and the sin whereby it came is called Fortunate and the world where this was enacted is the centre of worlds. Blessed be He!"

"The Tree was planted in that world but the fruit has ripened in this. The fountain that sprang with mingled blood and life in the Dark World, flows here with life only. We have passed the first cataracts, and from here onward the stream flows deep and turns in the direction of the sea. This is the Morning Star which He promised to those who conquer; this is the centre of worlds. Till now all has waited. But now the trumpet has sounded and the army is on the move. Blessed be He!"

"Though men or angels rule them, the worlds are for themselves. The waters you have not floated on, the fruit you have not plucked, the caves into which you have not descended and the fire through which your bodies cannot pass, do not await your coming to put on perfection, though they will obey you when you come. Times without number I have circled Arbol while you were not alive, and those times were not desert. Their own voice was in them, not merely a dreaming of the day when you should awake. They also were at the centre. Be comforted, small immortals. You are not the voice that all things utter, nor is there eternal silence in the places where you cannot come. No feet have walked, nor shall, on the ice of Glund; no eye looked up from beneath on the Ring of Lurga, and Iron-plain in Neruval is chaste and empty. Yet it is not for nothing that the gods walk ceaselessly around the fields of Arbol. Blessed be He!"

"That Dust itself which is scattered so rare in Heaven, whereof all worlds, and the bodies that are not worlds, are made, is at the centre. It waits not till created eyes have seen it or hands handled it, to be in itself a strength and splendour of Maleldil. Only the least part has served, or ever shall, a beast, a man, or a god. But always, and beyond all distances, before they came and after they are gone and where they never come, it is what it is and utters the heart of the Holy One with its own voice. It is farthest from Him of all things, for it has no life, nor sense, nor reason; it is nearest to Him of all things for without intervening soul, as sparks fly out of fire, He utters in each grain of it the unmixed image of His energy. Each grain, if it spoke, would say, I am at the centre; for me all things were made. Let no mouth open to gainsay it. Blessed be He!"

"Each grain is at the centre. The Dust is at the centre. The Worlds are at the centre. The beasts are at the centre. The ancient peoples are there. The race that sinned is there. Tor and Tinidril are there. The gods are there also. Blessed be He!"

"Where Maleldil is, there is the centre. He is in every place. Not some of Him in one place and some in another, but in each place the whole Maleldil, even in the smallness beyond thought. There is no way out of the centre save into the Bent Will which casts itself into the Nowhere. Blessed be He!"

"Each thing was made for Him. He is the centre. Because we are with Him, each of us is at the centre. It is not as in a city of the Darkened World where they say that each must live for all. In His city all things are made for each. When He died in the Wounded World He died not for men, but for each man. If each man had been the only man made, He would have done no less. Each thing, from the single grain of Dust to the strongest eldil, is the end and the final cause of all creation and the mirror in which the beam of His brightness comes to rest and so returns to Him. Blessed be He!"

"In the plan of the Great Dance plans without number interlock, and each movement becomes in its season the breaking into flower of the whole design to which all else had been directed. Thus each is equally at the centre and none are there by being equals, but some by giving place and some by receiving it, the small things by their smallness and the great by their greatness, and all the patterns linked and looped together by the unions of a kneeling with a sceptred love. Blessed be He!"

"He has immeasurable use for each thing that is made, that His love and splendour may flow forth like a strong river which has need of a great watercourse and fills alike the deep pools and the little crannies, that are filled equally and remain unequal; and when it has filled them brim full it flows over and makes new channels. We also have need beyond measure of all that He has made. Love me, my brothers, for I am infinitely necessary to you and for your delight I was made. Blessed be He!"

"He has no need at all of anything that is made. An eldil is not more needful to Him than a grain of the Dust: a peopled world no more needful than a world that is empty: but all needless alike, and what all add to Him is nothing. We also have no need of anything that is made. Love me, my brothers, for I am infinitely superfluous, and your love shall be like His, born neither of your need nor of my deserving, but a plain bounty. Blessed be He!"

"All things are by Him and for Him. He utters Himself also for His own delight and sees that He is good. He is His own begotten and what proceeds from Him is Himself. Blessed be He!"

"All that is made seems planless to the darkened mind, because there are more plans than it looked for. In these seas there are islands where the hairs of the turf are so fine and so closely woven together that unless a man looked long at them he would see neither hairs nor weaving at all, but only the same and the flat. So with the Great Dance. Set your eyes on one movement and it will lead you through all patterns and it will seem to you the master movement. But the seeming will be true. Let no mouth open to gainsay it. There seems no plan because it is all plan: there seems no centre because it is all centre. Blessed be He!"

"Yet this seeming also is the end and final cause for which He spreads out Time so long and Heaven so deep; lest if we never met the dark, and the road that leads nowhither, and the question to which no answer is imaginable, we should have in our minds no likeness of the Abyss of the Father, into which if a creature drop down his thoughts for ever he shall hear no echo return to him. Blessed, blessed, blessed be He!"

And now, by a transition which he did not notice, it seemed that what had begun as speech was turned into sight, or into something that can be remembered only as if it were seeing. He thought he saw the Great Dance. It seemed to be woven out of the intertwining undulation of many cords or bands of light, leaping over and under one another and mutually embraced in arabesques and flower-like subtleties. Each figure as he looked at it became the master-figure or focus of the whole spectacle, by means of which his eye disentangled all else and brought it into unity—only to be itself entangled when he looked to what he had taken for mere marginal decorations and found that there also the same hegemony was claimed, and the claim made good, yet the former pattern not thereby dispossessed but finding in its new subordination a significance greater than that which it had abdicated. He could see also (but the word "seeing" is now plainly inadequate) wherever the ribbons or serpents of light intersected, minute corpuscles of momentary brightness: and he knew somehow that these particles were the secular generalities of which history tells—peoples, institutions, climates of opinion, civilisations, arts, sciences, and the like—ephemeral coruscations that piped their short song and vanished. The ribbons or cords themselves, in which millions of corpuscles lived and died, were things of some different kind. At first he could not say what. But he knew in the end that most of them were individual entities. If so, the time in which the Great Dance proceeds is very unlike time as we know it. Some of the thinner and more delicate cords were beings that we call short-lived: flowers and insects, a fruit or a storm of rain, and once (he thought) a wave of the sea. Others were such things as we also think lasting: crystals, rivers, mountains, or even stars. Far above these in girth and luminosity and flashing with colours from beyond our spectrum were the lines of the personal beings, yet as different from one another in splendour as all of them from the previous class. But not all the cords were individuals: some were universal truths or universal qualities. It did not surprise him then to find that these and the persons were both cords and both stood together as against the mere atoms of generality which lived and died in the clashing of their streams: but afterwards, when he came back to earth, he wondered. And by now the thing must have passed together out of the region of sight as we understand it. For he says that the whole solid figure of these enamoured and inter-inanimated circlings was suddenly revealed as the mere superficies of a far vaster pattern in four dimensions, and that figure as the boundary of yet others in other worlds: till suddenly as the movement grew yet swifter, the interweaving yet more ecstatic, the relevance of all to all yet more intense, as dimension was added to dimension and that part of him which could reason and remember was dropped farther and farther behind that part of him which saw, even then, at the very zenith of complexity, complexity was eaten up and faded, as a thin white cloud fades into the hard blue burning of the sky, and a simplicity beyond all comprehension, ancient and young as spring, illimitable, pellucid, drew him with cords of infinite desire into its own stillness. He went up into such a quietness, a privacy, and a freshness that at the very moment when he stood farthest from our ordinary mode of being he had the sense of stripping off encumbrances and awaking from trance, and coming to himself. With a gesture of relaxation he looked about him. . . .

The animals had gone. The two white figures had disappeared. Tor and Tinidril and he were alone, in ordinary Perelandrian daylight, early in the morning.

"Where are the beasts?" said Ransom.

"They have gone about their small affairs," said Tinidril. "They have gone to bring up their whelps and lay their eggs, to build their nests and spin their webs and dig their burrows, to sing and play and to eat and drink."

"They did not wait long," said Ransom, "for I feel it is still early in the morning."

"But not the same morning," said Tor.

"We have been here long, then?" asked Ransom.

"Yes," said Tor. "I did not know it till now. But we have accomplished one whole circle about Arbol since we met on this mountain top."

"A year?" said Ransom. "A whole year? O Heavens, what may by now have happened in my own dark world! Did you know, Father, that so much time was passing?"

"I did not feel it pass," said Tor. "I believe the waves of time will often change for us henceforward. We are coming to have it in our own choice whether we shall be above them and see many waves together or whether we shall reach them one by one as we used to."

"It comes into my mind," said Tinidril, "that to-day, now that the year has brought us back to the same place in Heaven, the eldila are coming for Piebald to take him back to his own world."

"You are right, Tinidril," said Tor. Then he looked at Ransom and said, "There is a red dew coming up out of your foot, like a little spring."

Ransom looked down and saw that his heel was still bleeding. "Yes," he said, "it is where the Evil One bit me. The redness is of *hrū* (blood)."

"Sit down, friend," said Tor, "and let me wash your foot in this pool." Ransom hesitated but the King compelled him. So presently he sat on the little bank and the King kneeled before him in the shallow water and took the injured foot in his hand. He paused as he looked at it.

"So this is *hrū* ," he said at last. "I have never seen such a fluid before. And this is the substance wherewith Maleldil remade the worlds before any world was made."

He washed the foot for a long time but the bleeding did not stop. "Does it mean Piebald will die?" said Tinidril at last.

"I do not think so," said Tor. "I think that any of his race who has breathed the air that he has breathed and drunk the waters that he has drunk since he came to the Holy Mountain will not find it easy to die. Tell me, Friend, was it not so in your world that after they had lost their paradise the men of your race did not learn to die quickly?"

"I had heard," said Ransom, "that those first generations were long livers, but most take it for only a Story or a Poetry and I had not thought of the cause."

"Oh!" said Tinidril suddenly. "The eldila are come to take him."

Ransom looked round and saw, not the white manlike forms in which he had last seen Mars and Venus, but only the almost invisible lights. The King and Queen apparently recognised the spirits in this guise also: as easily, he thought, as an earthly King would recognise his acquaintance even when they were not in court dress.

The King released Ransom's foot and all three of them went towards the white casket. Its covering lay beside it on the ground. All felt an impulse to delay.

"What is this that we feel, Tor?" said Tinidril.

"I don't know," said the King. "One day I will give it a name. This is not a day for making names."

"It is like a fruit with a very thick shell," said Tinidril. "The joy of our meeting when we meet again in the Great Dance is the sweet of it. But the rind is thick—more years thick than I can count."

"You see now," said Tor, "what that Evil One would have done to us. If we had listened to him we should now be trying to get at that sweet without biting through the shell."

"And so it would not be 'That sweet' at all," said Tinidril.

"It is now his time to go," said the tingling voice of an eldil. Ransom found no words to say as he laid himself down in the casket. The sides rose up high above him like walls: beyond them, as if framed in a coffin-shaped window, he saw the golden sky and the faces of Tor and Tinidril. "You must cover my eyes," he said presently: and the two human forms went out of sight for a moment and returned. Their arms were full of the rose-red lilies. Both bent down and kissed him. He saw the King's hand lifted in blessing and then never saw anything again in that world. They covered his face with the cool petals till he was blinded in a red sweet-smelling cloud.

"Is all ready?" said the King's voice. "Farewell, Friend and Saviour, farewell," said both voices. "Farewell till we three pass out of the dimensions of time. Speak of us always to Maleldil as we speak always of you. The splendour, the love, and the strength be upon you."

Then came the great cumbrous noise of the lid being fastened on above him. Then, for a few seconds, noises without, in the world from which he was eternally divided. Then his consciousness was engulfed.